"I can't have you on the investigation any longer when it puts you at risk." The fact that she'd been letting him tag along was an embarrassing slip in protocol. **"It's too dangerous."**

Benjamin looked up with a subtle scowl. "What the hell are you talking about?"

"You're a civilian and it's not safe for you to be participating in the investigation now that people are shooting at us."

"I can take care of myself."

"It's a liability issue for the department," Luna said, holding firm, even though that wasn't the biggest reason. She would never forgive herself if anything happened to Benjamin on her watch. "Sorry."

"And what about you? That bullet could've been meant for you as much as it was for me," he reminded her.

"It's possible, but the risk comes with the job—my job, not yours."

"And I'm a retired marine. I think between us we can handle whatever the killer throws our way."

"We don't know that and I can't take the risk."

"I'm not running from anything."

"You're not running. I'm taking you out of the game."

Dear Reader,

Big Sky Country—I couldn't imagine a better setting for an intense romantic suspense anchored with a tragic murder and peppered with family secrets that force two people to cling to one another when the world stops making sense.

In life, everyone has a complex backstory, and I wanted Benjamin and Luna to share that complexity as they tried to untangle a tragedy that not only poked at their emotional wounds but also pushed them to grow.

I hope you enjoy the first of the Big Sky Justice series set in the fictitious town of Cottonwood, Montana.

Hearing from readers is a special joy. You can always find me on social media or you can always email me.

Happy reading!

Kimberly

Facebook: Facebook.com/kim.vanmeter.37

Email: alexandria2772@hotmail.com

DANGER IN BIG SKY COUNTRY

Kimberly Van Meter

HARLEQUIN
ROMANTIC SUSPENSE

HARLEQUIN®
ROMANTIC SUSPENSE™

Recycling programs
for this product may
not exist in your area.

ISBN-13: 978-1-335-73820-2

Danger in Big Sky Country

Copyright © 2022 by Kimberly Sheetz

For questions and comments about the quality of this book,
please contact us at CustomerService@Harlequin.com.

Harlequin Enterprises ULC
22 Adelaide St. West, 41st Floor
Toronto, Ontario M5H 4E3, Canada
www.Harlequin.com

Printed in U.S.A.

Kimberly Van Meter wrote her first book at sixteen and finally achieved publication in December 2006. She has written for the Harlequin Superromance, Blaze and Romantic Suspense lines. She and her husband of thirty years have three children, two cats, and always a houseful of friends, family and fun.

Editors are amazing unsung heroes. I am continually humbled by how the editors in my life refine, hone and polish what I give them. I am blessed with two amazing ladies from two different disciplines who are incredible human beings and consummate professionals.

Johanna, my editor from the start of my Harlequin career, you humble me with your expertise, your quiet and gentle wisdom, and your unwavering ability to lead with positive encouragement that never fails to make my work so much better. I cannot imagine life without you.

Marg, my newspaper editor, you are the kindest, most genuine person I've ever had the privilege to call a colleague and a friend. I marvel at the power of your memory and your ability to help others shine. You continually remind me why journalism remains vitally important in an ever-changing world. I cannot stress how much I value your influence in my life.

To editors! May we count them among our blessings!

Chapter 1

The cloying smell of decomp hit before Cottonwood police detective Luna Griffin was even ten paces from the front door.

Luna halted, covering her nose with the back of her hand, glancing around for signs of anyone around.

The place felt eerily abandoned, sending an unwelcome shiver crawling down her spine. Luna wasn't overly spiritual but she couldn't shake the feeling that her Macawi ancestors were standing in somber silence, whispering without words that something bad had happened there.

Someone had called in a wellness check but that smell, riding on the hot summer breeze, choked hope from her heart.

The constant buzz of cicadas seemed to make the climbing July heat stickier than usual as sweat dotted Luna's brow and dampened her pits in the stiff uniform that didn't allow for any airflow.

She gestured to her accompanying officer, Wes Standford, with a warning look. "I got a bad feeling," Luna told him, going to knock on the ornate double oak door.

"Yeah, something smells real bad," Wes agreed, wrinkling his nose with a worried grimace.

The Leicki ranchette was on the outskirts of Cottonwood, a plush, upscale place on several maintained acres that looked like a bougie ski lodge uprooted from Vail, Colorado, and transplanted in the wilds of Montana. It was one of several ranchettes in the Whispering Oaks properties, all built by the same builder looking to cash in on city people wanting the Montana ranch life without actually doing the work of a ranch.

It wasn't to Luna's tastes, but to each their own.

"Charlotte? Roger?" she called out in a firm voice. "It's Detective Luna Griffin." Unnatural silence answered. She swallowed and tried again. "We got a call the boys haven't shown up for Vacation Bible School for the past few days. Everything all right?"

Still nothing.

"Want me to go around back?" Wes gestured, but Luna shook her head. The hairs were standing up on the back of her neck. *Better to keep backup close in case things go sidewise.*

Another minute or so passed before she announced, "I'm coming in," sliding on her gloves to open the door. The fact that the front door was unlocked wasn't a huge shock—most people in Cottonwood didn't lock their doors—but when she walked cautiously into the foyer, tensed and ready, nothing could've prepared her for what she saw.

Broken glass from the shattered coffee table lay scattered everywhere and electronics destroyed with an almost palpable violence were flung from their original places. A male body lay facedown in a pool of congealed muck and blood spatter sprayed against the white, textured walls and the smell of death nearly suffocated the air from her lungs.

Covering her nose, she backed out slowly, waving the deputy away with a gargled, "Stay back! We need a forensics team *stat*."

"What about the Leickis?" he called out, confused. "Shouldn't we do a sweep to see if anyone's in there?"

Tears stung her eyes as she shook her head, knowing that was Roger in the foyer and the intensity of that smell meant no one in the house was likely alive. "Just make the call, Wes."

A young officer fresh out of the academy, Wes paled with a short nod. "Yes, ma'am," he said and hurried to get forensics on the scene.

Luna stepped far enough away from the house to escape the odor, leaning over to draw deep breaths into her lungs, but the smell seemed stuck in her nostrils.

Small town police work mainly was keeping the peace between the locals, calming tensions at a domestic call, so the mean drunk didn't end up making a mistake he couldn't take back, and dealing with what they deemed 'quality of life' crimes like burglaries, petty theft and vandalism.

In all the years she'd been on active duty with the Cottonwood Police Department, she'd never responded to anything as gut-wrenching as this scene.

Oh, Charlotte… What happened?

Her mouth watered as her stomach threatened to unload the bagel and cream cheese she'd stuffed down her gullet early this morning.

"They're on their way," Wes called out from his squad car. "Bringing in the team from county. ETA one hour."

She acknowledged him with a short nod. One hour seemed too long, but she couldn't risk going into the crime scene without the proper tools to process the evidence. Luna shook the tremor from her hands. She needed a minute to focus. Her brain kept screaming that something terrible had happened in that house and her childhood friend was likely dead.

She returned to her vehicle and turned the air on full blast. She couldn't afford to lose it, not with the rookie watching.

The icy blast calmed her agitated nerves so she could draw in another deep breath without it feeling trapped in her chest, but her heart slammed against her rib cage like a frightened bird. Wes was right—they should've confirmed it was all of the Leickis in the house, but Luna couldn't do it, not yet.

But she couldn't sit in her car and do nothing either.

Get it together, Griffin. You're in charge. Treat the scene like any other. You have a job to do.

Shutting off the car, she exited and gestured for Wes. "C'mon, we can do a perimeter search while we wait for forensics. Watch where you step, there could be evidence left behind."

"What the hell happened here?" Wes asked, shooting an uncertain glance at the house.

Her strangled "I don't know" was evidence enough that she wasn't up to talking and Wes wisely buttoned his lip and focused on the task. Her only saving grace was the driving need to find anything left behind that might help catch the bastards responsible.

As promised, within the hour, the place was crawling with the local forensics team and support from the neighboring town with more resources. Facing the house, she swallowed the lump in her throat. *Time to get this over with.*

Dabbing the menthol beneath her nose this time, she followed the lead forensics officer back into the house as they went room by room until they found all four of the Leicki family.

Just as she'd predicted, no one from the Leicki family had survived.

"Did you know them?" the lead forensics officer, Matty Barnes, asked when he noted her compressed lips and overall body tension.

"Yeah," she answered, her vocal cords threatening to cut off the short word prematurely. She cleared her throat and tried again. "Yes, Charlotte and I went to school together. She and Roger were good people."

A long time ago, she and Charlotte had been thick as thieves, but life had sent them on different paths, and their tight friendship had lost its grip on either of their lives. Beyond the superficial small talk at community events, their circles hadn't intersected often.

But Charlotte had always been the best of people. No matter how long it'd been between chats, she always had a smile and a warm hug for anyone—including Luna, who admittedly had turned into a hermit over the years, but Charlotte always acted as if no time at all had passed.

Charlotte always extended an offer to Luna to get together; Luna always found a reason to cancel with the intention to reschedule but never did.

Tears stung Luna's eyes all over again. "She was an amazing person," she whispered.

"The good die young," Matty murmured, crouching to take crime scene photos of Charlotte's body. "Sorry for your loss."

It seemed wrong to be standing over her cold, nearly nude body when she'd just seen Charlotte a few months ago at the Cottonwood Elementary Career Day sponsored by the Parent Teacher Club, of which Charlotte had been president.

Luna swallowed the lump in her throat and accepted the condolences with a nod. The cause of death appeared pretty straightforward with the gunshot wound to her chest, but the bruises and cuts on Charlotte's skin suggested she'd tried to fight her attacker.

It gave Luna some odd sense of satisfaction that Charlotte, who'd been the nicest person in Cottonwood, had fought like a wildcat to survive.

Roger Leicki, Charlotte's husband, was shot in the head, execution-style.

But worse than seeing Charlotte's body was finding the boys, seven-year-old Liam and nine-year-old Jeremy, slumped over in the corner of their bedroom as if they'd been trying to hide when the gunman came in and picked them off with two shots.

They were just babies, she wanted to cry.

"Who would do this?" she asked, mostly to herself, unable to get past the sickening reality of what'd happened in a town mostly famous for its annual chili cook-off in the fall. "This kind of thing doesn't happen in Cottonwood."

"It's definitely shocking," Matty agreed, moving to get a better angle. "They seemed like a normal family. Such a shame. The world's going to hell in a handbasket, you know?"

She nodded, trying to get her bearings.

Focus on the scene, not your relationship to the victim, she told herself, drawing on her training to get her head on straight. It took more deep breathing before her hands stopped shaking, but leaning on protocol helped her to dissociate from the trauma of the scene.

Pulling out her notebook, she left the forensics team to do their work and carefully walked through the house, noting every broken or misplaced item, searching for a clue that might've been left behind.

A robbery gone wrong? *Maybe*. She returned to Roger's home office. The room was similarly trashed, but the desktop computer remained. Computers were easy to move for quick cash, and yet, several items with a high-dollar value were left behind.

She paused at Roger's desk. A separate docking station lay to the right of the desktop computer, commonly used for a laptop, but a quick search of the room revealed no sign of the laptop. A safe in the wall was left open. She expected to see it emptied of valuables, but Charlotte's two-carat diamond ring that she only wore on special occasions remained in its jewelry box, as well as several fancy necklaces. Luna frowned, taking note. Strange to leave expensive jewelry behind if quick cash was the goal.

Luna didn't know what Roger did for a living, but whatever it was, it'd been enough to support his family in an enviable lifestyle on solely his income.

What secrets were hiding behind these four walls that'd ended up costing four lives?

Was it possible this was simply random bad luck? Or was the Leicki family targeted for some reason? Targeted for what, though? How could the nicest family in Cottonwood end up like this? The Leickis sponsored Little League teams and donated hefty sums of money to every cause Charlotte championed—of which there were many—and they seemed delighted to give back to the community in any way they could.

Luna wouldn't go so far as to call them saints but damn, they'd sure be in the running. Some people were generous for show but the Leickis had been genuinely kind and gentlehearted.

At least that's how Luna had known them. Maybe Roger was a relative unknown in the equation but not Charlotte. She'd truly known Charlotte, even if they'd chosen different life paths as adults; there was no way Charlotte had turned into a monster behind closed doors.

Tears gathered at the corners of her eyes, but she blinked them back. No one had prepared her for the emotional punch to the gut that something like this would feel.

Once word of the Leickis' deaths reached the community, a shock wave would travel through the small town. The gossip would start, and fear would spread like cancer.

One thing she knew for sure—after this, Cottonwood would never be the same.

Benjamin Reeves clicked off his cell, his hands shaking.

His little sister, Charlotte, was dead.

Her whole family was dead.

Two years ago at Christmas was the last time he'd seen them. Charlotte insisted that he spend the holiday with them. It was the first time he'd seen their new house, and Charlotte had been so excited to give him a tour.

He remembered being happy for his sister but perplexed, asking, "How can you guys afford this?" But Charlotte had just smiled and praised how brilliant her husband was.

He'd wanted to believe her, but the guy supposedly worked an IT job. As far as he knew, IT jobs weren't paying a mint to tinker with computers remotely.

Charlotte had pointedly returned that Benjamin could barely operate his smartphone, so he couldn't possibly understand how vital Roger's job was.

Fair point, he figured, and let it go. No sense in ruining Christmas, but that didn't mean his misgivings hadn't remained. And now? Those misgivings were front and center again. Somehow, this tragedy had to be Roger's fault.

He'd never been a fan of Roger's. It wasn't anything he could put his finger on specifically, more of a gut feeling that Roger was trying to be more than he was.

Like the kid who couldn't stand himself, so he was always trying to be someone else.

Then, when they'd moved into that giant house, Roger had all but bragged about his wealth, which had rubbed Benjamin the wrong way.

He wasn't envious—as a medically retired marine, he did all right on his pension—but it felt like Roger was compensating for insecurity.

And in his experience, insecure men often made rash decisions that rebounded in some way or another. He'd seen it enough in the military to know the signs.

Charlotte had defended her husband, saying Roger had a right to be proud of his accomplishments, and what could Benjamin say to that aside from, "Yeah, of course," and drop it?

Benjamin ground the tears leaking from his eyes. He should've pressed harder into Roger's business affairs, followed his gut. He winced as he rubbed the cramp from his bad knee. Maybe Charlotte and her family would still be alive if he hadn't capitulated to the social pressure to keep the peace.

The thing was, with Charlotte, he'd always felt compelled to tiptoe around her feelings because of his guilt for leaving her alone with their dad all those years ago when he shipped out to the Marines.

Sure, the past was the past, but he couldn't help but think that it was his fault she ended up with Roger in the first place. Maybe if he'd stuck around, he could've been there to make sure a weasely guy like Roger hadn't had a chance to woo his vulnerable sister.

A whole lot of maybes.

Didn't much matter now, he supposed.

Another tear leaked down his cheek to splash on his jeaned leg.

What could he do now? Benjamin suffered a wave of grief that overwhelmed him. The helplessness of the situation triggered his rage. He needed answers. Sitting here crying wasn't going to help anything. Rising, he wiped his eyes and blew his nose, channeling his grief into something he could work with.

Having an objective always helped narrow his focus and crowd out the noise in his head. That's what he needed right now—an objective.

The deputy on the phone hadn't given much detail aside from the fact that Charlotte was gone. Benjamin needed more information. He wanted to know every facet of the case to make sure no stone was left unturned.

He had to go to Cottonwood to handle the funeral arrangements. When he got to town, he'd find out what "Cottonwood's finest" were doing to bring his sister's killer to justice.

Benjamin's short, mirthless laugh said everything about his opinion on Cottonwood's cops. He didn't trust them to know their ass from a hole in the ground, much less navigate a brutal murder and find who did it.

He doubted much had changed at the good ol' Cottonwood Police Department since he'd left town, and that wasn't a positive thing. Small town cops were lazy, entitled and usually corrupt somewhere up or down the chain of command.

He remembered the old chief, a guy drunk on his own importance in a small town, who hadn't much liked Benjamin because of his father and assumed the apple didn't fall far from the tree—and that'd automatically made him a dick in Benjamin's eyes.

Small towns loved their cliques, and that certainly included their tight circle of law enforcement.

He wasn't about to let Charlotte's case get shuffled to the desk of some inept cop who didn't know what the hell they were doing.

If he didn't think Cottonwood's cops could get the job done, he'd take matters into his own hands.

Nothing was going to stand in his way of finding out who did this.

It was the least he could do to honor Charlotte's memory.

Resolved, Benjamin scrubbed his face with his palms and rose to pack.

Chapter 2

"There has to be something you can give me, Luna," Bonnie Turford, the single reporter/editor of the local newspaper, *The Cottonwood Tribune*, pressured, gesturing to the arriving news crews descending on Cottonwood like the plague. "You can't let me be scooped in my own hometown."

"I feel for you, Bonnie, but there's nothing to tell," Luna said against the prickle of anxiety dancing down her spine at the chief's expectation that she handle all media requests. Under normal circumstances, that would entail getting a press release to Bonnie before the next issue, but she wasn't accustomed to holding press conferences.

Then again, it wasn't an everyday occurrence in the sleepy town that an entire family was murdered in their home.

Luna rubbed at the sudden sharp pain between her brows and reached for the aspirin bottle on her desk. "I can promise you no one is getting scooped on anything because we don't have any new information to share."

But Bonnie wasn't convinced. "There's an armada of press out there. Why would they be here if you weren't about to announce something big? Do you have a lead on who killed the Leicki family? Do you think it was done by someone they knew or a stranger passing through?"

"Nice try, Bonnie. *A*, I don't have that information and *B*, I wouldn't divulge those kinds of details when the investigation is still ongoing. C'mon, you know that kind of information could tank the case and no one wants that. We all want the same thing—to see whoever killed the Leickis face justice. Am I right?"

"Of course," Bonnie agreed, but the dissatisfied pinch of her mouth gave away her irritation.

"Look, we've always kept the *Tribune* in the loop as much as possible, that's not about to change just because we've caught a little national attention. Trust me, as soon as the next juicy story comes along, we'll be forgotten." And not a minute too soon as far as Luna was concerned. "Until then, we have to ride the wave out."

"Yeah and in the meantime, the local paper gets to hope for scraps," Bonnie grumbled, tapping her pocket notebook against her thigh.

The knock at Luna's door was a welcome interruption until she saw past the officer to the tall, solidly built man wearing his grief with a stern expression.

It'd been years—probably close to twenty the last time she saw him—but there was no mistaking that set jaw and the reason he was there.

"There's a Benjamin Reeves here to see you," the young rookie announced unnecessarily.

Bonnie's head swiveled around to peer past Wes, and Luna knew Bonnie recognized the name, too. "Charlotte's brother? Didn't he leave for the Marines right after high school?"

She nodded, hating this part of her job. Someone else had

placed the call to Benjamin to break the news, but likely he was here to finalize funeral details, which would be as soon as the county coroner released the bodies after his report.

"Bonnie, we'll have to talk later," Luna said, rising.

"Maybe Benjamin would be willing to talk to his hometown paper," Bonnie said, but Luna's quelling look told her exactly how Luna felt about that idea.

"Let the man grieve. He just lost his only sister and nephews. Be better than that, Bonnie."

"I *am* better than that but they won't be," Bonnie said and pointed to the news crews outside. "Don't make me grovel for rotten fruit and I won't have to shake the tree."

Luna didn't much care for being threatened, especially by someone she'd known her entire adult life, but this case had put everyone on edge. She'd give Bonnie a pass on her poor attitude this time. "I'll be in touch," she promised Bonnie, ushering her out and gesturing for Benjamin to come in. Bonnie hesitated as she approached Benjamin, as if she might whip out a business card and press it into his hand, but she thought better of it and kept going, thank goodness.

This case was turning the entire town upside down.

"I don't even have the right words," she admitted to Benjamin, offering him a seat. She knew how to handle grieving next of kin from her training, but she'd never had to use it with someone she'd grown up with. In the end, she dumped the book training and went with the personal connection. "I still can't believe what happened," Luna said, fighting the closing of her throat. The image of Charlotte and her family still haunted Luna's dreams. She hadn't had a decent night's sleep since finding that awful scene. "I can't imagine what you must be going through right now."

Benjamin, always a good-looking kid, had grown into a man with enough seasoning to make a woman look twice if she were of a mind to notice. Luna didn't know where life had taken Benjamin after leaving Cottonwood, and it didn't seem right to ask now.

Benjamin, his sandy blond hair darkened at the roots from time, looked rough, as if he'd slept in his clothes and came straight to the police office after a long flight, but his bloodshot eyes spoke of bone-deep grief.

Her heart couldn't help but feel the spasm of pain.

"The officer didn't give much detail, just that they were found in their home, murdered by gunshot, apparently."

"Yes, that's the long and short of what we know so far," Luna answered, careful to keep the details brief and to the point. People often thought knowing elements of a tragedy would give them closure, but that was a lie. Too much information often layered on more pain. "I'm assuming you're here to finalize funeral arrangements?" At his short nod, she admitted, "Unfortunately, the bodies haven't been released yet but it shouldn't be too much longer. We've got the county coroner handling the autopsies, and they've put a rush on the report given the circumstances."

"I've rented an Airbnb just outside of town. I want to be here as soon as the bodies are released," he said.

"That's good," Luna said, oddly relieved he wouldn't be stuck in a hotel room. Somehow it seemed so much worse to be walled in a room with his grief than a small rental property. Hell, it was probably just as bad. There was no escaping grief when it wanted to stomp on your heart. "Is there anything you need from me?"

It was an offer made out of courtesy, but she wasn't prepared for the flat response.

"You can stop messing around and find out who the hell killed my sister."

Luna Griffin was supposed to be Charlotte's best friend. Why wasn't she tearing this town apart looking for the person responsible for killing her? From what he could tell, Cottonwood was the same backassward town he'd happily left behind the day he graduated, and that didn't fill him with a lot of hope that they could solve a case as brutal as Charlotte's.

He'd spent the bulk of his flight from Arizona to Montana going over every red flag that'd ever been raised over Charlotte's husband, Roger, so that by the time he landed, he was 100 percent convinced that Roger was at the heart of this tragedy.

And he wasn't about to be appeased by anyone—not even the striking brunette who'd grown from a gangly, awkward girl to someone he didn't recognize from his memory.

"Benjamin, I promise you we're doing everything we can—"

"Which is what?"

She stared, her almond-shaped dark eyes widening. "What do you mean?"

"I mean, what are you doing? I want details."

"I can't divulge details," she balked, surprised at his curt response. "You, of all people, should understand how this works."

"Cut the crap, Luna. I'm her brother, not some yahoo off the street or the press. I need to know that you're doing everything humanly possible to find her killer."

"What makes you think we wouldn't be?"

"Look, I'm not handing out gold stars for good intentions. I'm going to cut to the chase. It's likely you're in over your head with this case and I'd rather know that now before we get in too deep. If I have to, I'll hire a private investigator to find out what happened but I'm not going to sit around and hope for the best. Am I clear? So, let's get down to brass tacks—do you have any real leads or are you still staring at the evidence, totally lost? Tell me now. I need to know."

He wasn't sugarcoating anything. The subtle flare of

Luna's nostrils gave away her offense, but she wasn't bristling as most would under the circumstances. He gave her credit for keeping a cool head until her gaze narrowed as she pointed out in a clipped tone, "I promise you—*no one* has stopped thinking about what happened to Charlotte and her family since it happened. I found their bodies. My newest officer, Wes Standford, had to leave the scene to puke. I can't seem to reconcile the fact that I was just talking to Charlotte at Career Day a few months prior at Cottonwood Elementary and now she's dead. To put it bluntly, *you* moved away and put Cottonwood in your rearview mirror, which included your only family. Charlotte was part of *our* everyday lives. We feel the Leicki family loss in ways you can't even fathom, so don't come to me demanding answers as if we're not also grieving, because I can promise you, we are. I *promise* you, we certainly are, and it's not only insulting but insensitive to suggest otherwise."

Delivered cleanly, the emotional punch nearly caved in his sternum with a pain he didn't see coming.

Nothing she said wasn't true; that was the worst part.

Too many manufactured excuses to avoid this place when Charlotte had invited him for various holidays and birthdays rose in his memory, jabbing him with fresh guilt.

Yeah, it was his fault they were dead. He never should've ignored his instincts about Roger, but who was he to say anything to the sister he'd left to fend for herself when they'd only had each other? Some knots were too tangled to try and sort when it came to anything involving Charlotte and how he'd failed her.

His sweet sister, Charlotte, had done the best she could with the resources available. He couldn't judge her, never would, but now they were all gone and he was left with the pieces.

How was he supposed to claw his way out from beneath

the layer of dirt he was buried under when he didn't know which way was up?

All he knew was that he couldn't sit at home knowing his sister's killer was roaming free and the Cottonwood Police force was woefully ill-equipped to handle this kind of investigation.

He couldn't worry about stepping on toes or hurting feelings—even if Luna had hit the nail on the head with her assessment. There wasn't time to sort out those feelings, not right now.

Benjamin returned the look, holding her gaze. "Then you ought to be spending every waking hour chasing down leads, knocking on doors, and figuring out what kind of shady shit that worthless husband of hers was up to because if you don't, I will."

That caught her attention. "What do you mean? Roger? Everyone loved Roger. Why do you think he was shady?"

Benjamin didn't have proof, only a gut instinct, and he knew how flimsy that sounded, but he answered with a subtle shrug. "He rubbed me the wrong way. Something about him."

"Could it be that it was hard for you to see your sister all grown up?" Luna suggested with a perplexed frown. "Because there isn't anyone in town who didn't think the Leickis were a great family."

Travel fatigue caught up to him as frustration sharpened his voice. "I told you, it was a gut feeling. Once you've served active duty, you get a sense for people. It's that gut instinct that can mean the difference between life or death. The first time I met the guy, I felt he was shady."

"That's not much to go on," Luna said. "No offense, but your gut instinct isn't exactly a hot lead—even if it did keep you alive." She added, as if it seemed inappropriate not to, "Thank you for your service."

He waved away her gratitude with a grumbled "Yeah,

sure," needing to stay on topic. Benjamin shoved his hand through his hair, feeling grimy and covered in stale airplane germs. He wasn't getting far here. He needed to check into his rental and regroup, come at this from a different angle.

Luna sensed a window and took it. "You're tired, grieving, and you need to rest. Why don't you go, freshen up, get some take out and we'll meet up tomorrow when you're feeling more like yourself. I'm willing to share whatever I can, okay? I should have the coroner's report by tomorrow. I don't recommend family members reading the report but if you think you can handle it, I'll bend the rules for you."

He accepted her offer with a gruff nod. There was a certain level of logic and reason with her suggestion, even if he wanted to rage through the streets and shake every single person in this town and demand answers.

Her approach was probably better.

For now.

"I'll hold you to it," he said, jotting down his cell number on the back of one of her business cards he snagged from the desk. Pushing it toward her, he said, "Until tomorrow."

He didn't trust his mouth to say much more. Luna was trying to meet him halfway. It didn't make sense to bite the helping hand until he had a better handle on the situation.

Assess. Reevaluate. Retarget.

That was the plan—he just needed a clear head to see it through.

Chapter 3

Luna pulled into the driveway of her place and saw her youngest sister's car parked out front. Sayeh, a narcotics agent with the FBI in New York, wasn't one for obligatory visits home, much less impromptu ones, so seeing the older gas-guzzling Jeep immediately filled Luna with dread.

As she opened the front door and heard the instant tension between Sayeh and their adoptive father, Bill, she knew her gut wasn't far off.

She didn't start with "Hey, how's it going?" or "Good to see you, Sayeh," because Luna was too worn out from the day to mess around with useless chitchat when all hell was about to break loose. It wasn't often that Sayeh or Kenna came to visit, so that could only mean trouble wasn't far behind.

"What's going on? What are you doing here?" Luna asked. "Is everything okay?"

Their father answered before Sayeh could. "Everything is *not* okay. Your sister's been suspended from her job and she's homeless."

Luna gasped in shock. "What? What happened?"

Sayeh glared at their dad. "That's not entirely accurate. Leave it to Dad to blow things out of proportion."

"Were you not suspended?" Bill shot back.

"Technically, on administrative leave—"

"Pending an investigation!"

"That's just the legal jargon for the paperwork. It'll all blow over and I'll be reinstated but it's bad timing because my apartment is undergoing major renovations to satisfy health-code violations, which means, everyone in the building, not just me, had to vacate. So, technically, it's true I'm temporarily displaced, but it's not like I was *evicted* or anything like that, which puts me here for a few weeks," Sayeh said, ending with a wan, fake smile. "Surprise."

Luna frowned, thinking of how disruptive having Sayeh around would be to her routine, but she wasn't about to turn away her baby sister. She sighed, resigned to the situation. "Of course you can stay. I turned your old bedroom into a catchall for storage but you can make it work for a short while."

When their adoptive mother, Nancy, died a few years ago from cancer, Luna had given up her tiny rental to move back home with her dad to help him adjust to living without Nancy, but then, it'd seemed easier to stay.

And it wasn't bad. Luna and her father had always been close, so it wasn't a hardship to be home again, but that wasn't the case with Bill and Sayeh.

Sayeh was such a hothead and carried a chip on her shoulder that would topple a water buffalo. Time hadn't softened her disposition, and she always bumped heads with Bill, no matter the topic.

The idea of sharing a roof with these two again gave Luna an instant migraine.

"This isn't going to blow over like it's no big deal," Bill

warned Sayeh, returning to the topic that must've caused the tension in the first place. "You punched another agent in the face. That's assault. They take that sort of thing very seriously in the FBI. Hell, everywhere!"

"Trust me, he had it coming," Sayeh grumbled. "And when the facts are presented, that will become clear. In the meantime, I just have to sit tight and let my union rep do all the talking."

"You punched another agent?" Luna asked, dumbfounded. "Why?"

"I can't talk about it while it's still under investigation," Sayeh answered, "but you would've done the same."

"I highly doubt that," Luna returned, shaking her head. All she wanted was a cold beer and a shower. The family drama would have to get in line. "Okay, well, it's been a long day, so can I trust you two not to tear the house apart while I'm cleaning up?"

Annoyed, Bill shook his head and muttered under his breath before waving Luna off and shuffling out of the room. He disappeared out the back door to his workshop to work off some steam. Dad liked to tinker with woodworking in his retirement, and while he wasn't particularly good, it kept him occupied. That'd always been Mom's reasoning when Luna had questioned why she let him spend so much on a hobby that went nowhere.

"A man needs to stay busy," she'd said with a soft smile as she crocheted by the fireplace, listening to her favorite jazz CD. "Besides, he's getting better. Did you see that shoe he carved for me?"

Luna's gaze strayed to the clumsy carving that remained on the mantel right where her mother had placed it all those years ago and smiled despite the situation and her emotional fatigue.

Nancy had always been better at soothing Sayeh's temper than anyone else, and Luna certainly hadn't inherited her special touch. Luna was too straightforward and logical to try and navigate the twisted emotional tangle inside Sayeh's brain.

Now that her dad was out of earshot, she looked to her sister. "Do you really have to pick a fight the minute you step foot through the door?" she asked.

"He started it," Sayeh said, folding her arms across her chest. "I hadn't been here more than thirty minutes when he started in on me. He's the one who needs to temper his tongue, not me."

Sometimes there was no getting Sayeh to see reason, and Luna was too tired to try. "Okay, fine, be that as it may, I'm working a big case, and I can't afford to waste energy refereeing you two, so take it down a notch."

Sayeh's interest rose with her eyebrows. "Yeah? How big?"

Sayeh hadn't heard yet. Luna broke the bad news. "A few days ago, the entire Leicki family was killed in their home. Charlotte Leicki used to be Charlotte Reeves."

Recognition dawned. "Oh my God, I'm so sorry. I know you and Charlotte used to be close. What happened?"

"I don't know," she admitted, hating that there was so little information as of yet. "At first glance, it looks like a burglary gone wrong but I'm not sure if it's that cut and dry."

"What do you mean?"

Luna couldn't share much, especially when the case was still an open investigation. She shook her head, seaming her mouth shut. Sayeh understood.

"Are you okay?" she asked.

"Not really," Luna admitted. "I haven't really slept since finding them. I keep seeing their bodies, and I know that the potential of finding bodies is part of the job but until now, it'd never actually happened. Not like this."

"It's always harder when you know the victims," Sayeh agreed, her expression softening. "I'm sorry."

"I don't understand how something like this could've happened here," Luna said, shaking her head at the senselessness. "Cottonwood is a nice place. People don't have to worry about being murdered in their beds, not here. That's the kind of stuff you read about in the big cities. I know it's stupid but there was a comfort in believing Cottonwood was different."

"Sis, you've always viewed Cottonwood through rose-colored glasses. The fact of the matter is, Cottonwood has its share of darkness, too."

"Yeah, I know, but this dark? An entire family was murdered. The boys… They were picked off like rabbits in a field. Who could do that to two little boys?" Luna bit her tongue. She shouldn't have said that, but the image of Liam and Jeremy haunted her as much as seeing Charlotte brutalized.

"You'd be surprised how easily some people can compartmentalize," Sayeh said.

Luna knew that Sayeh probably saw this kind of thing all the time with the work she did with the FBI, but it was a shock to Luna.

"No leads?"

"Not yet, but we're still waiting on the coroner's report."

Sayeh reached out to rub Luna's shoulder in commiseration. "Man, that's a shit sandwich."

"It gets worse."

"How?"

"Charlotte's brother, Benjamin, showed up today looking like the devil pushed him here all the way from Arizona, demanding that we do more to solve his sister's murder. We're doing everything we can and to insinuate otherwise is flat-out uncalled for."

"Grief does crazy stuff to people."

"I understand that and I'm trying to be kind but he turned out to be a jerk. It's no wonder Charlotte had a hard time getting him to ever visit."

"Maybe he doesn't like Cottonwood for reasons that you're unaware of," Sayeh suggested.

"Maybe so, but that doesn't give him the right to crap all over my department because he's holding a twenty-year grudge against the town."

Sayeh shrugged. "Some things are hard to let go of."

"Well, I need to do whatever I can to get him to calm down and let us do our jobs so he doesn't end up in the way. Oh, and Bonnie Turford is breathing down my neck for an exclusive scoop for the *Tribune* but I don't want to talk to any press, much less the local newspaper that most recently wrote a story about how budget cuts had ended the beloved K-9 program."

"Everyone loves dogs," Sayeh said with a small smile.

"Yes, everyone does love dogs, and hopefully the Cottonwood PD gets the grant they've applied for so the K-9 program can continue. Otherwise, it's been axed."

"So how are you going to handle Benjamin?"

"I'm going to try to be accommodating as much as possible but he's going to have to understand there's only so much I can do. Everyone loved the Leicki family. No one wants to see justice for their deaths more than me. I don't know why he's coming at me like I'm the enemy."

"Don't take it personally," Sayeh said, grabbing her suitcase. "Like I said, grief messes with people. When he calms down he'll see that you're not the enemy."

"I hope so," she murmured, watching Sayeh walk down the hall and disappear into her old bedroom, an air of resignation clinging to her squared shoulders. Luna never understood why Sayeh hated Cottonwood so much, but she could only imagine how Sayeh must feel right about now.

Except that wasn't Luna's problem to solve.

She had bigger fish to fry.

Benjamin settled into the rental property, took a long, cool shower to rinse off the sweat and travel grime, and emerged feeling slightly more human and less volatile.

Maybe he'd come at Luna too hard. It wasn't her fault that she was in over her head. The most crime Cottonwood PD saw was a burglary and possibly drug-related incidents, but rarely something as horrific as what'd happened to Charlotte and her family.

He didn't want to think about it but couldn't help imagining how terrified they must've been.

Sweet Charlotte, always the peacemaker, always trying to make the best of a bad situation, had finally found herself in a position that she couldn't smooth over with charm and kind gestures.

She'd always been a baker.

Their dad, that rotten son of a bitch, never missed an opportunity to take his rage out on his two kids, but Charlotte found that plying him with sweets often dulled his anger. It was hard to scream at someone who'd just popped a freshly baked chocolate chip cookie in your mouth.

It wasn't a foolproof strategy, but it worked enough to save their hides a few times.

Benjamin wiped at his eyes. He had no doubt Charlotte had done her best to talk her attacker out of hurting them, but her pleas had fallen on deaf ears.

Who would want to hurt someone like Charlotte and the boys? He held on to the instinct that the buck stopped at Roger, but even so, the man had the soft hands of an accountant. It wasn't like Roger was running with a street gang in his spare time.

Or maybe that's exactly what he'd been doing. *Hell, who knows?* He'd give his soul for a chance to undo what'd happened to Charlotte and her family, but he'd have to settle for doing everything in his power to see justice served.

But even that solemn vow seemed flimsy in the face of his reality. He couldn't make up for squandered time when there was no more time to give.

How was he supposed to reconcile that truth in his heart now that she was dead?

Benjamin always thought there'd be more time to sort out the past, but that's what's crazy and cruel about the reality of passing time—there's never enough of what you truly need.

He walked to the kitchen and grabbed a beer from the fridge he'd paid extra to have stocked on his arrival.

Tomorrow he'd work on being more civil to Luna. She wasn't the enemy.

And maybe that adage, "You catch more bees with honey than vinegar," actually worked.

Might as well put it to the test.

Chapter 4

The following day Luna wasn't surprised to see Benjamin waiting for her to arrive at the station, but she was surprised by the two coffees in his hand from the local coffee shop. She would've preferred to get into the office and prepare for the day without a chaperone, but she wasn't above a peace offering.

"Early riser, I see," she said, exiting her vehicle.

"Career military drummed any other option out of me," he admitted, handing her the coffee with an apology. "I came at you pretty hard yesterday and I'm not proud of my behavior. I shouldn't have said what I said and that's no way to talk to someone who might be hurting just as bad as me."

The unexpected apology threw her off for a minute, and all she could do was nod, lifting the coffee cup with a receptive smile. "Thanks for this. And the apology." But she wished he would've waited for her call to meet her at the station. "I hope you didn't waste your time coming down to the station before the report is ready, though."

"I can appreciate that but I figured even if I beat the report, I'd like to talk to you about Charlotte—"

"I can't really talk too much about the case," she warned.

"I know, I mean, just about Charlotte before all this happened. Like you already mentioned, I wasn't too good about coming home to visit. I lost touch and I'd like to know a few things about her life, something other than what I'm about to learn about her death."

The earnest request struck a guilty chord. It was natural for Benjamin to assume that she and Charlotte had remained as tight as he remembered, especially when they'd both stayed in the same town, but the reality was embarrassing on her part to admit. However, this wasn't about her. Benjamin needed her compassion right now. She waved for him to follow her inside.

Once behind the closed door of her office, she wasn't sure where to start or how to share, but honesty always seemed a safe place to begin.

"I…um, well, you know Charlotte was always the social butterfly while I was more comfortable in the corner with a book in my hand," she started, biting her lip as she tried to find a way to explain why she only knew superficial details about the woman who'd once been her dearest and closest friend. "Honestly, I never understood why Charlotte liked hanging out with me. I always worried I was little too boring for her tastes."

"From what I remember, she adored you."

That simple recollection brought instant tears to Luna's eyes. She sniffed with a rueful chuckle, reminding him, "Charlotte adored everyone."

"No, Charlotte was *nice* to everyone," he gently corrected. "You were special in her heart. You knew the real Charlotte."

What Benjamin wasn't saying was Luna had known how bad things were at home, a fact Charlotte went to great lengths to hide from the rest of the town with bright smiles and an aggressively cheery disposition.

Luna jerked a short nod, accepting Benjamin's answer.

Maybe that was true, but the barrier had always been Luna. She hadn't been able to imagine why Charlotte would've wanted to hang out with her when Charlotte had always been up to her eyeballs in charitable event planning and rubbing elbows with Cottonwood's finest. To Luna, their worlds had diverged into completely different planets.

"Your sister was one of the nicest people I'd ever known," Luna said, drawing a deep breath before admitting forlornly, "I wish I'd made our friendship more of a priority."

"What do you mean?"

"After high school, we drifted apart, not because we had a falling-out or anything dramatic like that, but life took us in different directions. While I was preoccupied with my career, Charlotte had already met Roger and they'd started a life together. She was determined to be the best wife and mother, while I was focused on studying the penal code. We stopped having much in common aside from the past and we gravitated toward people more like the new people we were becoming. In the end, life took over and we lost track of each other's personal lives."

"I had no idea," Benjamin murmured, his brow creasing. "I'm sorry."

"I am, too," she said quietly. "We think we have the luxury of more time. You'd think someone like me would know what an illusion that belief is, and yet, here I am, regretting every cancelled lunch date because there won't ever be another."

"Trust me, I understand," he said with a haunted expression that plucked at her heart.

Luna felt a tenuous kinship between them in their shared regret. "You were always a hero in her eyes," she shared, hoping to give him something to ease his grief. "She was instrumental in starting the Veterans Day candlelight march down Main Street. She always carried a candle in honor of your service and made sure everyone knew that her brother had fought bravely for his country."

Benjamin blinked as if this information were news to him. For a long moment, he struggled to speak until he finally managed to say, "She never told me."

"That was Charlotte. She didn't do things for any reason but the right one. I can say that without hesitation. Half the charitable events in this town were either started or chaired by her. She loved giving back to the community in any way she could."

And someone had snuffed out that beautiful soul. *Why?* The plaintive cry reverberated in Luna's head as a surge of anger washed over her. Nothing made sense right now. Wiping at the gathering moisture in her eyes, Benjamin gave her the minute she needed to regroup. The time for grieving was later.

"I gotta tell you, last night it was hard to sleep when all I could think about was how I knew next to nothing about Charlotte's life when I should've known everything."

"Beating yourself up isn't going to bring her back," she said, even though hearing the words come out of her mouth made her feel like a hypocrite. "Charlotte wouldn't want that."

"Somehow that only makes it worse," he admitted. "I'm stuck in a loop of regret and anger that feeds on itself no matter how I try to stop it. That's why I need to do something to help. Anything. I know I'm asking a lot—trust me, I know all the reasons why I shouldn't—but it's the only thing holding me together right now."

That raw confession should've been the biggest, brightest red flag, but she understood his reasoning all too well. Her chief trusted her to handle this case because she wasn't one to play fast and loose with the rules, but she wanted to break the rules for Benjamin. She swallowed the catch in her throat, fighting for the right words. She had good reasons why a family member couldn't possibly be objective in a case like this and why it was better for their mental health and the outcome of the case to take a step back.

And yet, she couldn't make her mouth work. Not when those soulful eyes were racked with pain he couldn't express and he was practically begging her in the only way he knew how to help him find closure.

"You have to know that too much information might have the opposite effect on your healing," she said, picking her words carefully. "When I say that everyone loved your sister, it's not lip service in some attempt to ease your grief. I know people always try to say nice things about the dead because it feels disrespectful not to, but honestly, that's not the case with Charlotte. She was an amazing person. First to volunteer for any community event—I think she was the chairwoman for multiple committees—and she still found time to be a great mom to the boys. Of course, she was the PTC president for Cottonwood Elementary and she spearheaded the fundraising drive to build the new campus library. I think she managed to raise nearly seventy-five percent of the funds just by knocking on doors and presenting her case with smiles and a home-baked chocolate chip cookie—which were phenomenal, by the way."

"She was an incredible baker," Benjamin agreed with a sad chuckle. "Sometimes I thought for sure Charlotte put some kind of magic in her baking. Her oatmeal raisin cookies were out of this world and I don't even like raisins."

"Right?" Luna nodded with a smile, taking a minute to let the wave of pain wash over them both. Maybe memory lane wasn't a hot idea, but somehow it was better than what was to come. "But that's my point. I don't want your last memories of Charlotte to be like the ones I have locked in my head," she said, closing her eyes briefly against the flash in her memory. "I'm happy to share every good memory I have of Charlotte, but pushing forward with the need to know more about her death by digging into the investigation, I think, will only hurt you."

"I know you're probably right," he agreed with a grave expression, "but I also know I don't have a choice."

His quiet acceptance got to her. "Um, one thing about your sister was that she never begrudged anyone their absence. I mean, she never made me feel bad for being wrapped up in my own life. She always had a smile for me when we saw each other and her warmth never faded. Sometimes I think I took that warmth for granted," she admitted, her throat closing tightly. "Like it would always be there for me when I found time."

Benjamin understood. "Yeah, me, too."

They sat in silence, digesting their feelings about the hole Charlotte left behind until the soft ding of Luna's email notification popped up a few breaths later. The report was in. The moment of truth had arrived. Either she'd gently shut Benjamin out of the loop or she would ignore protocol and let him in.

"Are you sure you want to know what the report says?" Luna asked, giving him one last chance to choose a different path so she didn't have to.

But Benjamin didn't falter. When he nodded, steeling himself against the pain that was coming, she knew her choice was made as well.

"Okay," Luna said, knowing this was going to hurt way more than he realized, but she'd honor his request. "Let's see what the doc says."

Benjamin's gut hurt. He was no stranger to death. His last tour in Syria took out three men in his unit. He would've been among that count if not for fate choosing to blow out his knee instead.

But no one prepared for the brutal death of someone they loved.

"Roger Leicki, cause of death, gunshot wound to the head, execution-style; Charlotte Leicki, cause of death, gunshot wound to the chest, various defensive wounds on her chest, arms and legs; Liam Leicki and Jeremy Leicki, both causes of death, gunshot wound to the head." She paused, glancing at Benjamin, but he indicated for her to keep going. "Materials collected from under Charlotte Leicki's fingernails were sent to forensics for analysis."

Of all of them, Charlotte, the peacemaker, had fought like hell to stay alive. His bottom lip threatened to tremble as rage washed over him. He held on to his temper by the thinnest thread. "Was she…assaulted in any other way?"

"Benjamin…" She shook her head, reluctant to add to his burden, but he had to know. Luna understood and scanned the report, her gaze darting over the words with anxious tension. Finally, she sagged with visible relief, answering, "No evidence of sexual assault."

He let the breath he was holding go. *Thank God.* "Is there anything else?"

"Um, not really. Roger and the boys died instantly; Charlotte, within moments. Any suffering would've been brief, not that that's much of a comfort."

He gave Luna credit for softening the blow, but his heart felt caved in. "Thank you. I need a minute," he said, rising on stiff legs to walk outside. If he got his hands on whoever did this, he'd gladly go to prison for the acts of violence they were owed. The coffee washed like acid across his stomach, scoring his gut lining and reminding him that his body couldn't survive on high-octane caffeine anymore.

Just as he was breathing through a wave of pain, a man in a suit popped out from an unremarkable sedan, and a news crew appeared as if by magic. They must've been watching the station, saw him go in with Luna and then waited for the right time to pounce.

"Benjamin Reeves?" the man inquired as the cameraman pushed in on him. "What can you tell us about the search for your sister's killer? Do the police have any idea who might've had cause to murder your sister's family?"

"If you know what's good for you, you'll get that camera out of my face," Benjamin growled, pushing past him.

The man ignored Benjamin's threat and followed as he tried to get into his rental car. "Did you have any clue that your sister and her husband might be involved in something dangerous? Is there any possible connection between the Leicki murders and the murder of another socialite family in Billings?"

"What the hell are you talking about?" Benjamin barked, narrowing his gaze at the intrusive parasite masquerading as the press. "My sister was a good, God-fearing woman who didn't do anything to deserve what happened to her and her family. And she wasn't no *socialite*, she was a wife and mother who volunteered every bit of her spare time to help her community and those she loved. If anyone says otherwise, they can come say it to my face and see how that works out for them."

Before the reporter could lob another question at him, Benjamin slammed the door, hoping to catch a few fingers, and then accelerated out of the parking lot, leaving the reporter and his crew behind.

If they knew what was good for them, they wouldn't follow.

He was outside the city limits before he realized tears were tracking down his cheeks. Pulling over to the side of the road, the grief choking him as it bubbled out in ugly sobs, he cradled his face in his hands, hating that he hadn't been there to save her. He'd taken for granted that she'd always be there when he got around to being her big brother again. He'd been such a selfish prick that he'd lost any chance of knowing his nephews.

Everything in his world was on fire.

Oh God, Luna was right; knowing the details made everything so much worse.

The flames were licking at his mind, eating at his ability to form rational thoughts and feeding his need for revenge.

He'd tear whoever did this into a million tiny pieces. He'd willingly trash what was left of his life for the privilege of squeezing the breath out of whoever had pulled the trigger on Charlotte and her boys.

God help him, he'd sell his soul for the chance to feel their blood gushing over his hands as he wrung the life out of their body.

His body shook as he cried ugly tears born of regret, grief and rage.

He didn't know how long he sat on the roadside, but it was long enough to watch the sun climb the sky to anchor itself straight above as the heat index rose to prickly levels.

Sweat slid down his temples, but he didn't care. Dry heat didn't bother him.

What was he going to do?

There weren't any real leads in that report. The odds of finding the gun that shot his sister's family were slim to none. Chances were, whoever killed them had ditched the weapon immediately. It would take the kind of luck that only existed in fairy tales to recover that weapon anytime soon.

That weapon was probably deep in a lake or tossed in a river.

Benjamin wasn't the kind of person who accepted defeat readily. He had zero quit in him. Except some battles couldn't be won with grit and heart. Sometimes the odds were just stacked against you from the start.

He wiped his eyes and cleared his throat. Now that the

medical report was in, he was free to set up Charlotte's funeral arrangements.

Never in a million years did he ever imagine that he would outlive his sister.

Didn't seem right.

"I'm so sorry, sissy," he whispered, wiping at his nose as his grief leaked from every pore. "It ain't right. It just ain't right."

Chapter 5

"I don't have anger issues. I have issues with misogy-
nistic idiots," Sayeh fired back at their father from across
the breakfast table, which made Luna want to do an about-
face right back into her bedroom. Could they not spend
two minutes in each other's company without trying to
start World War III? Luna bit back her response and ignored them, going straight to the coffeepot. Sayeh turned
to Luna. "How would *you* handle a coworker trying to
grab your ass?"

Luna couldn't imagine any of her coworkers trying
something like that, but she sensed Sayeh was searching for an ally in this argument, and Luna wasn't sure she
could do that. Luna turned with a coffee mug in hand, in-
quiring, "Is that why you were written up?"

"Mostly," Sayeh hedged, adding, "although there may
be more within the report."

"More as in how much more?" Luna asked.

"It doesn't matter. He was wrong and I corrected him.

That's all that should count and if my union rep is worth his weight in salt, that's the argument that'll take priority."

"You can't go around punching people who piss you off," Bill growled.

"And why not? Seems a good deterrent for future bad behavior," Sayeh answered with a shrug.

"It's also a good way to lose your job," Bill said.

"They're not going to fire me over this," Sayeh said, but the faintest hint of uncertainty plucked at Luna's heart. Being the big sister, she couldn't help but want to champion Sayeh, but it was hard to be in her corner when she'd screwed up. "Besides, it's not an isolated event. I warned him if he kept pushing his luck, he was going to get popped. Play stupid games, win stupid prizes. That's how it goes."

"Did you report his inappropriate behavior to your superior?" Luna asked.

"Once," Sayeh admitted, chewing her cheek, adding, "but when nothing came of it, I knew it was never going to go far and I took matters into my own hands."

The wheels of justice moved incredibly slowly, even within the system created to administer it. Luna could only imagine Sayeh's frustration, but as a big sister, she was pissed that her complaint went nowhere.

But punching the man wasn't the answer either. When was Sayeh going to learn that you couldn't always sledgehammer your way to a solution? "When will you know more about your case?"

Sayeh exhaled a deep breath. "I don't know. I was told to sit tight and wait for word. Their exact words were, 'Take a vacation, Griffin, and cool off,' and I wanted to tell them to stick their vacation advice up their tailpipe but I didn't. I'd call that a win."

"Yeah," Luna agreed, but knew the victory was thin. "Well, not that I'm trying to side with anyone but maybe you could use a little downtime. The stress of your job is intense. Everyone needs a break now and then, even bad-ass narcotics agents." Luna ended with a wink that Sayeh grudgingly accepted with a smile. *That was encouraging.* Maybe it was safe to leave them alone. "Look, I need to get to the office. Can I trust you two not to bring the house down if I'm not here to mediate?"

Sayeh snorted. "Oh, get over yourself. Go to work. At least one of us needs an income these days."

"Hey, I have a pension that covers all my expenses," Bill said gruffly.

Sayeh chuckled, grabbing her coffee mug for a refill. "My mistake. I had no idea the Cottonwood Police Union had negotiated so well for its members back in the day when dinosaurs roamed the earth and inflation hadn't undercut everything with a dollar value."

Luna left them to bicker among themselves. She didn't have time to babysit.

Within thirty minutes, she was pulling into the station parking lot, immediately irritated by the crowd of reporters waiting. As expected, she spotted Bonnie with the local paper sending pointed looks her way, as if she were expecting some meteoric announcement, and if she didn't get one, Luna was to blame.

A reporter called out amongst the chaos. "Detective Griffin, today is the funeral for the Leicki family. Does that mean there aren't any more leads on their grisly murder?"

Her first instinct was to ignore all the noise and go straight inside, but she knew it wouldn't get any better, and she might as well get this part over with.

She turned to face the small crowd, absolutely hating the feeling of the cameras on her. "Per policy, I can't answer questions regarding an active murder investigation but I can assure the community that the Cottonwood Police Department is doing everything possible to find justice for the Leicki family."

"Was their murder drug-related—"

"No further questions," Luna said, cutting off the reporter and walking quickly into the station. She sank into her chair, rubbing her temple. It was too early for a migraine, but the sudden pounding in her head didn't seem to recognize that fact.

Wes poked his head into her office. "Sorry to bother you but the editor of the *Tribune* would like to speak with you. Should I take a message?"

If only Bonnie would be satisfied with leaving a message. She motioned for him to let her through but directed, "Let me know what time the Leicki funeral is set for, please. I want to pay my respects."

"Sure thing."

There was another reason she wanted to be at the funeral. Killers often got a macabre thrill from watching their victims' families grieve over their loved ones. Maybe there was a chance whoever was responsible might make an appearance at the funeral. Luna would watch out for anyone who seemed out of place in the small-town, close-knit community.

Bonnie walked into the office and slid into the opposite seat. "Nice statement for the interlopers but please tell me you've got something with more substance for the local paper."

"We're not playing favorites, Bonnie. What we have is what we've shared. C'mon, you know how this works. You're a professional. Why are you letting those outside networks get under your skin?"

"Newspapers are a dying breed," Bonnie said. "I can't compete with the immediacy of social media when I run a weekly newspaper. I have to offer something unique to my readers. There's no such thing as reader loyalty these days. Gone are the times when people bought a subscription simply because it was something they'd always done. The competition is fierce and cutthroat."

"I can appreciate the struggle but I can't jeopardize the case just to help the *Tribune*. You gotta understand where I'm coming from, too."

"I get it and I'm not trying to get in the way, I'm trying to write a story that has heart, something the community would appreciate and understand."

Luna recognized Bonnie wasn't the enemy and wasn't trying to create one either. She tried a different tactic. "What if you did a story that didn't focus so hard on their murders but their lives? The Leickis were pillars of the community. Surely there's something in the archives you can build on that celebrates who they were when they were alive, rather than focusing on their deaths."

"Of course, sure, Charlotte was on every committee known to man. It wouldn't be hard to dig stuff up to build on. The last time I talked to her she was gearing up to accept booth applications for the annual chili cook-off in the fall. She was real excited about some of the changes they were planning to implement with the new location."

"New location?" Luna asked.

"Yeah, I guess it wasn't common knowledge yet but instead of holding the cook-off at the fairgrounds, it was being moved to the Johnson Ranch. According to Charlotte, there's plenty of room and the barn was perfect for community craft booths. I remember thinking it would make really great front-page art."

"What's wrong with the fairgrounds?" Luna asked, confused. "The chili cook-off has been held there since I can remember."

"Yeah, and the facilities are old and falling apart. There's no money to fix up the grounds and I think when

Charlotte stumbled on the opportunity to have it some-place with a little more charm and class, she jumped on it."

"I didn't realize a chili cook-off required charm or class," Luna murmured, shaking her head with a small smile at Charlotte's bougie style. God love her, Charlotte was determined to turn Cottonwood into a touristy desti-nation town like something you see in the movies.

"When did old man Johnson agree to put his ranch in the commercial business of craft fair locations?" Luna asked.

"Not the old man, the son. He's got some real progres-sive ideas about how to revitalize the town, apparently. And maybe he was sweet on Charlotte. Lord knows, the attrac-tion between Charlotte and Roger was always a mystery."

True enough. Charlotte was known as a small-town beauty, while Roger had always been a bit plain and unas-suming, but they'd seemed happy. At least to Luna's eyes.

"Do you think Charlotte and Scott Johnson were..." Luna couldn't even finish the sentence. It seemed disre-spectful to say the words out loud. "I mean, probably not, Charlotte was crazy about Roger."

Bonnie shrugged, clarifying, "I don't deal in gossip but I can't say I heard anything inappropriate going on with those two. All I'm saying is that Scott Johnson isn't hard on the eyes if you're into that sort of thing and well, they make more sense as a couple than Charlotte and Roger ever did, that's for sure."

Bonnie rose, sensing she wasn't going to get much fur-ther on that topic. "You going to be at the funeral?" she asked. At Luna's nod, she said, "I'll see you there," and let herself out.

Luna let out the breath she hadn't realized she was hold-ing. She didn't like the idea that Charlotte may have been having an affair with Scott Johnson. She wasn't one to judge, but plenty of people in this town would if it were true.

Nobody was perfect.

But seeing as Scott Johnson may have been one of the last people to see Charlotte alive, it might be a good idea to visit him.

If only to rule him out.

Benjamin would rather crawl through glass than be where he was sitting right now.

His skin crawled as the scream he kept bottled inside threatened to erupt from his lips, but somehow with the grace of God, he managed to accept the line of condolences with a stiff nod and a silence that they attributed to his grief.

And yes, he was grieving, but his silence was filled with rage.

He couldn't exorcise the demons eating at him, no matter how hard he tried.

Even though his rental was nice, the bed was comfortable and he had no complaints about the place, he didn't think he'd managed more than two winks at a time since checking in.

He couldn't help but stare at each person with wary speculation, wondering if he was staring into the eyes of the person responsible for their deaths. Yeah, he knew all about how some killers liked to gloat, soaking up their victims' loved ones' grief like a fine wine, and he hoped to God they were stupid enough to show up today because he'd know.

He had the training to spot a liar.

Every muscle was tense as he cataloged every move by each person expressing their condolences.

Was that a tic in that man's eye? Was it guilt that made his hands sweaty? What about her? Who was she to his sister, and why did she look smugly satisfied by Charlotte's death?

Suddenly, Luna was silently by his side. The warmth of her body beside him settled his nerves with an invisible hand, as if she knew what he was doing and why because she was doing the same.

"It was a beautiful service," she murmured during a break in the receiving line. "Charlotte would've been proud. The snapdragons were gorgeous."

He was all thumbs with this kind of thing, and the overwhelming amount of details that needed attention had nearly put him into a tailspin of a different sort. "The lady at the funeral home took care of the flowers and stuff like that," he admitted. "I don't know what's appropriate for these things." But he cast an appreciative glance Luna's way with a sheepish "Thank you."

"Sarah understands what people need during the worst time in their lives," Luna said, nodding. "She's walked many a grieving loved one through the process. You were in good hands."

His throat threatened to shut. All he could do was nod.

Finally, the last person filed out and they were alone.

Given it was a service for the entire family, a large portrait of the Leickis was chosen instead of having caskets in the room. Besides, Benjamin didn't think he could've stomached sitting through the service with their bodies two feet away. Somehow it seemed easier to get through with a picture of a smiling family in the center as if everything was still okay.

Even though nothing would ever be okay again.

At least, not for him.

His eyes stung. A well of grief threatened to drown him. Just as he was about to exit at a clip, Luna's hand on his shoulder stopped him. He met Luna's gaze. He didn't

Chapter 6

Luna sensed Benjamin was about to break.

In her experience, men accustomed to bearing the load of a heavy burden didn't deal well with the realization that they weren't always strong enough for every problem thrown at them.

And she couldn't let Benjamin crumble without trying to help. It was the least she could do, she rationalized and ignored the warning, *Don't let it get personal*, whispering in the back of her head.

"Last time you bought me a coffee. Let me return the favor," she said. "One of my favorite coffee shops is only a short walk from here."

"I'm not really good company right now," he said.

"I didn't ask for good company. I offered a reciprocal coffee, not dinner and a movie."

A small grudging smile broke the stone of his expression as he gestured, "Lead the way, then," and they set off for the coffee shop.

The mom-and-pop was owned by an older couple who'd

moved to Cottonwood about ten years ago and had quietly made their mark on the town by providing a quality roast, the best apple fritters and a cozy atmosphere that felt like a rustic country store that was too charming for words.

It probably went without saying that it'd been Charlotte's favorite, too.

"Nothing like this in Arizona," he said, settling into the booth, his gaze doing a quick inventory. "Cute. The tourists probably love it."

"They do but the locals do, too," she said, holding up two fingers for Hannah.

An older woman with softly graying hair and a round face radiating warmth and kindness brought two steaming mugs within a minute. Hannah, the better half of the proprietor couple, smiled with understanding when she took one look at Luna's companion. "I have two apple fritters left from the morning rush. You interested?"

Luna nodded, and Hannah smiled and left to dish them up.

"They're the best," Luna promised. "Unless you don't like apples. Then I'll take yours to go."

Even though she saw the grief wrapped around him like a cloak, he chuckled. Luna knew loss but nothing at the level Benjamin was feeling. She wanted to reach out and clasp his hand to let him know he wasn't alone, but she stowed the impulse. Instead, she said, "It's been a long time since you've been back to Cottonwood. What have you been up to all this time? Aside from making a career for yourself in the military?"

"That's about the long and short of it," he admitted, pausing for Hannah to set the plates down. "I accepted a military retirement when I blew my knee out. I spent enough time in the service that my retirement income is enough to live on and when I want to make a little extra for projects or whatnot, I work for the local bike shop, repairing motorcycles."

"You ride?"

"Every chance I can get," he answered with a short smile. "There's nothing like the open road to calm the noise in your head. It always helped me to think when I needed to work stuff out."

"I wish I had something like that. Sometimes the noise in my head is deafening."

"It's important to keep doing things that keep the hamster running behind the scenes," he said.

Luna smiled, admitting, "I think my hamster is on its last leg." She paused to watch Benjamin take an exploratory bite. When he nodded with approval, she happily tasted her own. "So, why Arizona?"

He shrugged. "It wasn't anything like Montana," he answered.

The honesty was good, even if it made her sad that he hated this place so much that he'd purposefully chosen the opposite of his hometown. Reminded her of Sayeh. Luna knew a little about Charlotte and Benjamin's homelife, but only from what she'd glimpsed firsthand on the rare occasions she'd been allowed in the Reeveses' house.

But the memories were crystal clear.

Allen Reeves had been an angry drunk most days, bitter to the very end about the hand he'd been dealt in life.

Not many people had shed a tear when he died a few years after Charlotte graduated high school.

To Luna's knowledge, Benjamin hadn't even attended the funeral.

Best to keep the memories in a safe zone. Benjamin was suffering enough.

"Okay, I'll bite," Luna said. "No wife? No kids? How about a pet?"

His laughter tickled her in places that seemed inappropriate given the circumstances. "No wife, no kids, and doesn't seem right to subject an animal to my erratic schedule. So, just me."

"Sounds a little lonely."

"Nope. I like my own company. Too many people around gives me a headache."

She could understand that. Having Sayeh home again was messing with her routine, which made Luna feel bad for being irritated because her sister had only came home because she had nowhere else to go.

But then Benjamin flipped the script on her, lobbing the question back at her. "What's your story? No kids? No husband or boyfriend? Pets?"

Luna laughed, her cheeks flushing with subtle heat. "No to all of the above. I, um, came close to marrying when I was in my late twenties but I definitely dodged a bullet when I found him messing around behind my back with a coworker. We broke up and he left town with his mistress. Last I heard, he was fat, balding and a barely functioning alcoholic."

"Some people deserve each other," Benjamin said with zero regrets. "The best advice I ever stumbled on when I was still young and impressionable was when people show you their true colors, believe them."

She bit back a smile. That adage was one that she lived by and a primary reason she hadn't budged when Derek had tried to come crawling back, making big promises and falling all over himself with apologies.

He'd made his bed, and he could rot in it.

Luna cleared her throat, continuing, "And as far as pets go, well, I love animals but the idea of one more responsibility on my plate right now just doesn't appeal to me." She clarified a little further. "When my mom died a few years back, I gave up my apartment to help my dad around the house for a bit, and then I just ended up staying. We get along fine and he mostly takes care of himself but he's getting up there in age and I can't imagine leaving him to his own devices at this point."

Dawning broke in his expression. "Which also makes it hard to date," he supposed.

"Bingo," Luna answered with a short smile. "But to be honest, I like my routine and I'm not sure how open I am to someone else inserting their expectations and personal stuff into my life."

"Sounds kinda lonely," he teased.

She laughed. "Touché."

Benjamin finished his apple fritter, even going so far as to lick the icing from his fingertips with a murmured "Gotta admit, that was damn good," and his satisfied smile sent a spark of something straight to her stomach.

Like an electric butterfly.

Luna Griffin was an intriguing woman. The men in this town had to be stupid or blind to let a woman of her substance get away, but he was selfishly glad that she was free to spend her resources on Charlotte's case.

Well, that might not be the only reason he was glad she was single and unencumbered but the reason he felt comfortable admitting.

The thing was, he didn't have any business thinking about Luna in any other way aside from professional, especially not now.

The timing was shit.

And the last time he saw her, she was a gangly freshman in high school, all legs and arms and just as clumsy.

That memory seemed like a lie in comparison to the beautiful, capable woman sitting across from him, finishing off her fritter with a zeal he found alluring.

He appreciated the interlude, but he wasn't here to find

a girlfriend. Benjamin cleared his throat and regretfully broke the comfortable bubble between them.

"I have to meet with the attorney later this afternoon and go over Charlotte's will. As her only living relative, I'm the executor of her estate. Apparently, Roger didn't have any family, so it's just me to handle all the details of their assets."

Luna sobered, following his lead. "They couldn't have scheduled that for a day or two after the funeral? Big emotional events should be spaced out."

He shook his head, disagreeing. He just wanted to get it over with. "The faster the paperwork is processed, the faster I can put the house up on the market, get the estate sorted and put this whole nightmare behind me."

"I imagine the bank would be understanding about the mortgage right now," she said.

"No need," he said, surprising Luna. "That house is paid for. They didn't owe a red cent on that massive ranchette."

Luna didn't try to hide her shock. "By all appearances, Roger made a good living but I had no idea he made *that* good of money."

"Yeah, same," he agreed, deciding to put his cards on the table. "I know my intuition isn't a real actionable lead but it might be something worth chasing down at the very least."

He'd snagged her curiosity, possibly still processing the shocking information about the ranchette. She nodded, ready. "Okay, what do you got?"

"I have a feeling that whatever Roger did for a living wasn't what he said he did. There's no way an IT guy makes the kind of cash that pays off a fancy ranchette within a few years of buying it. Run his financials. Dig into his bank accounts and find out who was paying him."

"Charlotte never mentioned anything about what Roger did for a living?"

"Just that he worked with computers," Benjamin answered. "I tried to call bullshit but Charlotte was staunchly loyal and wouldn't budge no matter the angle I came at it with her. I should've pushed harder."

"You had no idea something like this was going to happen."

"Does that matter? I was her only family. It was my job to protect her and I failed. No sense in sugarcoating the truth."

"It's not sugarcoating, it's glossing over the fact that she was an adult and she was responsible for her own choices. You need to try and remember that."

No, it wasn't that simple. Luna didn't understand what kind of house they grew up in and how living in a constant state of fear and anxiety had created a bond that tethered them together, good or bad.

Which was why he deserved to shoulder the weight of his guilt for letting her down.

"I'll poke around into Roger's financials but I should warn you that it's not likely to turn up anything of value. For all we know, Roger could've been a wise investor, which provided some kind of windfall. Most people don't advertise when they've come into a lot of money, for obvious reasons."

Benjamin accepted her answer, but the set of his jaw gave away the guilt that he couldn't shake and nothing she could say would change his mind. Instead, she shifted the conversation to what was bugging her. "I don't know how to ask this without it sounding terrible, but I came across something that keeps tugging at my brain and I can't let it go."

"Chase down every lead, no matter how small," Benjamin said, prepared to support Luna's efforts. "You never know what could be the one detail that makes the difference."

Luna lost some of the tension in her shoulders at his support, relieved he was willing to listen. "Yes, I agree. I think I want to chase this down, if only to rule it out."

"What is it?"

"Do you think there's any chance Charlotte was having an affair?" She immediately cringed and started to apologize. "I hate even asking such a thing. Like you said, Charlotte was so loyal. I can't imagine, but, I don't know, there seems to be some whisperings that don't make a lot of sense."

Charlotte having an affair? Like Luna, he had a hard time picturing his sister being disloyal to Roger, but he also had to admit the possibility that things about his sister were unknown to him.

He chose his answer carefully. "What does your gut say about what you've heard? Is it idle gossip or does it come from a reputable source?"

"I would say that the source isn't someone known to spread gossip and prefers facts or speculation but I can't ignore that there might be something worth chasing down." She met his gaze, admitting in earnest, "I don't want it to be true but human beings aren't perfect and sometimes the stress of life gets to the best of us. I would never judge Charlotte even if it turned out to be true."

"Then you should pursue it," he decided, adding gruffly, "Not that you need my permission but I want to be able to rest believing every lead was run down, no matter how small or seemingly impossible. Otherwise, I'll never be able to put this to bed."

Even then, Charlotte's death would likely stick with him until the day he crossed the pearly gates himself, but he had to cling to something.

She may not have needed his permission but seemed relieved to have his understanding. He realized he hadn't asked her much about how she was handling Charlotte's death.

Aside from barking at her, that is.

"Are you okay?" he asked.

Luna's eyes welled, but she held herself in check. A brief nod later, she said, "It comes in waves. It helps to focus on the case," admitting, "but it's hard to sleep. I don't think I've managed more than an hour or two at a stretch, and it's starting to catch up to me."

Benjamin sensed it was a big deal for her to admit her struggles. Lord knew getting those words out of his mouth was like pulling a rusty bolt free from its socket. "You're doing all you can," he said. "We all are."

He could only hope it was enough.

Chapter 7

The Johnson Ranch was located about fifteen minutes outside of town, which probably made it a sensible choice for an alternative location for the chili cook-off, but Luna had a hard time seeing old man Johnson loving the idea of strangers tromping around on his property.

From her dealings with the old man, he wasn't exactly a people person. Luna didn't know his son very well. Scott Johnson hadn't grown up in Cottonwood but had returned to his father's ranch after college, bringing big-city ideas to the small town with various levels of success.

Small towns were notoriously closed-minded to progress, often eyeing change with suspicion, contributing to towns slowly withering away to nothing.

Cottonwood wasn't immune to the small-town curse.

Any time the town council talked about a new business venture, new agriculture, new development, it didn't matter—anything new and different—people got all up in a lather, protesting, going off half-cocked about "preserving the Cottonwood way of life" and grumbling about how city folk and outsiders were ruining everything good about the town.

Frankly, a little freshening up would be nice. Charlotte was right; the Johnson Ranch was beautiful, and the fairgrounds were a potential health-code violation that should've been demolished years ago and rebuilt, but there weren't the funds to make it happen.

Luna pulled up to the front and parked. The Johnson Ranch was a moderately sized working cattle ranch, and about this time of year, the ranch hands moved cattle from pasture to pasture to keep the cattle from overgrazing the land.

She'd called ahead to let Scott know she was coming, and he met her outside with an inviting smile that showcased nice, even white teeth and a sharp jawline that could cut paper.

"Thanks for being willing to talk on such short notice," Luna said, following him into his office inside the ranch house.

"Anything to help," he said, sliding into his chair opposite the massive desk. "We are devastated by the news. My God, who could do such a thing to such a wonderful family?"

"That's what we're trying to figure out," Luna assured Scott. Scott's spicy aftershave smelled expensive and made her nose twitch. Unfortunately, there was no way to finesse what she had to ask, so Luna went straight to the point. "There's no easy way to say this, but I have to ask. Were you and Charlotte having an affair?"

Scott shook his head, but he wasn't as offended as Luna thought he'd be. He leaned forward, clasping his hands together. "Not going to lie, there was interest on my part, but Charlotte wouldn't hear of it. She was loyal to Roger and I respect that. She was a good woman, and Roger was a lucky son of a bitch to have her."

Luna was relieved. "Do you know why anyone would think that there was something going on between you?"

"I sure do," he answered, surprising her. "I hate to say it but sometimes women can be catty creatures in the face of rejection."

"What do you mean?"

"Look, I'm not one to talk about personal stuff like this but given the circumstances, I feel there's no room to hold back if it means protecting Charlotte's character." He drew a deep breath. "I was seeing someone but when Charlotte and I started working on the details of moving the chili cook-off to the ranch, I started having feelings that weren't conducive to staying with the person I was dating. I thought a clean break was best."

"But you said Charlotte wasn't interested in dating you."

"That's true but that's not saying that I didn't want to keep trying my luck. I mean, we were working together a lot and I couldn't help being drawn to her. To know Charlotte was to love her, am I right?"

"She was one of a kind," Luna murmured in agreement but shifted against the "ick" from Scott's comment. Obviously, recognizing consent wasn't a huge concern in Scott's life if he continued to press his luck with Charlotte even after she turned him down.

Scott must've realized he'd hit the wrong chord because he was quick to clarify. "In the end, I respected Charlotte's wishes and backed off with no hard feelings but by that point I realized it'd never been a good fit between me and the other person. When I rebuffed her attempts at a reconciliation, she blamed Charlotte instead of putting the blame where it belonged, with me, and to be honest, that part bothered me more than the rejection. Charlotte didn't deserve anything but the best. I'm not one to wax poetic about anyone but Charlotte was the kind of person who made even people like me want to start being a better person. That's a rare individual."

"What do you mean, 'people like you?'"

His chagrined chuckle was telling as he admitted, "I'm not exactly known for my generous heart. I've always had a head for business and sometimes that's taken precedence over people's feelings when I'm dealing with situations. I'm trying to work on that aspect of myself but change comes slowly. Like I said, Charlotte made me want to be better and I'll always be grateful to her for that."

Luna accepted Scott's answer, realizing it probably took a lot for him to be vulnerable, but she had to get the ex-girlfriend's version of his story, too. No stone left unturned. "I'm going to need the name of your ex-girlfriend," she said with an apologetic expression.

"Is that really necessary? That's just likely to dredge up more bad blood and Charlotte doesn't deserve anything that could possibly tarnish her memory. She was a damn good woman."

"I won't let that happen," Luna promised. "But I have to corroborate your story."

"Of course," he said, understanding, but he wasn't happy about it as he revealed the name. "Brianne Wilton."

Luna vaguely remembered her—short, bleached blonde with a thing for bad boys. Last she heard, Brianne was dating the pool hall owner who got busted for running drugs through the business. Not precisely Scott Johnson's persona. "You got a contact number?"

"Sure, but you're going to have a hard time catching her. She's a travel nurse and her schedule is erratic. It's one of the reasons I realized it was never going to work between us. Maybe it's selfish of me but I need someone who's going to be around when I need them."

Maybe it was selfish, or he was just self-aware enough to know what he was looking for and didn't want to settle.

Either way, it wasn't her place to judge. After taking down Brianne's contact information, she returned to Charlotte. "Seeing as you and Charlotte spent so much time together for the chili cook-off preparations, do you know of anything happening behind the scenes of the Leicki family that might've been cause for concern?"

Scott shook his head. "They seemed real happy. Since I've had a little time to reflect, I think I was a little jealous. Charlotte was a good wife and Roger seemed like a real nice guy. They had the kind of marriage we all secretly want—the ultimate partnership, the true 'ride or die.'"

Luna looked up sharply, narrowing her gaze at his word choice.

Scott's flush of embarrassment prompted a hasty correction. "What I mean to say is, they were a good team. Damn, sometimes my dad was right on the money when he said my foot was always a better fit in my mouth than my tongue. I'm sorry."

Luna let the tension go in her shoulders. She couldn't keep being this touchy when it came to Charlotte. *Focus on the case.* "You can't think of any reason why someone might've broken into the house and killed the entire family?"

Scott's expression crumpled into helpless distress for drawing a blank. "I wish I had the answers. Sometimes the luck of the draw is cruel. I can't imagine a worse case of being in the wrong place at the wrong time. Best guess? Probably drug-related. If you ask me, drugs are ruining this country."

"Drugs?"

"When you hear about crimes like this, it usually turns out to be addicts trying to fund their next fix. The Leickis were comfortable and their wealth wasn't a secret. Sometimes people covet what they don't have and find the easiest way to get it for themselves."

An easy line to draw, except drug addicts usually grabbed the low-hanging fruit to pawn, and bypassing Charlotte's fat diamond ring seemed a red flag in the face of that theory.

However, it wasn't common knowledge that the perps left behind items typically taken in burglaries, and Luna wasn't about to share that intel now.

She wanted to talk to Brianne and find out if her story matched Scott's, even though it seemed highly unlikely Scott had anything to do with the Leicki murders.

No stone left unturned. Not even the smallest pebble.

"You stand to inherit quite a bit of money," the attorney said as he pulled the paperwork free from the folder. "Your sister had a separate fund created for you, as well as the boys, but seeing as the boys are deceased, the entire estate reverts to you."

Benjamin felt sick. He didn't want the money. Maybe he could find a way to donate it to a charity that Charlotte championed. It didn't seem right to enjoy one red cent of that money. Better to put it to good use elsewhere.

Curious, Benjamin asked, "Do you know what Roger did for a living?"

"Something in computers," the attorney answered without looking up from the paperwork as he sorted the stacks that needed signatures. "The man did well for himself. Well enough to dabble in the stock and crypto market. Your brother-in-law had a head for business."

That didn't sit well with Benjamin. He may have had a head for turning a dollar, but he sure as hell didn't consider that whatever he was doing was dangerous.

Sure, he didn't have proof yet, but his gut was never wrong.

He counted on Luna to dig into Roger's financials and find the real trail worth chasing—the money.

"I guess I went into the wrong career," he said. "I never realized computer work was so lucrative."

"You and me both," the attorney chuckled, adding, "but Roger did pretty well for himself. In addition to the stocks and bonds, crypto and of course the ranch, the cash assets are substantial."

"The money doesn't mean anything to me," he said. "I want whoever killed my family to pay for their crime."

The attorney sobered quickly. "Yes, yes, of course," he said, pushing the first sheaf of papers toward Benjamin. "I've marked each area that needs a signature."

Benjamin grabbed the pen from the marble penholder and started to sign but paused as he followed that thought process, saying, "Are you under any legal obligation to make a report of some kind if you thought your client was dealing in illegal business transactions?"

The attorney stilled, his gaze narrowing. "May I ask where are you going with this?"

"Nowhere, just asking. I mean, you said it yourself, you never thought computer work was this lucrative and yet, Roger was pulling down some serious cash. Weren't you worried that if he were involved with something shady that it could come back on you as his financial advisor and legal counsel?"

The attorney leaned back in his chair and steepled his fingers. "Mr. Reeves, I can assure you if I thought there was any illegal activity going on, I wouldn't sit on that concern. Mr. Leicki was an upstanding community member, a good father and husband. I had zero reason to question his character."

"Have you never heard of the saying 'Watch who you reveal your backstage face to'? Maybe you never saw the real Roger Leicki."

"I assure you, that's not the case," the attorney returned,

putting the subject to bed as he gestured to the paperwork. "Your signature, please."

The sudden frost in the room was hard to miss. Benjamin had rubbed the man the wrong way, but he didn't care. He wasn't here to make friends. If he needed to ruffle feathers, he'd shake up the roost everywhere he went. Someone in this town knew what had happened to Charlotte and her family; the key was to press on the right people.

But maybe he shouldn't go making enemies right away. He finished signing and offered an apology. "Hey, I'm sorry if I came on strong. It's hard to know what to think, you know? I didn't know Roger all that well and we didn't really connect when I was around. I loved my sister and I'm trying to make sense of something that doesn't make sense."

That helped soften the man's body language. "I understand. If I can help put your mind at ease, Roger was a good man—solid and dependable. Maybe he wasn't a hands-on kind of guy like you seem to be but he was a good provider and he adored your sister. No one loved Charlotte like Roger did. They had a love story worth remembering."

"Thanks, it's good to know she was happy," he said, blinking back the sting in his eyes. He rose, ready to leave. "You have my number if there's anything else I need to sign."

"Of course. It'll take several weeks to process but I'll let you know when the funds will be released."

Again, Benjamin didn't care about the money. Just talking about it made him want to puke, but the man was doing his job, so he wasn't going to make him feel bad about it.

He waved his goodbye and let himself out of the attorney's office, almost knocking over a blonde woman walking at a clip in heels and a short skirt down the sidewalk.

"Watch where you're going," she screeched as he caught her and pulled her upright, so she didn't go sprawling. She disentangled herself with a huff and a wrinkled curl of her lip until she saw him.

Then her attitude changed real quick.

She was mid-purr with flirty eyes when Luna's voice at his back interrupted introductions.

"Brianne Wilton? You're exactly the person I need to talk to."

Brianne's playful demeanor evaporated when she saw Luna. Straightening her skirt, she readjusted her purse on her shoulder with an annoyed expression to ask, "And you are?"

"Detective Luna Griffin with the Cottonwood Police Department. Would you mind coming with me to the station to answer a few questions?"

Benjamin eyed the salty blonde with new interest. Why did Luna want to talk to her?

"Questions about what?"

"It'll just take a few minutes of your time," Luna answered with a perfunctory smile.

"Maybe after, we could get a cup of coffee. We can walk together if you want," Benjamin offered Brianne with a smile, almost feeling Luna stiffen beside him. He wasn't interested in the woman, but her interest in him was plain as the nose on his face. If Luna needed her cooperation, he'd get it for her.

One way or another.

Even if it meant leading the woman on.

Chapter 8

Luna ignored the hot zing of awareness that raced through her at Benjamin's offer, choosing instead to focus on the victory of the moment. She needed to talk to Brianne Wilton about her involvement with Scott Johnson, and it was good fortune that she'd caught sight of the woman at the perfect moment. She'd left the station to grab a coffee and found Brianne and Benjamin talking outside in the main square.

She let Benjamin watch the interview from behind the safety glass. It wasn't protocol, and her chief had given her the side-eye, but Luna was given a lot of latitude with all the attention on the case, and her boss trusted her judgment. For now anyway. If she kept pushing her luck, that could change. She'd have to stay mindful that the blurred lines didn't become unrecognizable.

Brianne was superficially attractive, but a faint bitterness to her energy chipped away at whatever natural beauty she possessed. Luna could see Brianne being the kind of person to get catty about losing out to Charlotte. Whereas Charlotte's beauty had radiated from the inside out, Brianne's personality was like finding a rotten spot in an apple had ruined the entire fruit.

"What's this about?" Brianne asked.

"I need to confirm a few details about your relationship with Scott Johnson."

"Why?"

"Can you tell me about your relationship?"

"I can tell you that's my personal business and I don't know why the Cottonwood PD would want to know."

"I'm sure you've heard by now about the Leicki family being murdered," Luna said. "Scott Johnson was one of the last people to see Charlotte and he mentioned there might be some bad blood between you and him."

Brianne shifted in her chair, uncomfortable. "Yeah? So?"

"Can you share in your own words what happened between you?"

"What does my personal business have to do with the Leickis' murders?"

Luna drew a deep breath, praying for patience. This woman could make a saint snap. "Your name was brought up during a conversation with Scott, that you may have been upset about the way your relationship ended," she answered pointedly.

Brianne paled, appalled. "I didn't have anything to do with those murders. Did Scott say something about me that would make you think otherwise?"

"Please, tell me in your own words what happened between you and Scott."

"I mean, what's to tell? We broke up. As far as I know breaking up with a lying cheat isn't a crime, right? I don't understand why I'm being questioned unless Scott said something that would make you suspicious about my involvement with the Leicki murders, which is, frankly, ridiculous. I barely knew them."

"Scott thought you might be behind some disturbing rumors about Charlotte and him that recently surfaced. I'd like to know if it's true."

Brianne seamed her lip, her hard gaze narrowing as she stiffened with guilt, immediately defensive with her response. "Did he tell you that he was promising to marry me? That every single day he was treating me like a queen, acting like a ring was in my future and then all of a sudden, he just dropped me like a bad habit because of *her*? No warning, nothing. Just done. How was I supposed to feel about being dumped like that?"

"Your feelings were hurt," Luna supplied, giving Brianne room to keep talking. "That's understandable."

"That's an understatement," Brianne returned with a scowl. "I barely even knew who she was until she started sniffing around Scott, bringing him home-baked cookies and shit like that. Betty Crocker, my ass. I knew exactly what she was up to. My grannie always said the fastest way to a man's heart was through his stomach but I can't cook so I had to find other ways to get a man to notice me. It's pretty embarrassing to realize you got beat out by a woman bearing apple crumble pie."

"Charlotte loved to bake," Luna said. "She baked for everyone. Not just Scott."

"Yeah well, I know when a woman is scheming. It's a sixth sense thing."

"And you think Charlotte was interested in Scott?"

"Of course. Who wouldn't be? He's the best catch in this trash town. Good-looking, rich and still man enough to know how to handle himself in a fight. Sometimes rich guys get soft but not Scott—that man is pure muscle."

Luna didn't need to know about Scott's muscles. "By all accounts, Charlotte was happily married and the only reason she was spending so much time with Scott was because she was working with him to move the chili cook-off to the ranch."

"Look, I know everyone thought Charlotte was Little Miss Goody Two-Shoes but she wasn't all that sweet."

"And what makes you say that?"

Brianne spat back with enough heat to fry a circuit, "Because I caught her and Scott *kissing*!"

Luna tried to hide her surprise. That didn't sound like the Charlotte she knew. Disturbed, she pressed, "Are you sure?" hoping for a misunderstanding of some sort.

Brianne folded her arms across her chest with a glare. "You'd have to be deaf, dumb and blind to not see Scott's arms wrapped around the woman's body and his tongue down her throat. I know what I saw."

"Did you confront them?"

"Damn right I did. Jerk tried to play it off like it wasn't what it looked like but I'm not stupid. Charlotte ran off like the guilty whore she was and then, surprise, surprise, Scott wanted to get back together but I told him to piss off. No man treats *me* like an option. Ever."

That wasn't the version of the story Scott told. "So, if you're the one who turned Scott down, why were you mad at Charlotte?"

Brianne took a minute, and for a brief second, Luna saw a sliver of vulnerability as she admitted, "Because I thought I could love him. I mean, like *really* love him, not for his money but for the man I thought he was. For the first time ever, I was actually considering the whole 'family picture over the mantle' kind of life. I was considering sacrificing *this*—" she gestured emphatically to her flawless figure "—for kids. Can you imagine?" The disgust in her tone was hard to miss. "Like I said, everything seemed great. Until she came around." She sniffed a little, as the mask returned. "But whatever, his loss."

Brianne had the emotional depth of a puddle but Luna didn't sense anything dishonest about her answers. Privately, Luna was still reeling from the revelation of Scott and Charlotte's kiss. She knew the danger of putting someone on a pedestal but it was difficult to pull back from that inclination when it came to Charlotte now that she wasn't here to defend herself.

Luna drew a deep breath before asking, "Do you have anything that can back up your version of the story?"

Brianne smirked, unsurprised. "You want the receipts? I got them, right here." She pulled out her cell phone, quickly found what she was looking for, and thrust it at Luna to read. "Here they are, in all their cringey glory."

Luna scanned the text exchange with a troubled expression. Polar opposite from the story Scott had told her. Why would he lie? Was it just his ego, or was he hiding something else?

"Now tell me who's lying?" Brianne said, tucking her phone back into her purse. "I don't care what Scott told you. I'm telling you, they were hooking up or at the very least messing around and that's a fact."

Brianne's text messages were damning enough proof that Scott lied to Luna's face. Had he lied to protect Charlotte? But why?

"Thank you for your cooperation," she murmured. "You're free to go."

Brianne scooped her purse up and adjusted it on her shoulder, saying before leaving, "Look, I don't blame Charlotte for shooting her shot. I probably would've done the same if I were in her position, but it hits different when the shoe is on the other foot, that's all." She seemed to realize her attitude hadn't been charitable earlier and shifted her energy. "I'm real sorry to hear about what happened to Charlotte and her family. No one deserves to go out like that. Especially the kids."

Luna nodded in agreement. "We're doing all we can to find out who did it."

"Good luck," Brianne said, pausing to add, almost as an afterthought, "I'm not saying Scott had anything to do with Charlotte's murder but if you know Scott, you know he's got a temper. I was honestly surprised someone as soft as Charlotte could handle someone like him but I guess I was wrong. Anyway, not my circus, not my monkeys. Gotta run. I have a hair appointment in ten minutes. Guess coffee with the hot new guy will have to wait."

And then she was gone.

Luna joined Benjamin in the room behind the glass.

"My sister wasn't having an affair," Benjamin said, his expression stony. "She wasn't that kind of person."

"Brianne saw something between Scott and Charlotte, even if it was just a kiss. It was something. Something that Scott conveniently left out."

"So let's go back to this Scott guy and see if he needs his memory jogged."

By the menace in Benjamin's tone, Luna had no doubt Benjamin would happily use his fists to help Scott with his memory, and that was the last thing Luna wanted, especially if her chief caught wind of how much access Luna was allowing Benjamin on this case. She said, "With this new information, it's enough to bring Scott in for formal questioning. If he was having an affair with Charlotte, it puts him in the crosshairs for a motive."

Benjamin didn't want to wait. "Let's bring him in now. No sense in waiting."

"I have a few more people I want to talk to before I bring Scott in," Luna said, cautioning Benjamin to slow his roll. "I know it feels like the process is interminably slow but cases need time to build or else the perps get off on a technicality."

"I'll save the state a few bucks on a trial. One bullet will solve everything. All I need is a clear shot."

Luna cast a sharp glance toward Benjamin at his growled threat. "I'm going to pretend I didn't hear you say that," she warned, gesturing for him to follow her into the office and hoping no one had caught his little quip. Once inside, she closed the door with a stern look. "Don't make me regret letting you in so closely on this case, Benjamin. If I was smart, I'd keep you on the outside because you're too emotionally involved but I thought I was doing you a kindness. With comments like that, it makes me wonder if I screwed up. I can't have you talking like you're going to go vigilante. One screw up from you could cost me my job because I'm the one vouching for you."

Benjamin's expression darkened as a storm raged across his face, but he reined in whatever was on his tongue and jerked a short nod in understanding. "Sorry, that was out of line," he admitted gruffly, his cheeks pinking slightly. "Won't happen again."

Mollified, Luna accepted his apology, choosing to move on. She'd made her point—no sense in stomping it into the ground—but a general uneasiness remained that made her second-guess her instincts. If Benjamin let his emotions get the better of him, he could tank her entire case. There were solid reasons why people close to the victims were left outside the investigation circle, and she'd never before found herself with a reason to break that protocol. Chewing the side of her cheek, she shared, "I want to talk to the other chili cook-off committee members about the move to Johnson Ranch. If anyone would know what was happening behind closed doors, it would be those working closest to Charlotte."

Benjamin was immediately on board, ready to go. "Daylight's wasting. Let's do it." When she hesitated, Benjamin paused with a frown. "Everything okay?"

No, she wanted to answer. He'd given her a good reason to insert some appropriate distance between him and the case, but the fact that she didn't want to was worrisome. Instead of ripping the Band-Aid off cleanly, she shook her head and went with a warning instead. "You can come but only if you promise to behave yourself. I can't have you threatening people, no matter what we find out. Can I trust you to control yourself?"

"I'll do my best," he said.

"I need something better than that flimsy offer."

Benjamin inhaled a long breath, as if weighing the options of his potential handling of her request, and slowly nodded, saying, "I won't do anything to jeopardize the case."

Luna accepted his answer with a short nod. "Good. Then, yes, you can come." She locked up her office and they headed out. She told herself that having Benjamin close was better than having him roaming the streets trying to do his own investigation, but there was another thought—completely unwelcome and far more discomfiting—that lurked in the back of her mind.

And it had everything to do with Brianne Wilton identifying Benjamin as a suitable target.

Somehow that made her hackles rise when it shouldn't matter at all.

Messing around with Benjamin wasn't an option. Ever.

Benjamin grudgingly admired the way Luna stayed unruffled under pressure. His blood pressure had spiked the second that woman had started bad-mouthing Charlotte, but Luna had stayed cool as a cucumber. She would've done well in interrogation if she'd gone the military route.

He felt terrible for letting his mouth run away with him. She was right to call him out, but he was embarrassed for letting his emotions get the better of him. Everything about Charlotte's murder case had him on edge.

After a quick phone call, they found one of the committee chairs for the chili cook-off, Tim Parsons, who also happened to be volunteering down at the senior center today, serving up lunches to the senior citizens.

Tim, a city retiree with a slim build, a balding head and an infectious laugh seemed to have a smile permanently etched on his face, making him the perfect volunteer for most community events. He also threw himself into each event with a zeal that most people couldn't match, so he was always first on the volunteer call list.

Luna waved and smiled at Tim, who motioned for a helper to relieve him. Then he removed his apron and joined them. "Hello, sugar, you're looking like the picture of health these days," he said to Luna, his gaze darting to Benjamin. "And who is your gentleman friend?"

"Tim, this is Benjamin Reeves, Charlotte's older brother. He's in town for the time being."

Tim's expression dimmed, and for the first time, Luna saw Tim's smile fade to nothing. "Sad business. I'm sorry I missed the funeral. It's my private shame, but I cannot stomach that final goodbye. It's too much. Much too much."

"I don't much like them myself," Benjamin said, letting the old guy off the hook. "I'm sure Charlotte would understand."

"Yes, I'm sure she would. Your sister was an angel. Straight angel. Never known anyone with a bigger heart, that's for sure."

"I appreciate that," Benjamin said, his throat threatening to close. "Means a lot to know she touched a lot of hearts."

"That she did." Tim paused a minute before venturing, "What can I do you for?" trying to find his bearings again. "Surely you didn't come to eat beans and corn bread because that's what we're serving today, though, I'll admit, they're pretty good. Had a bowl earlier. Had to taste test for quality, of course."

"Actually, I was hoping to talk to you about the chili cook-off plans," Luna said, surprising Tim.

"Surely there are more important things to work on," Tim said, confused. "Bless your heart for caring so much but I think we'd rather you spend your energy on solving that terrible crime. It's sitting on the whole community like a dark cloud."

"Bear with me. I need to ask you something that might seem a little inappropriate but I can promise you, it's important."

"Well, shoot, okay then. I'll do my best."

"Was there anything going on between Charlotte and Scott Johnson that might've been inappropriate?"

"Honey, I don't traffic in gossip," Tim said gravely. "Shame on whoever might've suggested that our sweet Charlotte was anything but an angel."

"Having an affair doesn't make people evil," Luna reminded Tim quietly. "It just makes them flawed humans, like everyone else."

Tim bit his lip, bothered by the conversation. Either he knew something, and he didn't want to share, or he was so torn up about the idea of Charlotte being less than a saint that he couldn't deal. Benjamin didn't know which way he hoped the sail turned.

Finally, Tim's mouth firmed as he shook his head. "Nope, I didn't hear nothing about Charlotte being inappropriate. She was a loyal married woman and loved her husband. She'd never do anything to bring shame on her family. Never."

Even though Luna saw the text exchange between Scott and Brianne, Brianne might have seen something and misinterpreted what'd happened. Maybe Scott had tried to kiss

Charlotte, but then Charlotte had set him straight and sent him on his way.

Benjamin asked Tim, "So, is the chili cook-off still going to be held at the Johnson Ranch?"

"Oh no, Charlotte changed her mind two weeks before she died. Now we're working on getting some repairs done to the fairgrounds in time. We've managed to find some volunteers to do some of the work so we might just make it."

Luna frowned. "Wait, Charlotte changed her mind?"

"Sure did. Shocked us all. But we figured it was probably a logistic thing and frankly, some of the committee members weren't thrilled at the idea of having it at the Johnson Ranch anyway but no one was going to tell Charlotte no. Shoot, she had a way of getting people onboard with plans that they weren't in favor of but seeing as she'd already set in motion switching back to the fairgrounds, it was an easy decision. Thankfully, the committee hadn't signed any contracts yet with the Johnson Ranch so there was no legal obligation to stay with the ranch."

"Thank you, Tim, that's helpful," Luna said, nodding to Benjamin, sharing the same thought. It seemed like that Scott fellow had a few things to clear up from his earlier talk with Luna.

And Benjamin wanted to be behind the glass when that interview went down.

Chapter 9

Luna's mind was elsewhere after dinner, lingering too long on Benjamin if the truth be told when it should've been on her scheduled interview with Scott Johnson tomorrow.

Lying about an affair didn't make someone a killer, just as lying about the details of a breakup to protect a fragile ego didn't make anyone a killer either.

But the fact that he'd lied to her face without batting an eye chewed at the back of her mind.

And yet, her thoughts were on Benjamin.

She'd felt a hot surge of jealousy when Brianne had practically served herself up on a platter as an all-you-can-eat-buffet for Benjamin's enjoyment, and that bothered her.

It was unprofessional to think of Charlotte's brother in any way that wasn't strictly related to the case.

But he was a hard man to overlook.

A sigh escaped her mouth as Sayeh walked past, causing her to stop in her tracks and double back. "That sounds promising," Sayeh said, settling on the sofa beside Luna. "Was that heavy sigh personal or professional?"

"It was nothing I want to talk about."

"Ah, personal," Sayeh surmised, nodding. "Please feel free to elaborate."

Luna gave her sister a look. "I'd rather not. It's nothing. My headspace is all over the place right now."

But Sayeh wasn't giving up. "C'mon, throw me a bone. My brain is atrophying here and boredom is threatening to destroy what's left of my sanity after spending hours on end with Dad. Have pity on me."

Despite herself, Luna chuckled. It'd been a long time since she'd had anyone to talk with about "girl" stuff, and it wasn't like she and her sisters regularly got on the phone and gabbed, but maybe she'd lost track of how important it was to have a sounding board. If Luna had made their friendship a priority, Charlotte would've happily filled that role. Luna had always worn the badge of *workaholic* proudly, but in the light of Charlotte's death, her preoccupation with work felt like a hollow win.

What a sad mess. A hiccup of grief burned under her breastbone. Sayeh seemed to understand and softened her smart-ass attitude. "You can talk to me. I'm the best at keeping secrets, I promise," she said with a slight tease in her voice. "What's going on?"

She shrugged, admitting, "I guess I've started to realize that my work/life balance is a hot mess." Even worse than her dismal social life was her growing attraction to Benjamin, but how could she divulge that little nugget when she was the big sister and supposed to be setting the example?

"It can't be that bad," Sayeh promised, nudging her. "Spill it. You'll feel better."

Maybe Sayeh was right. Talking about her feelings might help them go away. Likely some twisted form of grief caused her to be attracted to Benjamin right now, she rationalized. If that were the case, she could handle waiting out the uncomfortable tide of feelings until he inevitably left town.

But it'd been a long time since she'd been attracted to anyone who left her flustered and out of sorts. She wasn't some lovesick teenager, and it wasn't a good look to act like one.

"It's this case," she blurted, biting down on any mention of Benjamin. *Chicken.* "It's messing with my head."

Sayeh seemed disappointed it wasn't juicier but nodded. "Cottonwood isn't exactly a crime hub. Cases like this don't happen often. It's natural to be overwhelmed."

Sayeh as the voice of reason? Good Lord, that had to be the first sign of the apocalypse. "I used to wish there was a little more action to chase after but I feel naive for thinking something so reckless. I want life to go back to the way it was before this happened—quiet and boring."

"A case like this has a way of leaving a permanent mark," Sayeh said sadly. "Nothing will ever be the same. I'm sorry."

Luna knew Sayeh was right, even though Luna was fighting the knowledge.

"Any new leads in the case?"

"Not exactly, but there are some troubling things that've popped up."

"Like what?"

She shouldn't talk about the case with anyone aside from investigators but despite her anger management issues, Sayeh was an accomplished FBI agent and Luna could use some fresh eyes. What the hell—she seemed to be playing fast and loose with all the rules lately, so what was one more? "Scott Johnson lied to my face about his relationship with Charlotte. They might've been having an affair."

"Most people lie about that," Sayeh quipped. "No one

likes to be held accountable for their actions or be called out as the bad guy. I mean, how's it going to look to find out that he was having an affair with the recently murdered woman? Even if he's only guilty of being a douche, the suspicion alone could kill his reputation in a small town."

"True," Luna murmured, the gears turning. "But is the flip side of that argument that he lied because he was responsible for Charlotte's murder? Seems unlikely. What would his motive be?"

"Jealousy? Crime of passion? Men have flipped their lids over less," Sayeh said.

"Yeah, but to kill Charlotte's entire family? Seems a little much for a crime of passion."

Sayeh saw Luna's point. "Were they business partners or something?"

"No, Charlotte wanted to move the chili cook-off away from the fairgrounds and the Johnson Ranch had the classy look she was going for."

"So, they hadn't really known each other before negotiations started for the cook-off?"

"Not that I can tell." Luna added another troubling point. "Scott also didn't share that negotiations had fallen through for the cook-off before Charlotte's death. Now, the cook-off is back at the fairgrounds. Don't you think he would've mentioned that when we were talking? Seems weird to leave that out."

"Sounds like a shady guy," Sayeh agreed. "I'd dig a little harder into his background, see what shakes out."

"He's coming in tomorrow for formal questioning," Luna said. "I want to see if he comes clean and then I'll get a better idea the direction I need to go. I don't want to go making an enemy if I don't need to."

"Can't be afraid of that," Sayeh said. "You're the law. It's a lonely field for a reason."

"Maybe for someone in your career, but this is Cotton-wood. I see these people every day, chat with them in the grocery store, and end up bidding on the same fundrais-ing baskets. Small towns don't work the same as big-city politics. The dynamics are far more entangled."

"I remember," Sayeh returned quietly. "Which is an-other reason why I wanted to get out of this place. How do you breathe with so many people in your business?"

"I don't mind," Luna answered with a short smile. "I like feeling connected."

Sayeh let it go, returning to the case. "What did the hus-band do for a living?"

"Some kind of computer guy. Not really clear on his actual job but tomorrow I plan to make some calls in to his place of employment. Hopefully, they can explain to me in layman's terms what his job entailed."

Sayeh caught the troubled frown. "What's that for?"

"It's probably nothing, but Benjamin doesn't seem to think that Roger was getting paid simply to do computer work. I guess he wasn't a big fan of Roger's but he doesn't have much more than a hunch for me to chase after."

"There's big money in computer work, especially the high-tech stuff."

"Yeah, that's true. I guess I just need more information about what he did before I start chasing leads that go no-where."

"Probably wise," Sayeh agreed, switching gears so quickly Luna almost fell for it. "So, what's the real reason you're preoccupied tonight?"

"I—um, it's nothing. Just tired. It's been a long day. I think I'll turn in early," she said, rising from the sofa with a smile. "Thanks for the chat. I needed that."

Sayeh let it go.

Which was good, because Luna wasn't ready to talk about what was going on in her head.

It would pass if she gave it enough time.

Anyway, she had plenty to focus her attention on.

Like her interview with Scott Johnson.

Benjamin's nerves were strung taut. He needed to find something to occupy his mind that didn't involve the case or Luna, for that matter.

One thing he knew for sure—sitting in that rental by himself didn't do much to silence the noise in his head or lessen the slowly increasing sense of panic that Charlotte's killer was out there somewhere, laughing with the smug certainty that no one was going to catch him or her.

Also, another growing issue left him uncomfortably aware of a certain small-town detective.

Hell, it'd been a long time since anyone had turned his head like Luna did—he wasn't exaggerating when he told himself the feelings were unwelcome and yet they took up residence in his head anyway.

How could he not notice a woman like her? Tough as nails, yet somehow still kindhearted, those deep dark eyes enough to happily drown in if given half the chance.

And that bothered him.

Best way he knew to distract himself from a bad idea was to seek out a new one.

He stepped into The Cattlemen Pub, a local brewery that hadn't been around when he'd been a resident of Cottonwood, and gave it a good look.

Playing a little too hard to the touristy side of town, but he didn't hold that against the place, especially when he heard it was a great choice for a burger and a cold beer, which sounded like the right decision at the moment.

He stepped up to the bar and ordered a pale ale, swiveling on his stool to people-watch.

Country music playing overhead from hidden speakers, coupled with laughter and the buzz of conversation, created an atmosphere that soothed his ragged nerves. By the first sip of his beer, he was feeling better about his decision to venture out, which he never could've imagined he would be willing to do in this town ever again.

But this Cottonwood seemed different than the one he'd left behind—another jarring realization that had him thinking in all sorts of ways.

Charlotte had always been after him to give Cottonwood a second chance. But he hadn't been willing to listen. Bless her ever-loving heart; even with his closed-off attitude, she'd never stopped trying.

But it couldn't be all roses and strawberry pie—someone in this place had killed Charlotte—so he wasn't about to wipe the slate clean on account of a decent brewery.

Cottonwood was batting a thousand in the "Shitty Memories" game of life and Luna was its only saving grace as far as he was concerned.

A table of women briefly snagged his attention, their raucous laughter giving "Girls' Night Out" vibes, but not even the curvy redhead flashing him a flirty smile did much to hold his gaze for long.

Nothing like Luna. *What the hell is wrong with you? Snap out of it.* Thinking about Luna Griffin in any way but professional was a one-way road to messed up. He was here for one purpose and it wasn't where his mind kept stubbornly going.

He sighed. *Gonna be a long night.*

Another man took the stool beside him, slight in build but wiry with muscle. He flagged the bartender, gesturing to Benjamin, saying, "Whatever he wants, next drink's on me," with a solemn expression.

Immediately wary but not wanting to be rude, Benjamin said, "I appreciate the hospitality but what's that for?"

"I promise you I'm not weird or coming on to you." The man extended a hand in welcome, introducing himself. "My name's Hank. I'm the ranch manager for the Johnson Ranch. I'm taking a wild guess that you're Ms. Charlotte's brother."

"I am," Benjamin confirmed, silently marveling at the power of the local grapevine. No doubt tongues had started wagging the minute he stepped onto Main Street. "How'd you know Charlotte?"

"We all knew Ms. Charlotte on account of her spending so much time with Mr. Johnson for that chili cook-off planning—right nice lady—and we're all sick inside at her passing. Word spread that you were in town and, well, you stand out so I put two and two together, figuring you were her brother."

"Nice to meet you, Hank. It's always good to hear how loved Charlotte was in this town."

"Ain't no one gonna speak bad about Ms. Charlotte. She used to bring those fancy French cookies to the ranch, enough for everyone to share. She never left no one out. She was something special."

A lump rose in Benjamin's throat. "That was Charlotte. Always thinking of everyone."

"Yeah, yeah, definitely. God broke the mold with her, you know?"

"Seems like."

"Cops got any leads on who did that terrible thing to her family?" he asked, his brow creasing in earnest. "I'd volunteer to be on the firing squad if they found who done it."

Tomorrow Luna was talking to Scott Johnson again. It seemed a stroke of good luck that the ranch manager was feeling chatty. Maybe he could divulge something about his boss that might prove useful.

"You and me both," he shared, lifting his glass for a drink. He didn't want to leak anything that might be important, not that they knew much, but Benjamin knew better than to take the risk. "They're working real hard on the case," he said. "They don't share many details with me, though."

"No? Surprising. You being the big brother and all. I don't know how you keep from shaking the information out of that woman detective. I tell you what, if Ms. Charlotte had been my kin, nothing would stop me from finding out what happened."

"She's doing her job and I stay out of her way," he said, protective of Luna. Not that she needed his protection, but he couldn't stop the immediate stiffening at even the slightest criticism. "So, working with Scott Johnson, what's that like? He a good boss?"

"Can't complain. The work is steady and the pay is fair. In this day and age, that's all you can ask for, right? Damn economy ain't no joke. Everyone's out there doing what they gotta do to survive but there's pride in a good day's work, you know?"

Benjamin nodded in commiseration but swapping complaints about inflation didn't interest him. If Hank didn't have anything useful to share that he could pass on to Luna, he wasn't into chitchatting either.

But Hank switched gears without Benjamin's prompting. He leaned in with a short look around him before saying, "Look, I just want to say, Ms. Charlotte was the best of people and we're all sick over what happened. Between you and me, I have a hard time thinking it was anyone local who did this. It had to be some drifter coming in and gone by morning because nothing else makes much sense. You know, like some random twist of fate that no one could've seen coming. A few years back I heard about some family in Billings that was murdered in the dead of night, without a single clue. Same as Ms. Charlotte. Turned out some parolee hopped up on drugs did the thing and had no memory of it the next day. I'm telling you, you can't trust nobody these days."

Benjamin shook his head. "My gut says whoever did it is right here in this town."

"What makes you so sure?" Hank asked, surprised.

"Just a feeling."

Hank digested Benjamin's comment, then released a heavy sigh. "You're right, could be. You never know."

"Either way, the truth will come out. It always does," he said with more confidence than he felt. "All it takes is one good lead to bust open a case."

Hank chuckled ruefully. "I want to believe that but Cottonwood's not exactly swimming in that high-tech forensics stuff they have in the city. Not likely they're going to find that one tiny speck of dirt that holds the key to finding who did the deed but I sure wish they would. Like I said, Ms. Charlotte didn't have a mean bone in her body."

Benjamin accepted the sentiment and Hank grabbed his beer as he slid off the stool. "Nice talking to you. I'm sure I'll see you around again sometime. Small town and all."

"Thanks for the drink," Benjamin said, watching the man leave and join a group of guys at a crowded table. They must all work at the Johnson Ranch, he mused, returning to his beer.

It felt good to know that Charlotte had touched so many lives in a positive way, but it hurt, too.

The ghosts of this town had chased him out and kept him far away from the one person who'd mattered.

Realizing he wasn't going to find what he was looking for at the crowded brewery, especially when curious stares kept drifting his way, he ordered the signature burger to go. As much as he'd thought he wanted a change of scenery, being around a bunch of people wasn't doing it for him either.

He paid his tab, grabbed his to-go bag and headed out, but as he approached his rental car, he noticed with a start all four tires were flat.

No, not flat.

Slashed.

He knelt beside the driver rear tire for a closer look. A clean jab with a sharp knife had punctured the sidewall. A quick inspection revealed the same technique for each tire.

Who the hell would do that? *Small-town punks with nothing better to do.*

Or was someone trying to send him a message?

Benjamin did a slow pivot, surveying the parking lot, looking for anyone who might've lingered, but whoever did this was long gone.

It was probably kids being jerks, he finally concluded as he pulled his cell to call a tow truck, but the prickling at the back of his neck felt like a warning he shouldn't ignore.

Chapter 10

Benjamin didn't know how he felt about the possibility that Charlotte had had an affair with the guy Luna had in the interrogation room. Once again, he observed from behind the darkened glass, his arms folded across his chest as he listened.

He had that slick attorney look that Benjamin immediately didn't like. It reminded him too much of military administration making decisions without any tactical experience that inevitably killed people.

But unlike Roger, who'd been a gangly, somewhat unattractive man, this guy was handsome in that rich kind of way.

A man like him wouldn't have any issues snagging the attention of any woman he put his sights on, maybe even Charlotte.

Hell, Benjamin didn't know enough about his sister to honestly know whether or not she'd stray. He wanted to believe that she wouldn't, but life was full of contradictions, and being an adult was messy.

Luna's voice cut into his thoughts as he tuned back into the interview.

"Scott, you had to know that Brianne wasn't going to back up your version of the breakup. She said that she caught you and Charlotte kissing. Why'd you lie?"

Scott's jaw worked as if he was prepared to lie again, but he held back, compressing his lips into a fine line as if struggling with something. Then, he came clean with a chagrined chuckle. "Okay, the truth is, maybe I wasn't so honorable in my initial approach to the situation, and when it came time to tell the story, I didn't like the way I came across."

"Altering the story doesn't change the facts, it only delays the discovery," Luna said. "What's the truth? What really happened? Were you and Charlotte having an affair, something that Brianne discovered?"

"Charlotte and I weren't having an affair," he said, but admitted, "Brianne did catch us kissing, though."

"Would you mind clarifying?"

"I'd rather not."

"I'm going to have to insist."

He sighed. "It's real simple. I was interested and Charlotte wasn't. I misread a situation and reacted by kissing her, which is right about the time Brianne walked in, but it wasn't reciprocated on Charlotte's part and I felt like a real jerk afterwards."

"How did Charlotte react?"

"She was embarrassed," he answered, "and worried that Brianne might tell Roger. I assured her that I'd make sure Brianne didn't say anything and immediately went to take care of the problem."

"Which is when you tried to make up with Brianne?"

"In a knee-jerk reaction, and in hindsight, I'm grateful she turned me down," Scott said. "It wasn't my finest moment. I was trying to placate Brianne to protect Charlotte but it ended up pissing Brianne off more and making the whole thing worse."

Sometimes men could be blindingly stupid. Luna put that aside for the moment. "You also didn't mention that the chili cook-off location change to the Johnson Ranch had been cancelled before Charlotte's death. Any reason why you didn't mention that?"

"Didn't seem important. We have business deals fall through all the time. Why would that one, a particularly small and unimportant one in the big scheme of things, warrant much attention?"

"If Charlotte was in any way involved, let me make those decisions. Is there anything else you'd like to share at this time? Perhaps to clarify or provide what might've been missed the first time around?"

Scott paused, bristling ever so slightly. "I came down here to help but this feels a lot like a different kind of questioning, Detective Griffin. Should I be calling my lawyer?"

"Do you have something to hide?"

"No."

"Then why would you need your lawyer?"

"Because this feels less like friendly cooperation and more like targeted interrogation."

Luna held his stare. Benjamin admired her strength, never wavering despite the growing hostility in the man's gaze. "We appreciate your cooperation. I'd like to believe we all have the same goal—finding the person responsible for the Leicki murders—and your willingness to be transparent is a big help."

Buttering the bread with such precision, playing to his ego. Benjamin watched the man's every move, every twitch. He didn't come off as overtly guilty—pissed off and insulted, but not guilty. However, accomplished liars knew how to mask their true emotions.

"Of course I want to help. That's why I'm here," Scott returned with a faint scowl. "But let's try to remember, we're all on the same side."

"And as such, we should endeavor to be honest with one another going forward, yes?"

"I don't like feeling schooled," he warned.

"I don't like being lied to."

The terse standoff between the two built tension, yet Luna held her ground. Then, she went full throttle, shocking Benjamin.

"I'm going to need your whereabouts on July 16 between the hours of 8:00 p.m. and midnight." She ended with, "And Mr. Johnson, if you can't account for your whereabouts, you might want to call that lawyer."

Hot damn, that's how you get things done.

Luna was taking a big risk—one the chief wasn't going to be happy about—but her instincts told her to press forward. Ordinarily, she might've pulled back but it was something Sayeh said about the law being a lonely profession for a reason. She couldn't be afraid to step on toes, even if those toes belonged to rich, influential men with a lot of reach.

There came a time for every person in law enforcement when a case dropped into their lap to test their mettle. It just so happened that her chance came at a personal cost. Finding Charlotte's killer was going to require stepping on toes—hell, maybe even smashing those toes into the ground, if need be.

And she was willing to do it.

She joined Benjamin in the interrogation viewing room. The pride in his eyes sparked an unwelcome but sweet warmth in the pit of her belly that she immediately stomped to ash.

"You might've made an enemy with that Johnson guy

but it was damn beautiful to watch you in action," Benjamin said with an unapologetic grin that sent trickles of awareness through her body. She flushed and ducked her head, waving away his praise, but he wasn't going to let it go.

"No, I'm being serious. You've shown me in so many ways that I was wrong about your ability to handle this case and I'm embarrassed that I doubted your skills."

"Benjamin, I appreciate the vote of confidence but let's not get ahead of ourselves. We're a long way away from finding anything that connects anyone to Charlotte's murder," she warned, not wanting to get his hopes up. Letting Benjamin down wasn't something she wanted to contemplate. "I want to catch who did this, just as much as you, but the reality is that I doubt it was Scott Johnson."

"How so?"

She shared her thoughts. "Well, I have a sneaking suspicion when I check his alibi, he'll come out clean as a whistle. He didn't even bat an eye when I asked him to account for his whereabouts. It doesn't make sense. Even if Scott and Charlotte were having an affair, it would take a sociopath to kill her entire family in a crime of passion. I think Scott might be a narcissist but I don't think he's a killer."

"Not even to protect his ego?"

"It would be a stretch."

Benjamin took a minute to chew on her answer, finally admitting, "I get it. Maybe I did get a little too excited when you caught him lying but it's frustrating to have nothing so far. I guess I needed a little hope to cling to. I met his ranch manager last night at the local brewery, a guy by the name of Hank. It seems everyone in town has an opinion on this case."

"Yeah? How so?" she asked.

"Hank was telling me it had to be the work of some homicidal drifter, same as that case in Billings or something like that, because it seemed highly unlikely a crime of that nature had been committed by a local."

"That's what we'd all like to think," she admitted. "Did he say anything about Scott as a boss?"

"A little. He said Johnson's a decent boss. The pay is good and the work stable. Usually when people get the chance to bitch about their boss they take it but Hank didn't have nothing bad to say. I guess that's a point in his favor, even if I still think the guy's an ass for chasing a married woman."

"I don't blame you," she said with a frown. "I'd like Scott Johnson to be guilty of something but I can't put my finger on what that could be. I have this feeling I can't shake though that I need to keep putting the pressure on."

"If it's there, don't ignore it. That feeling has kept me alive more times than I can count," he said.

Part of the insulation she felt from danger in her field was the relative comfort of a small bubble, but this case had shattered that illusion. Now everything had the potential for something far worse. Nothing felt safe.

As if reading her mind, Benjamin shared, "Yeah, something happened last night at the brewery that's been chewing on my backside and each time I try to brush it off as nothing, it keeps coming back."

She frowned with concern. "What happened?"

"When I left the brewery, I found all four tires on my rental slashed. At first thought, dumbass kids without any appreciation for the cost of the damage came to mind but there's something about it that doesn't feel right."

Luna agreed. "One tire makes sense but all four? That's excessive. Also, it would take more than one person to get the job done without being noticed. Seems planned out. I don't like this."

"I don't like to jump to conclusions but it creates more questions than gives answers," he admitted.

"Why would someone try to intimidate you?" she asked, troubled. "I don't like this at all."

"I'll be fine," he assured her, "but maybe this means you're getting too close to the person responsible for Charlotte's death and if that's the case, they can try and scare me off all they want because it ain't gonna work."

Benjamin's innate strength plucked at a long-silenced chord inside her, one she thought had disintegrated with dust and disuse but was vibrating with an intensity that made her feel alive again. She swallowed, her toes curling in the privacy of her shoes, struggling to find her bearings again. "I—"

But Benjamin must've picked up on that subtle tune because he jumped on it. "Let me make you dinner," he said.

"Dinner?" she repeated, dumbfounded. "What do you mean?"

He chuckled. "I mean, you and me enjoying some adult conversation over a decent meal prepared by yours truly. I promise I know my way around the kitchen. You won't die from my cooking."

She laughed at the unexpected humor. "I'm not worried about your cooking skills," she assured him. *I'm worried about how you make me feel when it's inappropriate given the circumstances. Politely decline.* "Um, I guess that would be okay. Sounds innocent enough," she said, ignoring her own advice. "Should I bring anything?"

"A robust red would be nice," he suggested. "I'm making steaks."

"Okay," she agreed, still spinning from her reckless decision. "Six thirty good?"

"Perfect."

She watched as he left the station, leaving her to wonder

how far down the rabbit hole she was willing to go when it came to Benjamin Reeves—because at the moment, she was free-falling straight to the earth's core.

And she didn't feel nearly as bad about it as she should.

Chapter 11

There were good decisions and there were decisions that weren't good but felt amazing—enjoying dinner with Luna fell into the latter category. The problem with those kinds of decisions was that they were contagious and had a tendency to multiply like daisies in a field.

The more time he spent with Luna, the more time he wanted to.

Dinner was finished and yet he wasn't ready to end the night. They left the table and sat next to each other on the sofa.

"Need a refill?" Benjamin offered, grabbing the wine bottle from the coffee table.

Luna hesitated, but the interest in her eyes gave away her answer before her mouth did. "Sure," she relented with a smile, holding out her glass as she admitted, "I probably shouldn't, but for the first time in a while I feel like I can breathe and it feels good."

"The case?"

"That and some personal stuff at home." She paused, glancing around the rental, quick to take the focus away from herself. "This is a nice place. People are making a nice side income renting out these old cabins. Tourists love the Montana experience."

He wanted to press but didn't. "Yeah, summer is an easy sell. Let them come back during winter and find out just how great it is to be snowed in for days on end with no electricity and nothing but a woodstove to cook and boil your water. I don't miss that experience at all."

"I know all about that life," she agreed, laughing. "We have a generator for exactly that purpose. My last big purchase was a snowblower for the driveway because my dad is too old to shovel and I hate doing it myself. Best money spent."

"Sounds like it to me."

"Tell me about Arizona."

"It's dry in the summer and where I'm at, it doesn't snow. Best part." He grinned, finishing off his glass. "Well, that and there's plenty of road for when I want to take the beast out to clear my head."

"And by beast, I assume you mean your motorcycle?"

"That's right," he confirmed with a proud nod. "A 2015 Victory Gunner, limited edition. Best adult purchase of my life. She's never let me down."

"I know next to nothing about motorcycles," she admitted, shooting a playful glance his way, "but I like the way your face lights up when you talk about yours."

Was she flirting with him? God, he hoped so. Otherwise, he was reading all the wrong signs. Bigger question, should he be flirting back? The warmth in the pit of his gut shut down his good sense. Was that a subtle blush pinking her cheeks as she ducked her gaze?

"Whoa, that wine went straight to my head, I think,"

she said, fanning herself with embarrassment. "Not sure what came over me. Sorry."

"No apologies needed," he said gruffly. "I don't mind."

She met his gaze for a long moment before looking away, clearing her throat. "Well, it's important to fill the well. Doing stuff that makes you happy," she clarified, returning to the subject of his motorcycle.

"Filling the well? Never heard of that. What does it mean?"

Luna was happy to explain, brightening as she said, "Oh, actually it's something Charlotte used to tell me on the rare occasions that we were able to chat. She was always after me to find a hobby that 'filled the well,' usually after reminding me that working to live wasn't the way to create a life." Luna chuckled at the memory, even though she winced with the recollection. "She was the kindest person. Always looking out for everyone else. I'm not just saying that either. You know, people often feel obligated to say complimentary things about people who died but Charlotte was the real deal. Nice to a fault."

Benjamin sobered. "Yeah, she was always like that. Makes me wonder if that's who she was by choice or by circumstance. Our dad was a real piece of crap. Charlotte was always the peacemaker, trying to calm Dad's temper so he didn't fly off the handle and knock us around. She was real good at figuring out what people needed."

"That she was," Luna murmured.

"Maybe if I'd had half of that gift, I would've spent less time going rounds with the old man. I can't stand a bully and that's all he was."

"I'm sorry. I remember him being a jerk and that's probably putting it nicely."

"Too nicely if you ask me. I'll say it for you—he was an asshole."

She nodded. "Yeah, seemed like it."

Benjamin's chuckle ended on a sigh. "But you know, Charlotte was so talented at trying to find the good in people. I loved that about her."

Luna admitted, "She was my best friend and I let life get in the way of our friendship." Tears crowded her sinuses. She wiped at the sting in her eyes, apologizing. "I'm sorry, I don't mean to ruin a lovely dinner."

He surprised her by gently wiping the sudden tear snaking down her cheek, assuring her, "You're not ruining anything."

They were sitting too close. He should put some distance between them, but he didn't want to. She smelled like apples and cinnamon. The scent teased his nostrils and made him want to lean in for a deeper sniff. "You smell good," he admitted in a husky whisper as they leaned toward one another, their lips angling for contact.

"Thank you," she said softly before meeting him the rest of the way, straight to his mouth.

Electric sparks tickled his insides and made him forget all the reasons why it wasn't a good idea to get too personal. Professional lines were important to keep straight but he couldn't recall why—at least not at the moment.

Luna was more damn beautiful than he ever remembered. Or maybe it was the maturity that sweetened the pot, but he couldn't stop staring all through dinner. Hell, he tried to keep his head in the right lane—what kind of jerk would think of kissing his dead sister's former best friend?—but he kept veering off course.

And then, that sliver of vulnerability was his undoing.

All good intentions went out the window. He had to kiss her.

And now that his lips had tasted hers, he didn't regret a second.

He could only hope she felt the same.

Remember that crossing boundaries always goes wrong.

More wise advice he wasn't going to follow. Not to-night anyway.

What were they doing? A sudden avalanche of anxi-ety threatened to ruin their stolen moment as Luna pulled away.

He understood but added, "There's something about you that I can't seem to shake and trust me, I've tried."

There was some relief knowing she wasn't alone, but a part of her wished he would've shut her down hard be-cause then it would've been easier to ignore her feelings. "It seems wrong, and then again, not. How does that make sense?"

"I don't know but it does," he said. "I know all the rea-sons why we shouldn't do this. Hell, we're not kids and letting hormones get the better of us isn't a good look on adults, but I haven't felt this kind of pull toward another person in longer than I can remember."

Luna nodded, putting a little more distance between them, trying to clear her head. "It could be grief. I mean, we have to be honest about the reality of what's happen-ing. We're both mourning Charlotte's death, and the need to be close to someone is a natural reaction to the reality of our own mortality."

Applying logic and reason to the situation was probably the right course of action, but it certainly didn't feel good.

"Probably," he grunted, but his troubled frown ques-tioned her logic. Still, he concluded with a disappointed "So, we should probably agree not to let this happen again."

She nodded, immediately unhappy about it. "Yeah, that would be the smart thing to do."

Noooo, that sounds like an awful plan. She wanted to taste those lips again and again until she lost the memory of any other lips. Couldn't exactly say that, though.

"I've never been accused of being particularly smart," he said, glancing her way. "But I guess there's a first time for everything."

Luna chuckled, enjoying his wry sense of humor in the face of something emotionally uncomfortable, but they needed to keep what was important in front of their feelings before things got out of hand. She straightened with a forced lightness to her tone. "Right, so, it was great, no complaints, but best to keep things professional." *Yay for emotional maturity.*

"Yeah."

"Yeah." A beat passed, and she could practically feel the disappointment growing between them.

He snagged her gaze, venturing, "Or…we could say to hell with the rules and just enjoy each other for the night."

Wild hope leaped in her chest and her palms slicked with sudden moisture as awareness prickled throughout her body. "Just for the night?" she repeated, feeling like a teenager about to break all the rules. "You think that's something we could handle?"

"We're mature adults. I think we could handle it," he assured her, believing it himself. "Neither of us are looking for that person to ride off into the sunset with, right?"

"God, no."

"Then, I think we can handle what happens between consenting adults."

The slow smile spreading across her mouth was all the encouragement Benjamin needed. He rose and held his hand out, inviting her to come with him. "The bed is much nicer than this old couch," he said.

If she was going to back out, now was the time, but she wasn't going to. She slid her hand into his as she rose. "I'm too old for making out on a couch," she said with a seductive grin. "Show me this bed."

He scooped her into his arms, carrying her the rest of the way to his bedroom.

"Such a gentleman," she murmured.

"When it's appropriate," he returned with a grin.

Something between them felt meaningful, more significant than a one-night stand.

Luna ignored the warning tingling at the back of her mind.

They could do this and remain professional.

And the best way to prove it was to put action behind the words.

Chapter 12

Luna hadn't meant to fall asleep in Benjamin's bed, but her eyes popped open at first light, realizing her sister and dad were probably going out of their minds with worry. Snatching her phone, she winced at the multiple missed calls from her sister and immediately checked the voice mail.

"Hey, uh, hate to be the bearer of bad news but something happened and Kenna showed up last night with Ty. She's got a nasty shiner. Details when you get home. Hope you're getting laid and not just falling asleep at your desk."

Luna's cheeks flared with heat, cursing under her breath for oversleeping. What had happened with Kenna that she'd bolt with her son back home? Seemed pretty damn serious. *Of all the friggen lousy timing.* Trying not to wake Benjamin, she eased from the bed, but years in the military had made him a light sleeper, and his eyes opened. "Everything okay?" he asked, his voice thick with sleep. Damn, he was sexy. He rubbed his eyes. "What time is it?"

"Everything is fine, I just overslept. I hadn't meant to stay all night. I have to get home."

"You want some coffee?" he offered, starting to get up, but she stopped him.

"No, I'm good. I really have to go. Family stuff to deal with." Scooping up her clothes, she quickly dressed. "Thank you…for everything. It was great."

That curve of his mouth made her want to kiss him all over again. *No, stop.* What they'd done was a onetime hall pass. "Okay, catch you later, dude."

Dude?

Even Benjamin's eyebrow rose in question.

"I'm sorry, I'm new to this," she blurted, trying to get out of there before she further embarrassed herself. "Bye!"

And then she hustled to her car, anxious to get away. She could only imagine what was running through Benjamin's head right now. This was an excellent example of why she didn't have one-night stands. What was the etiquette? How did one handle the morning after with any grace? That was probably a conversation for Sayeh's expertise, but Luna was awkward when talking about sex with her sisters. They didn't have that kind of relationship. She didn't have anyone she could talk to about those kinds of situations, which only made Luna realize just how much she'd insulated herself against social situations by using her career as a shield.

Probably something she ought to work on.

Later.

She walked into the house, relieved no one was awake just yet, and practically ran to the shower as if she were following her usual routine. By the time she finished, she had walked into the kitchen to find the house awake, sitting around the breakfast table.

Luna saw Kenna's black eye as she met her sister's miserable gaze over her coffee mug and instead turned her attention to her nephew, Ty, whom she hadn't seen in a few years.

"Auntie Luna," Ty shouted, jumping from his chair to wrap his arms around her waist.

"My favorite nephew!" Luna exclaimed, hugging him tightly. "Look how much you've grown! You're going to be taller than me soon."

"Probably," Ty said with an unabashed grin. "But that's okay, girls are supposed to be shorter than guys."

"Who said?" Sayeh piped in, glancing at Kenna. "Who's filling this poor boy's head with misogyny?"

"Don't start, Sayeh," Kenna implored with an eye roll, though the exhaustion in her face was hard to miss. What had her sister been through? And who the hell had busted up her face like that?

"I'm just saying," Sayeh returned with a shrug.

Coffee. STAT. Caffeine was required to deal with both sisters at the same time. She went straight to the kitchen and poured a mug, taking a moment to savor the jolt. She'd slept well, so well that she'd completely knocked out after round two. Her cheeks heated at the private thought, and she was immensely grateful Sayeh hadn't seen her reaction because the woman would never let her live it down without spilling details.

Okay, time to catch up on current events.

With perfect timing, their dad walked in and gestured to Ty. "C'mon, grandson, let's get the morning chores started."

"Can I drive the old truck?" Ty asked, excited.

"You sure can. Gotta learn sometime."

"Dad, he's only ten," Kenna reminded Bill, but they were already out the door.

Sayeh waved away Kenna's concern. "That old truck doesn't go faster than twenty miles per hour. He'll be fine."

Luna sat across from Kenna and got straight to the point. "What happened? Are you okay?"

Before Kenna could answer, Sayeh cut in. "Clearly she's not okay. Some jerk knocked her around. The question is, which jerk this time? And did she leave whoever did this to her or is she going to give him a second chance to knock her lights out, because let's face it, Kenna has the worst taste in men."

"Sayeh," Luna barked, not in the mood for her commentary. "Let Kenna talk."

Kenna's eyes watered, her feelings hurt, but she didn't bite back. "I left him. I left everything. I don't have anything but the clothes on our backs. We can't go back. It's home or…" She gulped, not finishing, but they got the idea.

Even Sayeh heard the difference in Kenna's voice. This time she meant it.

"Let's file a police report," Luna suggested gently, reaching for her sister's hand. "A paper trail is best for these kinds of things."

"I don't want anything to lead him back to me. I can't afford any kind of paper trail. Trust me, it's better that we just disappear."

"What kind of trouble are you in?" Sayeh asked.

"I have to do what I can to protect Ty," Kenna said by way of answering. "A fresh start is best for the both of us."

"It must be pretty bad if coming home to Cottonwood was your best option," Sayeh quipped.

Luna silently agreed, but she could tell Kenna wasn't going to share. Whatever had happened was going to remain behind her sister's lips, and Luna didn't have the time to pry. Instead, she focused on the now. "If this is a fresh start, let it be that, at least for Ty's sake, okay?"

If there was one thing they could agree upon, it was their shared love for that boy. Sayeh nodded, and Kenna followed. Satisfied, Luna exhaled and assured her sister, "We're here for you and Ty. Is there anything we should know about this guy? Like is he likely to follow you? I need to know if he's a threat."

She shook her head. "He doesn't know where I'm from. Thank God," she added under her breath before her gaze darted between her sisters. "I'm sorry. I really thought he was different."

Sayeh softened, reaching for Kenna's hand to squeeze it gently. "Hey, who am I to judge? My last boyfriend is being investigated for tax fraud. No one's perfect. Maybe all of our pickers are broken."

Luna silently thought of Benjamin and wondered if Sayeh was right. She was not looking to date Benjamin, but her track record wasn't stellar either.

"So we won't date," Luna said with false cheerfulness. "Strong, independent women don't need to date these days. We've got other things to occupy our time."

But of the three sisters, Kenna had the softest heart. It's likely why she always fell for the guy who couldn't be trusted or the one who spent more time waving red flags than anything else. She always wanted to believe they were going to be different.

And they never were.

"I won't press the restraining order if you truly feel you're going to be safe here and that whoever did this isn't going to follow you," Luna said.

Kenna nodded. "I paid cash for everything to get here and cut up all my credit cards that were under his control. As far as he's concerned, we simply disappeared in the middle of the night."

"Okay," Luna said, relieved. "Then let's embrace this as your fresh start. I've got some arnica you can put on your bruise that should help it heal more quickly and we'll see what we can do to find you a job and get Ty enrolled in school for the coming year. Luckily, we've got some time before school starts so it should be fine."

Kenna smiled with gratitude, her eyes filling with tears. "Thank you."

"Of course." She would never abandon her sisters for anything. They were a package deal, even if that package was a hot mess most days. Luna glanced at her watch, noting the time. "I have to go. Sayeh, help Kenna get settled in her old bedroom." She pulled a credit card from her wallet. "And take them clothes shopping. Whatever they need."

"You don't have to do that," Kenna started, but it was her pride speaking, and they both knew it. Luna smiled, and Kenna wiped at her eyes, nodding. "Thank you."

Sayeh, on the other hand, scooped up the card with a grin. "Let's go shopping."

Luna left them knowing Sayeh would probably drive up her credit card bill just for the fun of it, because she was born under a difficult star and never missed an opportunity to be a jackass.

Ah, the joy of having sisters.

Benjamin popped into the police station a little after lunch, doing his best to appear as if he hadn't been watching the clock for an appropriately timed visit. He didn't want to seem too eager, nor did he want Luna to be the subject of small-town gossip, but he couldn't stop thinking about her since she bolted from the house that morning.

Sure, it was probably a good thing she left when she did because he'd been more than willing to go another round or two, and that wasn't the right way to start a casual situation.

But there were other reasons he wanted to see her that had nothing to do with the state of his groin, and that's what he was focusing on as he bounded up the steps and strode into the station.

He was becoming a regular at the station and barely registered an eye blink as they motioned him back to her office. Benjamin knocked lightly on the doorjamb, ignoring the leap in his gut when she met his gaze. It was harder than he realized to shelve those memories of last night, but it had to be done. They both needed to focus.

"Good morning," she said with a professional smile. "You have the look of a man on a mission. What's up?"

Benjamin went straight to it. "The other day, I went to Roger's business manager and personal attorney to sign all the paperwork for the estate and I gotta tell you, there's no way Roger was just doing IT work unless he was working for the Queen of England on the down-low. He had way too much liquid for someone who worked on a computer for a midsize company."

Curious, she asked, "What kind of money are we talking?"

"The house was paid for—"

He'd already researched that the market value of those ranchettes was at least a million five. Although she kept her expression neutral, he could tell her spidey-sense was tingling, same as Benjamin.

"—and there were several accounts, one for each boy, Charlotte, with at least one hundred thousand between the three, several crypto accounts and some real estate purchases outside of Billings. Looks like undeveloped land, maybe to develop later into housing units, not sure. But my point being, there's no computer gig paying that kind of money."

"You're not wrong," she admitted, frowning. "It was on my schedule to talk to Roger's former employer but it seems like that's become the priority. I'll check into it."

"I'm ready when you are."

The way Luna's gaze shifted toward her chief's office betrayed her hesitation to include him. After last night, everything probably felt inappropriate between them, even a simple car ride.

"While you drive, I can give you some more details on Roger's financials that might be useful," he offered, keeping his expression neutral. She was a good cop and he didn't want to make her question her judgment, but he also wasn't about to be put on the sidelines for a stupid reason.

His logic seemed to work. Luna grabbed her keys, saying, "Then let's go for a drive." And he didn't even try to smother his grin for winning the silent battle raging behind those dark eyes.

Time for some real answers.

Nothing was going to stop him from being in the loop—not even the rules.

Chapter 13

According to what Luna knew, Roger worked for a company based out of Billings, Montana, only a half hour drive from Cottonwood. The easy commute was something Charlotte often mentioned when she'd been talking up Roger's great career. Luna had never begrudged Charlotte her crowing because Luna made it a point to never stomp on someone else's pride and joy.

But maybe a few people in the community had whispered nasty gossip about Charlotte out of jealousy, and Luna had always ignored them as "Negative Nellies," which her mom used to say when dealing with catty people.

Asset Protection was a high-tech computer security company hired by other big companies to create firewalls and cyber protection against financial hackers. The gray building was ugly, square and unremarkable in every way, but Luna supposed that was the point. Standing out wasn't their goal. They provided a service that depended on quiet efficiency without fanfare.

Her badge got them in quickly to the owner, Lawrence Chapel, a man who still believed in clocking in every day alongside his team, preferring to be hands-on rather than delegating too much to his staff, which worked for Luna because that meant they wouldn't be bounced from one person to the next for answers.

Lawrence rose to greet them with a sturdy and solid handshake during introductions. Immediately, Luna and Benjamin noticed the military memorabilia indicating Lawrence was a proud veteran. Benjamin straightened ever so slightly, a nod to a fellow serviceman, and the two seemed aware of each other's energy in a different way.

Lawrence started in without preamble. "I was sorry to hear about Roger and his family. If there's anything we at Asset Protection can do, don't hesitate to ask."

"We appreciate your cooperation. We're all pretty shook by this case," Luna admitted. "Things like this don't happen in Cottonwood. We're a quiet town and that's how we like it."

"It's a beautiful place," Lawrence said without argument. "Someday, if I ever retire, Cottonwood is on the short list."

"I know this is going to be hard but we need to ask some personal questions about Roger and the work he did here," Luna said.

"Ordinarily, I would have you talk to our HR department but like I said, I want to do whatever I can to help, though I'm not sure what we can do that might assist your investigation. Ask away."

"We appreciate that," Luna murmured, shooting a quick look Benjamin's way before continuing. "We recently discovered that Roger was quite flush, so much so that it seemed odd that he was making the kind of money needed to acquire the kind of assets he had."

Lawrence's brow furrowed, his mouth pursing with open confusion. "I wasn't close enough to Roger to share those kinds of confidences with him. When Roger left Asset Protection three years ago to freelance, I assumed it was to start up his own consulting business. By your statement, I have to assume that he must've been successful."

"Wait, he left three years ago?" Luna repeated, dumbfounded. "Are you sure?"

"Of course I'm sure," he answered without a doubt. "We were sad to see him go. He was a solid guy, dependable and we never had client complaints about his work. I didn't want to lose him. Even offered him a raise but from the sounds of it, I couldn't compete with whatever he was trading up for. To be honest, you've got me curious where he ended up."

"So are we," Benjamin quipped darkly. "There seems to be some confusion as to who employed Roger."

Did Charlotte know that Roger wasn't with Asset Protection, or had she been protecting her husband's secret? And if so, why lie about where he worked unless she didn't want anyone to ask questions? This new information dropped a ball of anxiety into Luna's gut.

"He didn't give any indication what he'd be doing or where he was going?" Benjamin asked.

"No, and I didn't ask. He seemed happy and ready to make a move and I wanted to support that kind of initiative. Roger might not have been the kind of man most would've taken seriously but he was smart as a whip and that's how people underestimated him. I was really rooting for him."

Luna read between the lines. What Roger lacked in muscle, he'd made up for with his mind. Maybe that's what'd drawn Charlotte. Her father had been built like a brick wall, and he'd used that strength against those weaker than him, including his children.

Working backward, she asked, "What did Roger do for Asset Protection?"

"He was in charge of creating and managing firewall protections for several of our larger clients. He handled all security protocols, protecting software, data and the hardware against any cyber threat, as well as created safety protocols for potential breaches."

"All of that could be done from his home office or did he have to be here?" Luna asked.

"He did some of the work here, but mostly he worked from home using our secure network."

For three years, he'd been working on his own. Where? Who'd been paying him? And for what? She'd need to put forensic accounting onto this case, but they didn't have that kind of resource available, which meant she'd have to ask the county for help.

Which could also take months.

But what choice did she have?

Benjamin asked, "Would you have heard if another company similar to yours hired Roger?"

"Absolutely. We're a pretty tight network. Everyone knows everyone in this game. If someone would've hired Roger, I would've heard about it."

"If that's the case, who would need to hire someone like Roger for his particular set of skills and would be willing to pay a lot of cash for his services?"

Luna could tell Lawrence was reluctant to answer, but he was true to his word and didn't hold back. "Nothing legal," he admitted, sighing. "Here's the thing. The world is evolving at a rapid rate, and everything's going digital, even the crime. You've got people making millions off a series of digital art prints of monkeys or gorillas, or some stuff like that, and where there's money, there's criminals. It's like the Wild Wild West on the digital plane. People like Roger, who understand the new landscape and how to play the game, are likely in high demand for both sides of the playing field."

"You think Roger is the kind of guy who'd willingly work with criminals?" Benjamin asked.

"I'd like to think no, but when you're talking about an obscene amount of money waved in front of your face I've seen better men do worse," he admitted. "I want to believe he wouldn't. Like I said, I really liked the guy but who knows?"

"He was very likable," Luna murmured in agreement, thinking. "So, just playing devil's advocate, what kind of business in this area do you think would be the easiest to fall into?"

"Pick your vice," Lawrence said. "Drugs, prostitution, gambling, human trafficking—that stuff has always been around and now, it's going high-tech. No one keeps paper trails anymore. Easier to have everything on an encrypted server with a self-destruct function, if worst comes to worst and you have to destroy the evidence. Then, you walk away clean as a whistle and start all over someplace else."

"Almost makes crime sound like a walk in the park," Benjamin said.

"Sure, until you're caught. Businesses like mine don't pay half as well and I sleep real well knowing no one is looking for me. The big reward of fast money comes with big consequences. Somehow, somewhere, someone's paying the price and taking the fall."

And people end up dead.

Luna couldn't ignore what her gut was telling her. Benjamin was right—Roger had been up to no good, and whatever it was had likely cost him everything.

Damn it, Roger. What the hell were you doing?

She pulled a business card from her pocket and handed it to Lawrence. "We appreciate your candor and your willingness to help. Means a lot. If you remember anything else that might be helpful, please don't hesitate to call, day or night. That's my cell."

Lawrence nodded and pocketed the card. "I hope you find who did this. They were a nice family."

Benjamin and Lawrence exchanged quiet looks of respect, a wordless exchange that spoke of understanding, sorrow and the need for justice, and Luna admired both men for their solid sense of right and wrong.

But the case was nowhere near being solved.

If anything, it just became more complicated.

Benjamin was silent for most of the ride back to Cottonwood. He hadn't wanted to be right about Roger, but the facts seemed pretty clear. Still, for his sister's sake, he'd wanted to be wrong. Not that it mattered—even if their murders had been a twisted hand of fate and completely random, they were still dead.

And they had no idea how to find who Roger had been working for.

Luna must've read his mind. "We need a forensic accounting team to go through Roger's finances," she said, "but we don't have those kinds of resources and it could take months for the county to free up the resources to help. I know that's not the best news but I want to be honest with you."

"I figured as much," he said, thinking. He might know someone who could help, but it wouldn't be through official channels, which meant anything they turned up wouldn't be admissible in court. But he didn't give two shits about court right now. He just wanted answers. "I know your hands are tied. It's not your fault."

He wanted to make sure she knew that he didn't blame her for the slow-moving wheels of bureaucracy, but he also hoped she understood when he went around the law for answers.

"Yeah, but somehow it feels like it's my fault," she said with a heavy sigh. "I've never found myself hamstrung by our meager resources before, but then we've never really had to deal with anything like this."

"Don't beat yourself up. You're sharp and you're doing the best that you can. I know that," he assured her.

"It's hard to wrap my head around the knowledge that Roger was living a double life. What keeps circling my brain, though, is wondering if Charlotte knew. Makes me wonder what else Roger was hiding. Am I going to find a secret mistress or something? It hurts my heart to even think about it. I know it's probably stupid but I used to think Charlotte and Roger had the kind of love story that was textbook cute. He was a math nerd and she was the pretty small-town girl but somehow they made it work. If I find out that Roger had a mistress... I think I'll lose whatever hope remained that true love is still possible."

"You'd really take it that hard?" he asked, bemused.

She hated to admit it but yes. "Sometimes I can be a closet romantic. Don't tell anyone."

"Your secret is safe with me," he said, thinking about Roger and Charlotte. "To be honest, I have no idea how someone like Roger landed Charlotte to begin with so I doubt he was a player."

"Money is the great equalizer. Clearly Roger had cash to play with. Who's to say he didn't have a stable of women at his beck and call?"

Benjamin chuckled. "I thought you just said you were a closet romantic?"

Luna shared a small smile, but it faded quickly. "Each time I turn around, this case has me questioning more about everything I thought I knew about this town and the people in it," she admitted with a heavy exhale that made him want to hold her hand in support, but he held back. "I know people are complex and no one truly knows what goes on behind closed doors but damn, I don't know what to think about the stuff we're learning about Roger and Charlotte's life."

He understood, because even though he hadn't thought

much of Roger, he'd loved his sister more than anyone, but he'd done a crap job of showing it. The only relief he could hope for was solving their murders.

"Charlotte was well-known in town, well-liked, even. There has to be someone who knows more than they're saying. We need more than someone interested in spreading catty gossip—someone who actually cared about her to come forward and talk to us."

Luna looked ready to cry, saying with frustration, "I should've been the one who knew what was going on. When we were kids, we were inseparable. It's not okay that I know next to nothing about her personal life. Each time I turn around I feel like I'm hearing things about a stranger because that's what she'd become. I'm such a shit friend for taking our friendship for granted."

Benjamin hated the anguish he heard in Luna's voice. "Don't do that to yourself. It's not your fault," he admonished. "It's hard to keep track of other people when you become an adult. If anyone should've been more connected, it's me. That blame falls squarely on my shoulders."

She shook her head, just as adamant that he wasn't to blame. "You didn't live here anymore. I did. There were opportunities to get together but other things became more important. But I never stopped caring for her. God, I hope you know that. She was my closest friend and I let her down. I feel that in my bones and I can't shake it."

He sighed, seeing where this was going, and he didn't like it. "Look, we're both going to feel a certain way about how Charlotte died and why, and there's likely nothing either of us can say to change that feeling, but all I can say is, I'll never believe that you should shoulder any of that guilt ever, and that's that."

"Same," she murmured, risking a glance his way. "So, how do we get through it?"

"I don't know," he confessed, adding with a hint of frustration, "but what I do know is that until we find who did this…there's never going to be any hope of feeling any different."

It was the stark truth, even if it wasn't fair to either of them.

But it wasn't fair that Charlotte and her whole damn family were in the ground either, so no sense in playing that card. Hell, this was the kind of thing that no one got off scot-free from in the end.

And he'd already accepted that fact.

He looked at Luna. He probably shouldn't, but the offer was on his tongue before he could stop it.

"Want to swing by my place tonight? I could make spaghetti."

She didn't hesitate. "Yes, but I can't spend the night this time."

"Fair enough. You can bring the garlic bread and the wine. I'll take care of the rest."

And just like that, it was settled.

It felt too easy between them, almost natural. Wasn't that a red flag or something?

Hell, who cared? Neither was looking to settle down and raise kids together.

It was just spaghetti and sex—and they could both use the release.

But if she ended up falling asleep in his arms again, he wouldn't be mad about it either.

Chapter 14

After work, Luna headed home to shower and clean up before going to Benjamin's but was surprised when her father caught her midstride toward the bathroom.

"Luna, can I talk to you for a minute?"

She paused, concerned. "Of course, everything okay?"

He gestured for her to follow him out to his shop, which only made her more perplexed. Once the door shut behind them, Bill leaned up against his lathe, shoving his hands in his pockets, and Luna immediately thought it was about her sisters.

"I know it's probably stressful having Kenna and Sayeh back in the house, but it's only temporary," she assured him.

He waved off her concern. "Kenna will figure things out. She's always had a tough time of it with finding the right man, but your mom always said Kenna had a good heart and good hearts eventually find a home. Your mom wasn't wrong on much so I lean on her words when I'm not sure which end is up."

Luna smiled, wishing her mom was still here. She could use a bit of that quiet wisdom herself. She regarded her father with a frown. "What's wrong, then?"

Her dad looked flustered, unsure how to start, which wasn't like him. "It's this case you're working," he finally admitted with earnest concern. "Honey, I gotta tell you, I've got a bad feeling about it all. There's a dark cloud hanging over Cottonwood that I've never felt before and it's got me worried about you."

Well, she did not see *that* coming.

"About me? Dad, I'm a detective. I'll be fine," she said. "It's my job to solve Charlotte's murder. People are depending on me. You, of all people, should understand that."

Bill was a retired lieutenant with the Cottonwood PD. He knew all about community expectations but his agitation seemed unlike him.

"I do, I do, but this isn't your run-of-the-mill case, a burglary or even assault—this is murder. A whole family died. I don't like knowing that you're in the thick of this. You don't know that whoever did this might start looking sideways at your asking questions."

"Dad," Luna ventured, baffled and a little hurt. "Do you think I'm not capable of handling myself? That I'm in over my head?"

"No, no, of course not," he said quickly, his cheeks flushing. "I'm just worried is all. I don't want anything happening to you. After losing your mother, I can't stomach the idea of losing you, too."

Relief flooded her. Now it made sense. She gentled her voice to calm her dad's nerves. " I appreciate your concern but trust that I know what I'm doing, and I'll be fine, okay? I'm very thorough and I will catch whoever did this. I promise."

His lip trembled ever so slightly, and she suffered a pang

of guilt for not being more sympathetic. Dad wasn't young anymore, and sometimes the fear of losing those closest to him created anxiety. She tried again. "It's all very scary, but it'll work out somehow. Secrets never stay buried forever. Eventually, someone screws up and leaves behind a clue."

"I know you want to solve the case and I know that you're a good detective, but what if that young family were just up to their eyeballs in things they shouldn't have been messing with? Bad people are unpredictable. Isn't there anyone else who can handle this case? I don't want you getting caught in the crosshairs of someone else's trouble."

"Dad, it's my case," she said stiffly. "No one is taking it from me."

Never in her life had her dad ever acted this way and it scared her. "What's really going on? This isn't like you."

Bill stared, looking trapped and unsure of what to do, but then his gaze cleared, and he wiped at his forehead before waving away her question with a gruff "I'm just an old man. What do I know?" He looked away with a sniff. "Watch yourself. You don't know who's involved with this mess, and it could end up going a lot deeper than you realize. You won't know who to trust if it gets to that point."

A chill danced down her spine as she watched her dad leave more questions than answers in his wake.

What the hell just happened?

Maybe she ought to cancel with Benjamin.

But she didn't want to.

She spent most of her life considering the needs of others before she considered her own and she was due a bit of selfishness, but she was dancing dangerously close to the line she swore never to cross. Boundaries were there for a reason, and until Benjamin came along, keeping the course had never been difficult. Now? It seemed breaking the rules was becoming second nature.

A part of her wanted to go after her dad and figure out what had really caused his fear. Was it simply the press of age at the back of his mind reminding him of his own frailty that prompted him, or was it something else? Her dad was straight as an arrow but something had lurked in the shadows of his gaze that caused her to question more than just his mental health.

And that feeling—foreign and intrusive—kept her lingering with indecision until she walked into the house and saw Kenna. The bruising under her eye was beginning to fade but remained an ugly reminder of what she'd been through.

"What's wrong?" Kenna asked, biting into a banana. "You have that look on your face like something is chewing on your toe."

"Dad seems off. Do you think he has the beginning stages of dementia?" she wondered.

"Dad doesn't have dementia," Kenna said. "He was just teaching Ty to drive."

"That's a skill set stored in long-term memory, which is the last thing affected by dementia," Luna answered, still considering canceling on Benjamin.

"He's fine," Kenna said with a smile, as if Luna were silly for even thinking it. "You in tonight?"

Luna hesitated. Now was her chance to do the right thing and cancel. *One and done, remember? Not, one-and-two-and-maybe-one-more-for-good-measure.* But she wanted to see Benjamin. There, she said it. "No, I have plans tonight," she answered, making her decision.

"Have fun," Kenna said with a wink as she left the room.

Luna stared after Kenna with suspicion. Had Sayeh told Kenna about Benjamin? Luna had never actually confirmed her involvement with Benjamin but that "sister intuition" was hard to trick and Sayeh was as sharp as a tack. Damn that girl and her mouth. Ugh. She'd deal with that later. She was already late.

* * *

Benjamin heard the knock at his front door and hollered, "Door's open, come on in," as he maneuvered hot sauce around the noodles. Luna walked in carrying a bag of French bread and a bottle of wine, looking like a million bucks in jeans and a casual T-shirt, her hair loose and free.

"Smells good," she said, going to open the wine so it could breathe before she started cutting up slices of bread. "I've spent so long eating like a bachelor that I'd forgotten what home-cooked food is like. Neither my dad or myself are skilled in the kitchen. Well, I mean, except for pancakes. My dad tries his best to make blueberry pancakes sometimes."

"You don't like to cook?"

"No, I do not," she answered with a chuckle. "I mean, I can probably do an adequate job but it's not my favorite activity."

"What's your favorite?" he asked, not intending to make it ring with innuendo, but that rising blush in her high cheekbones made it worth it.

She laughed and sidestepped the question with a shake of her head. "Keep it clean for now," she warned playfully, setting the table for them. They worked together well, something he'd never encountered before. Usually, he was reluctant to have strangers in his space, but that was the thing—Luna didn't feel like a stranger even though he'd barely paid much attention to his little sister's friend when they'd been kids.

He chuckled, bringing the spaghetti and placing it on the small table. Luna poured the wine and sat opposite as he dished them up. It didn't occur to him not to serve her plate until after, and he paused, unsure if he'd just offended her. "I'm sorry—"

"You don't need to apologize. It's very sweet," she assured him.

Benjamin took his place and shook his head, admitting, "I'm feeling all out of sorts. Like I've suddenly forgotten how to be an adult and yet, I'm real comfortable around you at the same time."

"I feel the same way," she said. "I called you *dude* earlier."

"Yeah, that was weird and cute at the same time."

"I never in a million years thought I'd be called cute at thirty-five years old," she said, laughing. "But I'll take it."

They laughed through dinner, shared stories and kept their minds away from the case. They needed the break. It wasn't that Charlotte's case wasn't always in the back of their minds, but they needed a breather from the stress of chasing down leads that were so slim and disappointing.

So when Luna started to share about her sisters, he was eager to listen.

"It's not that I'm not happy to spend time with my sisters but we're a little rusty in that department. We've always been independent of each other and now, when they need me the most, I can't seem to make those connections feel less awkward. Makes me feel like a bad sister."

Benjamin recalled a sliver of detail shared by Charlotte back in the day. "You and your sisters are adopted, right?"

"Yeah, Bill and Nancy were distant cousins of my mother's. We were born on the reservation but when we were little, our parents died in a fire and Bill and Nancy were our only living relatives so we came to Cottonwood. They thought it best to give us their name for a fresh start."

"What was your original name?"

"Proudfoot."

"Luna Proudfoot. It fits you," he said, rolling the name around his mouth a minute before asking, "How old were you?"

"I was six, Kenna was four and Sayeh was two. I have memories of our parents but my sisters don't. Well, I take that back. Kenna has very vague, shadowy memories, more like those of a fading dream, but Sayeh doesn't remember anything."

Benjamin nodded, wanting to know more. "What kind of fire? Was it accidental?" He pulled back, realizing it probably seemed a little pushy wanting so many details. "Look at me putting you under a hot bulb. You don't have to answer if it's not something you want to share."

But Luna didn't mind. "It's okay. It was a long time ago and I don't remember much. The details are hazy. I mean, my biological parents had their demons and it's hard to say what really happened that night because no one survived the fire but drugs were suspected. We were with a babysitter the night our trailer burned down. The fire burned so hot that the bodies were damn near disintegrated. Those old trailers are so flammable they burn hot as crematoriums."

"You're lucky to be alive," he said.

"Yeah, that's true. It could've easily gone a different way," she agreed, sighing. "I wish I had better memories of my time with my biological family but it's a hard life on the reservation. They need access to better resources, funding, healthcare, recovery services, and there's just not a lot available. It's no wonder Indigenous peoples have to fight stereotypes all the time. It's not apples to apples when it comes to opportunity and that's just the truth. There's a lot of poverty, and impoverished people with few resources don't usually find a way out of their situation. It's a self-perpetuating cycle that's heartbreaking."

"No argument from me," he said. "I hate seeing what's happened to the Indigenous peoples. I wish there was more we could do to help."

Luna nodded, the mood dampening, admitting, "I've always felt a little estranged from my heritage even though I'm the only one with memories of our time on the reservation. The thing is, my memories aren't good. I remember being cold, hungry, scared, and sleeping on a bed that crawled with cockroaches. It's not that I don't appreciate my heritage—because I am proud of who I am—I just wish things had been different so I didn't have to reconcile my heritage against such terrible memories."

Benjamin saw the conflict in her expression and understood even though he couldn't claim any particular heritage to be proud of. He wasn't sure, but he recalled his father saying they were part Irish or Scottish. Who knew? The old man had been drunk most of the time. They could be German for all he knew. Charlotte had always been after him to do an ancestry DNA kit so they could trace their roots, but he'd never gotten around to doing it. Maybe he'd do it now in Charlotte's memory.

Whatever Luna's lineage, she radiated a level of beauty that stole his breath the longer he looked at her. She glanced his way and caught him staring. She blushed, ducking her gaze. "What?"

"You're damn breathtaking," he admitted. "And the longer I look at you, the bigger the problem becomes."

Her stare dropped inadvertently to his groin, and he chuckled ruefully, saying, "Not that problem." He clarified by tapping his head. "This problem."

"What do you mean?"

"I like you way too much, and the more time I'm around you, the more difficult it becomes to remember why I shouldn't get too attached."

Understanding dawned. She smiled above her wineglass, assuring him with a sexy look, "Don't worry, Benjamin, I won't let you fall in love with me."

"Yeah? And how would you stop it?"

She rose, setting her wineglass down carefully, before approaching him. "Because we both know that this is bound to implode at some point. We're too different, too set in our ways, and definitely not cut out to ride off into the sunset together."

Solid points. And yet...

He pulled her gently into his lap, and she curled her arms around his neck. "And what if that's not enough to stop what's happening between us?"

"It has to be," she murmured as she brushed her lips against his.

"Because why?"

But before she could answer, the sound of shattering glass interrupted the moment and sent them both diving for cover beneath the table.

The sound of tires peeling off into the distance told them whoever was responsible was leaving like a bat out of hell, and there was no catching them.

"What the hell was that about?" Benjamin growled as he climbed to his feet, going to the front room where a small bullet had punched through the glass, burying itself in the cabin wall that'd narrowly missed hitting them.

"Don't touch anything," instructed Luna, going into police mode. She grabbed her cell and quickly called dispatch. "We need a forensics unit out to 1916 Sugar Wood Drive. Someone just shot at the window and could've killed me or Benjamin Reeves. No ambulance needed. Just the forensics team."

She clicked off and looked to Benjamin, her dark eyes wide, her thoughts playing across her forehead, mirroring his own. So much for any loving tonight.

Someone had just tried to kill one of them.

Chapter 15

Luna paced her office, waiting for forensics to return with the ballistics from the bullet, unable to stop thinking about how close they'd come to meeting their maker. Whoever shot that bullet had been happy to take out either her or Benjamin, which meant that Benjamin wasn't safe anymore.

The wheels were turning fast. She'd been willing to write off the slashed tires as a cruel prank by punks but after this incident, it seemed highly unlikely the two were unrelated. A dark chill anchored her thoughts. What if the bullet had found its target tonight?

She turned to Benjamin, knowing he wouldn't like what she was about to say, but it had to be done. "I can't have you on the investigation any longer when it puts you at risk." The fact that she'd been letting him tag along was an embarrassing slip in protocol that could've had disastrous consequences, and it was past time to rectify her oversight. "It's too dangerous."

Benjamin, lost in his thoughts, looked up with a subtle scowl. "What the hell are you talking about?"

"You're a civilian and it's not safe for you to be participating in the investigation now that people are shooting at us."

"I can take care of myself."

"It's a liability issue for the department," she said, holding firm, even though that wasn't the biggest reason. She would never forgive herself if anything happened to Benjamin on her watch, but she didn't know how to verbalize her fears without sounding overly attached. "Sorry."

"And what about you? That bullet could've been meant for you as much as it was for me," he reminded her.

"It's possible but the risk comes with the job—my job, not yours."

"And I'm a retired marine. I think between us we can handle whatever that jack knob thinks he can throw our way."

"We don't know that and I can't take the risk." She added, "And we don't know that it's not a woman who took the shot."

"Man, woman, jackalope, it doesn't matter. I'm not running from anything."

"You're not running. I'm taking you out of the game," she clarified for his male pride. "It's not the same."

"Stop," he said, irritated. "You sound like a broken record. It could've been a bunch of stupid kids messing around. Let's not jump to conclusions."

"I don't believe in coincidence. Not like this."

"Luna—"

"No, I can't let anything happen to you."

Her eyes burned with sudden tears, but she held them back. She wasn't going to negotiate on this point. Benjamin saw that she wasn't going to budge and swore under his breath, but he didn't press any further. He grabbed his jacket and headed out. She was prepared to let him leave without saying anything further, but the minute he'd left the building, she was hurrying after him. *Damn it.*

"You shouldn't go back to the rental," she said, catching up to him.

He turned, his lips compressed. "And where should I go? Your place? Are you offering up your bed?"

She pulled up short, her breath catching. "N-no, I mean, that would create a lot of questions that I don't have time to deal with right now," she answered, blanching at the very thought of her sisters peppering Benjamin for personal information the minute he walked through the door. "But a hotel wouldn't be a terrible idea…"

"I'm already paying for a rental. Why would I pay for a hotel room?" he asked.

She saw his point. So what was her solution? She didn't have one. All she had was a bundle of feelings quickly knotting like a tangled mess of hair. "I don't think you should be alone," Luna said, wincing at how terribly she was communicating. She'd suddenly regressed to a seventh-grader and forgotten how to adult. She drew a deep breath and tried again. "I'm sorry, you're right," she admitted, trying for complete transparency. "I can't stop thinking about how you could've been killed and I'm sick to my stomach, okay?"

"Why didn't you just say that in the first place?" His expression gentled with understanding. He reached for her, drawing her to him. Even though she should've pulled back, she wanted to feel his touch. "It's natural to knee-jerk react to situations that feel out of our control and threaten something or someone we care about, but it doesn't make sense to shut me out of this investigation when you're already scraping the bottom of the barrel with resources."

"It isn't right to put our limitations on your shoulders,"

she said, frustrated. "Especially if helping could get you killed."

"I could've been killed a hundred different times when deployed—still didn't stop me from serving my country, so some punk-ass coward shooting through windows isn't going to stop me from helping find justice for my sister." He gently thumbed her cheek, searching her gaze. "Now, if you want to keep me safe, I wouldn't be opposed to you spending the night, if that's what you're offering."

Was that what she was offering? She didn't know what she was doing aside from acting recklessly and out of character. What was it about Benjamin that made her weak all over? She frowned, annoyed at the situation and the pull between them. "You and I both know we're breaking all the rules and rules are there for a reason."

"Some rules are stupid."

"Not these."

He shrugged. "Agree to disagree. Come with me and keep me safe."

A smile tugged at her lips, even as she wanted to stay firm. "What happened to you being able to take care of yourself?"

"You made me realize how vulnerable I am," he quipped, not taking this situation nearly serious enough but his attitude was contagious. Why was he so damn handsome? When he reached for her, she didn't resist. He tried a different approach, offering, "How about some logic? It's useless to sit at the station when nothing will be processed until morning, which leaves you here pacing for no good reason, and since I'm not going anywhere if you're not, that means we're going to watch paint peel all night when we could be taking advantage of a soft bed."

"Compelling argument," she conceded, thinking out loud, adding, "Or I could sleep on the couch, thereby keeping you safe and avoiding anything inappropriate."

"You're in my bed, beside me," he corrected as his hold tightened around her. "It's the most efficient way to keep me safe."

A shiver danced through her. "You're impossible," she said in a low, breathy tone. "But convincing."

A low chuckle smacking of victory followed a throaty "Get your stuff," and she bounded up the stairs to close up her office.

The butterflies in her stomach tickled as they fluttered around, and she had to shut down the feminine purr that wanted to follow.

She was an out-of-control steam engine barreling down the tracks knowing full well a dead end awaited at the end of the line, but she couldn't seem to make herself stop.

No matter the crash that would follow.

Luna was concerned about protecting him, but he'd been just as pressed about someone shooting at her. An odd sense of protectiveness washed over him, and he'd wanted to wrap her in Kevlar so he knew she'd be safe.

But that was as ridiculous as her wanting to kick him to the curb for his protection.

And he couldn't exactly admit to it either. She was already keyed up; he'd needed to find a way to settle her nerves in a manner that wasn't going to set her off in the wrong way.

He may have made light of the situation but internally, it was a different story. He didn't like the idea of someone shooting at either of them but it made him see red that someone might've taken a shot at Luna.

And there was only one reason he could figure that someone would take that shot—either to scare Luna or take her out to stop the investigation.

That meant Charlotte's killer was still in Cottonwood.

He'd never believed their murders were committed by a random psycho passing through town. He knew some people felt safer thinking it was accidental, bad luck, but he'd never bought into that theory.

The reality was that someone in this town was involved, and they were trying to intimidate him and Luna into closing the investigation.

It had to be someone who knew they'd talked to Roger's former employer and found out that he hadn't worked there for years.

They didn't know that intimidation tactics didn't work for him. He'd stared into the gaping maw of destruction before, and death didn't scare him.

Now, Luna getting hurt? That was a different story. The feelings growing for Luna were complicated and messy, definitely not what he wanted to focus on, but hard to ignore.

For now, he was content to have her in his bed. At least he knew she was safe with him.

Once back at the rental, he spent a short time using cardboard to temporarily block up the broken section in the glass until the repairman came, and then, he and Luna headed for bed.

They were tired, drained from the tension of the night, and neither had much steam for more than holding each other, which was fine by Benjamin.

"You've never been married," she said, breaking the silence.

"No."

"Any particular reason why?"

He sighed. "I'll be honest, when I was younger, I spent most of my time running away from my childhood, which was easy to do when enlisted. Then, when I realized I was a hot mess I actually started to do the healing work I needed, but by that point, I was pretty content with my life and didn't see the need to change it. I figured if the right person came along, I'd cross that bridge when I came to it. As it happened, that bridge never materialized."

She chuckled, admitting, "I'm impressed that you got therapy. Not a lot of military guys are willing to do that, even if they need it."

"Hey now, who's playing into the stereotype?" he teased, but she was right. "Naw, I've seen too many buddies sink into addiction trying to blot out their pain so I didn't ignore my own when I saw things heading in the wrong direction, but before you give me too much credit, it might be that I'm too damn stubborn to let myself turn into a statistic, so I got help."

"You don't have to justify the way you helped yourself for me to admire the end result."

"Fair enough."

"Remember that boyfriend I told you about before?"

"Yeah, the one who ran off with a coworker?"

"Well, he was more than my boyfriend. We'd been engaged."

"Ouch."

"Yeah. I think the hardest part was everyone knowing what'd happened. Maybe I was projecting but I always thought people were looking at me with pity in their eyes for being the poor woman whose man ran off on her. I guess the saving grace was that he didn't leave me at the altar, which totally would've been worse."

"Only cowards run off in the middle of the night. He should've had the balls to tell you that the relationship was over."

"Yeah, he wasn't great," she admitted. "I'm glad it didn't work out but at the time I was devastated."

"I used to hate the saying 'everything happens for a reason' but sometimes it does seem that way."

She smiled against his chest. "I've always hated that saying, too."

He had a hard time imagining anyone walking away from Luna for someone else. That guy had been an idiot, but that was his loss because she was in his arms now.

Almost subconsciously, his arms tightened around her. Luna's contented sigh felt like a warm hug around his soul.

That was the problem. He wanted more, but more of what? He lived in Arizona, and she lived here. He had zero interest in moving back to Cottonwood. This place was the place of his nightmares. It'd been hard enough to drag himself back a few times for family dinners with Charlotte.

"I can hear the gears moving," she teased.

He didn't want to ruin the moment with the sudden dampening of his spirits, so he responded by brushing his lips across hers in a tender kiss. She shifted, her hand sliding down his stomach to rest lightly above his groin. That tantalizingly close touch was enough to drive the fatigue from his body and the turbulent thoughts from his brain.

When he hardened at her gentle touch, she teased, "I thought you were tired?" moving to straddle him. He reached up to caress her back, drawing her to his mouth. Her tongue darted to meet his as her hot center ground into his stiffened length.

"Suddenly, I'm wide awake."

Her light laughter was sweet like summer rain, but it did something to his head that he couldn't control.

He growled as his hands filled with her backside, drawing her closer. He wanted to experience her all around him. "You're beginning to feel like the most dangerous addiction I've ever faced down," he murmured against her mouth.

"Likewise," she said, her hair coming down to tickle his chest. "But that's a problem for another day, okay?"

"I'm on board with that plan," he said, rolling her on the

bed, pressing against her softness, ready to forget everything but this moment.

All that mattered was now.

Tomorrow would come soon enough.

Chapter 16

"Detective, we've got someone in interrogation that you might want to talk to," Wes said, poking his head into her office the following day.

She looked up, interested. "Yeah? Who is it?"

"Some guy patrol picked up for a traffic violation but they found power tools in the back of his truck listed as stolen from the Leicki house the night of their murder. Thought you might want to get in on this."

That got her attention. "Who is it?"

"The name's Mark Duncan, apparently some kind of independent contractor. Said he bought the tools second-hand but he doesn't know who he bought them from."

She rose quickly and went straight to the interrogation room.

The man, middle-aged with a beer belly and a ruddy complexion from spending too much time outdoors, scowled from his chair, fidgeting in his cuffs and looking guilty as hell, but guilty of what?

"Mark Duncan, I'm Detective Griffin. Can you tell me where you bought the power tools found in your truck?"

"I already told the first officer. I bought them used from some guy off Craigslist. I didn't think it was necessary to get personal details for a goddamn miter saw and a drill set. I saw the deal and I took it, okay? I paid cash and I never saw the guy again."

"Did you know those items were listed as part of a crime scene?" Luna asked.

"What are you talking about? What crime?"

"The murder of the entire Leicki family."

The man paled beneath his sun-weathered skin. "I didn't have nothing to do with that. All I did was buy the tools. Hey, look, I'm just an independent contractor trying to make a living and times are tough, you know? Sometimes I buy used tools. It's not a crime. We all do it. How was I supposed to know they were stolen?"

"Where did you meet up with the guy to make the purchase?"

Mark chewed his bottom lip as if he were reluctant to answer because he knew how it would look, but he relented. "A parking lot after hours, but I've bought plenty of tools from guys trying to make fast cash. It's not my place to judge why they gotta have the money, you know?"

"You didn't think for a second that the tools might be stolen?"

"That's not my business," he retorted sullenly. "A guy's gotta eat."

"Well, it's your business now, isn't it?" Luna said. "We're going to need your phone to trace the number used to make the sale."

"I don't know why I'm being treated like a criminal when I didn't do nothing wrong."

"You purchased stolen property. That's a crime."

"Yeah but how was I supposed to know? It's not like they were sporting stickers saying 'Stolen property.'"

"Most people buy their professional tools through official channels, with receipts."

"Yeah, well, like I said, everyone's gotta eat and tools are expensive. Sometimes you can't always buy through the stores. It's not like I wouldn't want to do it that way but, hell, you don't know what it's like out there right now. With the price of materials going through the roof, and no one wanting to spend a dime on quality work, you cut corners where you can."

"I sympathize with your situation but that doesn't change the fact that you're in possession of stolen property that was taken from a murder scene."

"That's my damn luck," he muttered. "So what's going to happen now?"

"We're going to process the stolen property, dust it for possible prints that might still remain, as well as take your prints, and once we can determine your whereabouts on the night of the murder, we're going to process you for acquiring stolen property."

"Hold up, what do you mean? I didn't have anything to do with no murder."

"And if you can provide an alibi for the night in question, we'll be happy to simply process you on the property charges." She looked him square in the eye. "Do you have an alibi for the night of July 16?"

Mark shifted in his seat, trying to find a more comfortable position. "I live alone. No one but my dog, Roscoe, was with me and something tells me he don't count."

"No, he doesn't."

"This is some bullshit," he muttered. "I didn't have nothing to do with those people getting killed."

"If you're innocent the evidence will prove it."

"And how exactly is that going to work if I don't have anyone who can vouch for me?"

"Hopefully your prints aren't on the crime scene."

Mark stared, a bead of moisture collecting on his lip as he tried wiping it away with his shoulder. "It's hotter than Hades in this box. Jesus, don't you have air conditioning?"

Luna ignored his complaint. "Is there anything you'd like to tell us before we start going through your phone?"

"I didn't know the stuff was stolen," he insisted.

"The law doesn't discriminate against ignorance," she said without sympathy.

"This is messed up," he said, shaking his head. "I swear to God, I didn't have anything to do with any murder and I damn well didn't know that the tools were stolen. How the hell did you even know they were stolen?"

"Roger Leicki was a fastidious individual. Not only did he register all of his tools, he kept an organized file of every tool's paperwork. We found the paperwork for the miter saw and the drill set, but didn't see the corresponding tools and figured that they'd been stolen at the time of the murders. All it took was running the serial numbers against the database to confirm they were the ones stolen from the scene."

"Hold on one damn minute," he said, shaking his head. "You don't know when those tools were stolen. They could've been missing way before they got killed. What proof you got that it's connected at all?"

"As I said, Roger was a man who liked doing things in an orderly fashion. If the tools had been stolen previously, he would've reported it and we don't have any record of Roger Leicki reporting any kind of theft at his residence ever."

"Seems kinda flimsy if you ask me but you're making the rules, not me."

"Did you know the Leickis?" Luna asked.

"No?"

But it was the way he quickly answered that made her pause. "Are you sure?"

"Yeah, of course I'm sure."

"If I find out you're lying, it won't go well for you."

Mark swallowed but compressed his lips before demanding, "I want to talk to my lawyer. I got rights."

"You got something to hide?"

"I ain't saying another damn word until I talk to a lawyer."

Luna bit back a frustrated sigh. "Fine." She motioned for Wes to come and get the suspect. Nothing more would happen with him until they had more to go on. Maybe with some luck, they'd find Mark Duncan's prints on more than just the stolen tools.

After a career in the military, Benjamin had accumulated a few friends in high places and some friends who didn't mind doing the odd favor that was technically outside the lines of legal.

One such friend, Codi Ellers, served with him in the Marines but went chasing after more money in the private sector in financial security. If you wanted to get technical, Codi was the most sophisticated hacker he'd ever seen, but when she wasn't playing on the deep web, she was running financial security programs for major corporations.

She ran a dangerous game—if any of her big employers knew the stuff she was doing on her own time, they'd probably bust her ass—but Codi thrived on the adrenaline rush of not getting caught, and nothing would make her stop.

Benjamin fully expected Codi's luck to run out at some point, but that wasn't today, so it was a problem for another time.

He needed a favor only Codi would be willing to do.

She picked up on the first ring, which was saying some-

thing because when he called, the call usually went straight
to voice mail.

"This has got to be good. You never call anymore. I'm
starting to think we aren't still friends."

"Shut up, you're the one who's never around. The fact
that you're not in jail yet is a mystery."

"Can't catch the leaf on the wind, baby," she said with
laughter in her voice. "No, but seriously, why you calling?
Everything okay?"

"Actually, no," he answered with a heavy sigh, sharing
the news about his sister. Then, finishing, he said, "The
guy was getting paid for something shady, but the local
police department would need bigger resources to dig into
his bank accounts to see where the money was going and
coming from. There's only one person I could think of
that might be able to find what Roger didn't want found.
What do you say?"

"Is there money involved?" she asked.

"I can pay you a few bucks for your trouble," he said.

She laughed. "I'm kidding. I can't have you paying me
for illegal work. That's a federal crime, homie. I'll poke
around and see what I can find. I'll need some details."

"Whatever you need," he promised. "Just name it."

"I'll need basic personal information, name, age, birth
date, Social Security number and mother's maiden name,
if possible."

"I can get that. When can you start digging?"

"As soon as you get me the intel. I'll have you send it
through an encrypted channel to my private server."

She was speaking gibberish, but as long as she knew what
she was doing, Benjamin didn't mind doing the paint-by-
numbers routine. "You got it. Give me a day to get the info."

"Cool." She waited for a beat, then asked, "Hey, man,
in all seriousness, how are you holding up?"

"You mean is my mental totally trashed? Hell yeah, I'm

holding it together by a string but there's no time for a breakdown right now. I'm not going to rest until I find out who did this."

"What about the cop on the case? You don't have faith in the local police?"

Luna he believed in, but her resources were thin and stretched to the snapping point already. He wasn't about to rest the fate of Charlotte's case on the shoulders of a department that could barely handle a handful of crime incidents on any given night. "Let's say, small towns are great for ambience but shit for solving a murder. They don't have the stomach for that level of violence, or the expertise."

"The downside of Mayberry, I guess."

"Yeah, it's what they don't put on the brochure."

She chuckled but said, "You know, you never had much to say about where you grew up but something told me you didn't have a lot of good memories. I hope being home isn't messing with you too hard."

It was, but it helped to have Luna around to distract him, not only in a sexual way. He enjoyed her company. Her sharp wit kept him on his toes, which was something he hadn't realized he appreciated until he saw Luna again.

"It's all right," he said, leaving Luna out of it. "I appreciate your help in this. I know I shouldn't ask but—"

"Hey, knock it off. I can count on my hand the number of people I owe my life to and the first four fingers don't count. Anything you need, you got. You hear me?"

Benjamin's throat threatened to close. Their unit had been assigned to an evacuation control center in Kabul. A surprise insurgent attack had nearly cost them their lives. Codi took an almost fatal hit to the kidney as insurgent fire erupted all around them. Benjamin dragged her away from the fray, saving her life. That incident had earned Codi her medical discharge, and she'd found herself in the private sector with her unique skill set.

He didn't like to talk about that deployment. He'd managed to save Codi's life, but not everyone in their unit survived that day.

And that was all they needed to say about that.

"Thanks," he murmured. "I'll be in touch."

He clicked off and took a minute to breathe through the wall of tension that always threatened to squeeze the air from his lungs when he thought too long about that deployment. He used all his tools to get through the moment.

Thank God for therapy.

Now, he had to find the information Codi needed to start digging.

Chapter 17

"Scott Johnson has an alibi for the night Charlotte was killed," Luna told Benjamin with a frown. Not only had she taken a swing at one of the richest men in town, but her swing had also missed its mark, and now she'd made an enemy. She didn't want to think about how this would bite her in the ass later. She supposed she'd cross that bridge when she came to it.

It was nearing the end of the day, and Benjamin popped in, as it was becoming his habit to see if she was coming to his place for dinner, when she got the bad news a few minutes prior.

Benjamin wasn't surprised but he'd hoped for a stroke of good luck to fall their way. "Even if the guy was guilty, there's no way he'd have blood on his hands. A man like that would hire someone else to do his dirty work."

"But there's literally no motive for Scott Johnson to kill Charlotte and her entire family. It doesn't make sense."

"Yeah, that's the part that's been eating at me, too. We're

missing something, a crucial element, and it's driving me nuts thinking it might be something right in front of our faces."

Leaving them vulnerable. They could be walking past Charlotte's killer every day and not even know it. That part kept her on edge.

She rubbed at the sudden pain between her brows. "Yeah, same. That's my biggest fear, to be honest." Luna didn't want to admit just how much she worried that Charlotte's case might go unsolved because she'd somehow missed something important.

"It had to be personal, right?" Luna mused out loud, trying to mentally dig through the clues. "Killing an entire family. Maybe to send a message? But a message to who?" Frustration ate at her with sharp teeth. "Damn it, what are we missing?"

Wes appeared in her doorway, dropping a report on her desk. "Mark Duncan's fingerprints came back all over the Leicki garage. He lied about not knowing them."

"The contractor?" Benjamin recalled with a questioning look.

"Yeah," Luna confirmed as she read the report. "Looks like I'll be having another conversation with Mr. Duncan. Luckily, he's still in custody so we won't have to go searching for him."

"On a property charge?"

"We pressed the potential murder charges because he couldn't confirm his alibi for the night of the murders. He couldn't make bail so his ass is still at county. I'll pay him a visit tomorrow. See if he's ready to change his story about how he didn't know the Leickis."

Benjamin checked his watch, coming to the same conclusion she had. If either had a choice, they would've preferred jumping in the car and driving to county lockup to talk to

Mark Duncan that very second, but it was too late, and it would have to wait.

As if on cue, her stomach growled, reminding her that she'd skipped lunch. Benjamin took that as a sign it was time to punch out. "I picked up take-and-bake pizza tonight. Hope that's all right with you."

It was on the tip of her tongue to say, "Fine with me," but it wasn't fine. Not that she didn't love pizza; it was that he automatically assumed that she was going home with him. Where did this stop? They couldn't afford to play house, not when the stakes were so damn high. When she didn't answer, he turned to regard her with a brow raised in question.

"Or…not?"

"This is getting out of hand," she muttered, shaking her head.

"I'm not married to the idea of pizza. We can get something else."

"It's not the pizza, it's this." She gestured between them emphatically. "It's a problem."

"How so?"

"You know why. Lines are getting blurred. Before you know it, I'll just be staying at your place every night. I might as well keep a toothbrush in your bathroom."

"Makes sense to me," he said. "Can't ignore your dental hygiene."

"That's not funny." She wasn't in the mood for jokes. "I don't know about you but if we keep doing this I'm going to get attached and when you leave for Arizona, that leaves me in a bad spot emotionally, which is something I've spent a lot of effort avoiding. And that's not the only thing bothering me," she admitted.

He sobered, taking her seriously. "What else is there?" he asked.

"Charlotte," she blurted out.

He wasn't sure how to take that. "Can you clarify?"

"I shouldn't be enjoying sleeping next to her brother when she's dead. It's not right," Luna admitted, feeling a curl of shame heating her cheeks. "It feels wrong."

By the shift in his energy, she sensed she wasn't alone in that guilt. His silence gave away the weight pulling on his shoulders, too. He didn't know what to say and maybe that was a good thing. It shouldn't be an easy thing to brush aside.

"Yeah, exactly," she murmured.

"Luna—"

"No, I think I need some space to put my head on right," she said, backing away. "I'm mentally drained and I'm all over the place, which means I need to regroup. The last thing I should be doing is laughing and having a grand ol' time with you over pizza and beer when Charlotte and her family's killer is still at-large. I—" *hate myself for being so damn weak when it comes to you* "—think I need some alone time."

"This evening took a turn I didn't see coming," he admitted in a quiet voice. Was that hurt in his tone? Did it matter? She couldn't let that sway her. Disappointed, he conceded, "If that's what you want," but he lingered for a long moment as if he wanted to pull her into his arms and kiss her good night.

She yearned to feel those lips against hers but that was part of the problem. When he realized she wasn't going to budge, he waved, climbed into his car and drove away.

She released a short breath, glancing around to make sure no one was watching, and then got into her car to drive home.

"I'm sorry, Charlotte," she murmured, suffering the pangs of guilt like sharpened sticks skewering her gut. "I didn't mean to sleep with your brother. I swear I'm doing everything in my power to find who killed you and your family. Please don't haunt me because your brother is hot and I was weak."

Her cheeks burned a little at talking to herself, but she felt slightly better for trying to make amends, even if it was all in her head. The thing was, she wasn't particularly spiritual, which was always a big surprise for those who usually exclaimed, "But you're Native American. Spirituality is part of your culture!" and it only made her feel that much more disconnected from her roots.

Kenna had always been the most connected to her spiritual side. When they were younger, she was always hiking and spending time outdoors when Luna had been more interested in reading quietly and being left to her own devices. Sayeh had been the athletic one, spending her time being competitive on a field somewhere rather than reading or socializing.

And now Luna was talking to herself in the car on the off chance ghost Charlotte was hanging around and watching.

Would Charlotte approve of whatever was happening between Luna and Benjamin? Hard to say. Charlotte had been the sweetest, most accepting person Luna had ever known, but she didn't know how she would've reacted to this current situation.

She might've hated it.

She might've loved it.

Tears sprung to Luna's eyes. Damn it, they'd never know.

Benjamin felt the moment Luna's energy changed.

He couldn't say that he didn't understand where she was coming from. He'd always been better at compartmentalizing than most because of his childhood, and then his time in the military had honed that skill to a fine point.

There were moments when holding Luna in his arms, enjoying the bliss, the guilt came crashing down, threatening to wrench every good feeling away from him, but he held fiercely to the one thing that brought him joy right now.

Maybe it was selfish of him and Luna was right. They needed to cool things down so they could gain perspective. Playing house was bound to leave them in a bad spot when it came time to get back to their real lives. He wasn't staying in Cottonwood and Luna wasn't leaving. He chuckled with dark humor at the hopelessness of the situation. He couldn't imagine Luna living anywhere but here. She was anchored to this place like an old oak. He'd never ask her to give up that part of herself.

And he'd never move back.

He exhaled loudly, shaking his head. This was a shit sandwich he hadn't prepared for, but then how do you prepare for the experience of Luna Griffin? The girl had blossomed into a force of nature and he was helplessly drawn to her. The chemistry between them was nothing short of magnetic.

Look at him, spouting off in his mind like a poet, but it was the truth.

Even though he could understand her reasoning, it hurt when Luna withdrew.

Hell, that was a can of worms he knew he ought to leave alone.

Yeah, this was probably best—a little distance was good to reset the brain.

He had stuff to do anyway. The stack of financial paperwork from Roger's attorney needed to be combed through for Codi, not to mention he had to prepare for tomorrow, which would be a mental kick to the nuts.

He'd planned to talk to Luna about his plans for tomorrow, but now it would have to wait. After Cottonwood PD released the crime scene, he'd had professional cleaners from Billings come to the house and take care of the mess left behind from the murders.

The things you learn that you never wanted to know.

Crime scene cleanup was a specialized type of cleaning service. Blood had a way of getting in the nooks and crannies, and it required a professional with chemicals you couldn't buy at the local hardware store to wipe away the evidence and sanitize everything.

Even though the house was clean, in his mind, it would forever bear the stains of Charlotte's blood, and he'd rather spend the night behind enemy lines than walk through those doors ever again.

But it couldn't be helped.

Codi needed him to find that personal information for her to do her thing, so that's what he was going to do.

He had a feeling Luna wasn't going to like his favor from Codi, but he didn't mind coloring outside the lines if it meant finding information that otherwise would've been lost to them. He knew how hard it was to get resources, especially with budget cuts and short-staffing issues.

The thought of walking into that giant house, knowing that's where Charlotte had taken her last breath, made him sick to his stomach. He would've been happy to sell that house and never step foot in it again. He had never been impressed by big houses or fancy cars, but Charlotte had always needed to prove something.

For all her sweetness, there'd been something inside Charlotte pushing her to prove that she had risen above her childhood. Why it mattered to her what the small-town people thought of her, he would never know, but Cottonwood had become as much a part of Charlotte's DNA as anything else. Maybe as much as he had run away, for her, it was her touchstone.

God, he hated that. And he also hated that she had died here.

Benjamin grabbed a beer and sat on the porch. As he tipped the beer back, his thoughts drifted into territory he tried to avoid because it brought a never-ending loop of unanswered misery.

He still didn't know what to think of Roger. Even if Roger hadn't been the shady guy Benjamin had suspected, he sure as hell hadn't been smart. At least not smart enough to realize that messing around with dirty money was bound to leave a stain.

Would anything have been different if he'd tried harder to build a relationship with Roger?

Maybe if he'd been a better brother-in-law to Roger, he could've counseled him on whatever harebrained scheme he'd cooked up. Or perhaps it wouldn't have mattered at all. Maybe Roger would've done exactly what Roger was going to do, and fate had already written their story.

Hard to know.

Roger could've been a great guy, but his choices had doomed them all, and nothing Benjamin could've said or done would have changed the outcome.

Ah, hell, he hated that idea that nothing could've saved them, but then again, maybe that was a mercy because if nothing could've changed what'd happened, perhaps he could let go of some of the guilt that was crushing him.

Who knows?

He was thinking in circles at this point. At least when Luna was with him, he could focus on something far more enjoyable than the crap that was looping the drain in his head.

Was that fair to Luna? It wasn't her job to keep him sane. Already, the idea of returning to Arizona seemed a foreign concept, even though he wanted to leave this place and never return. Except leaving Cottonwood meant leaving Luna, and that created a deeper conflict.

Why? Why her?

Life sure had a funny way of screwing with people, and he'd just about lost any lingering sense of humor when it came to weathering messed-up situations.

Even though it was probably too late to start the pizza, his stomach didn't much appreciate that the only thing in there was the beer he'd just finished.

He rose to get the pizza started when he saw a pair of headlights on the road slow, as if the car was preparing to turn down the driveway, but instead it idled without making the turn. The road wasn't heavily traveled so there was no traffic to hold up anyone. The hairs stood up on the back of his neck. "Make your move, coward," he said in a low tone, every muscle tensing. He didn't have a gun but he had two fists and a mean streak.

But whoever was driving must've had second thoughts because a few seconds later, the car drove away and the lights faded into darkness again.

Could've been a lost traveler, he realized sheepishly as his adrenaline drained. Damn, this whole situation had him seeing the boogeyman in every shadow.

Maybe he ought to go to bed early, forget the pizza.

He was ready to put an end to this day anyway.

Chapter 18

The following day Luna got to county lockup as early as possible. She knew the county wouldn't let Benjamin tag along, and in light of their conversation last night, she thought it best that she go alone.

Moments later, the jailer brought a cuffed and leg-shackled Mark Duncan into the interrogation room, and his sour expression wasn't a big surprise.

"This is some bullshit and you know it," he spat as he dropped heavily into the metal chair across from her. "You got that judge to jack up my bail so there was no way I could get the money together but you know I didn't do shit to deserve getting put here."

Luna didn't waste time defending herself and moved to the fingerprints. "You lied to me," she said. "You told me that you didn't know the Leickis but your prints were found all over their garage. Care to explain?"

Mark Duncan's mouth trembled, but he insisted, "I don't know what you're talking about. You probably planted my prints there because you ain't got no case and you need someone to take the fall."

"Don't waste my time. We're not going to play this game where you spout off improbable scenarios to deflect from the fact that you're a liar. Now the bigger question is, are you a killer, too?"

He paled, exclaiming, "I didn't kill no one!"

"You have exactly five seconds to tell me why your fingerprints are all over that garage."

"I… I—all right, fine, I wasn't lying when I said I didn't know the Leickis, but I did some work for them."

"What kind of work?"

"They wanted someone to build one of those fancy gazebos. The wife had some idea of having summer parties on the ranch and kept going on about how a gazebo would be good for the ambience or something like that."

That sounded like Charlotte. She'd loved entertaining. "Go on."

"I told them I could do it for ten thousand and they gave me the job."

"Seems kinda high for a gazebo."

"I gave them a deal. The cost of lumber alone nearly ate up all my profit," he said with disgust. "Anyway, I was starting the job and realized I'd left my drill back at my place and would have to go back to get it but the husband didn't want to lose any production time and offered for me to use whatever he had in the garage."

"That was kind of him."

"Yeah, it was real decent," he admitted. "So, I mean, I saw all of those great tools and that guy didn't know how to use half of the shit that he had in his garage but he had the money to buy the toys, you know?"

"So you thought in return for his kindness, you would steal the man's tools?"

Mark Duncan glowered. "I didn't take nothing from that garage. I bought them, sure, but I didn't take them."

"But you knew they belonged to Roger Leicki," she supplied.

This time Mark Duncan didn't dance around the truth, admitting, "I recognized them as the same tools I'd seen at the Leicki place."

"How so?"

"They were brand-new, except for a few distinct scratches on the external housing. Best guess is that the guy probably dropped them because he didn't know how to use them. Happens all the time."

"So, you knew they were stolen."

Mark wasn't going to get around that fact, but he was still trying to make himself look less like a bad guy. "Look, *I* didn't steal anything. I can't control how people get their shit. I was taking advantage of an opportunity and if you're going to arrest me for that you'll have to arrest every single independent contractor in this goddamn town because everybody does it. It's just my damn bad luck that the tools I purchased came from a house that turned out to be a murder scene."

Luna sensed the truth in his declaration. Did she believe that Mark Duncan killed the Leickis? No, but if he'd lied about one thing, he'd likely lied about something else.

"If you didn't steal the tools, who did you get the stolen merchandise from?"

"I already told you, I don't know who it was. I met the guy in a parking lot after hours. It's not like we were exchanging numbers to date or something."

She sighed. "You're going to have to give me something better than that if you want to walk out of here."

"I can't give you what I don't have. I'm telling you you can't pin that shit on me. I'm not a goddamn killer."

"You're a liar and an opportunistic weasel. How do I know you're not a murderer, too?"

He scowled. "Look, they called me to build a gazebo for them and I did quality work. They didn't have no complaints when the job was done and even suggested that I might come back and do some more projects. Why would I screw up the chance to get more jobs, especially when the guy paid cash?"

"Ten grand seems a lot for a gazebo."

"Well, it ain't. You clearly haven't bid on any construction projects before."

"True." She met his gaze. "All right, do you have anyone who can corroborate that you worked the job and then left?"

Mark Duncan's expression lit up. "Yes! I hired a kid to help me out. His name was Johnny something," he paused to pull the name from his memory, remembering with a snap of a finger, "Johnny Richards."

The name didn't ring a bell. "And where can I find this Johnny?"

He shrugged. "Hell if I know. I didn't know the kid. I needed some help and I needed somebody who was willing to work for nonunion wages and his name came up."

"In other words you wanted to pay him dirt under the table."

"Look, you don't understand how hard it is out there to make a living so keep your judgment to yourself. I paid the kid what he was worth."

Luna wasn't sure about that, nor did she care. She wasn't after Mark Duncan for being a shitty slave driver. "Let's say I can get a hold of this Johnny Richards, and he corroborates your story that you worked for the Leickis and did what you say you did, do you remember seeing anyone at the Leickis while you were there?"

"What do you mean?"

"Did you see anyone at the house? Like business associates? Did Roger Leicki have anyone at the house? Did you see anyone lurking on the property, anything like that?"

"I didn't notice anything and I wasn't exactly invited in the house. I just did the work and left."

Luna sensed that Mark was being honest about that, at least. If Johnny Richards corroborated Mark Duncan's account, it was unlikely they would be able to make anything stick currently holding him at county.

Not that she wanted an innocent man to take the fall for someone else, but it was frustrating to know they had so little to build a case on.

She tried a different tactic. "Is there anything that could help you, help us?"

Mark's gaze narrowed. "Meaning?"

"You're telling me that you didn't have anything to do with the Leicki murders but you're in possession of their stolen property and you lied to me about knowing them or even being on the property. Give me something I can work with if you really are innocent."

Mark swallowed and stared down at his cuffed hands. "I'm sorry I lied. I didn't think it was going to be a big deal buying those tools. Rich guys like Roger Leicki can afford to replace that shit like it's nothing. I didn't know when I bought the tools that the guy had been killed."

He shifted in his seat, continuing, "I'm just a guy trying to make ends meet. I've got two ex-wives, I never see my kids, I can barely make my child support payments and I know that sometimes I make my own problems but I'm not a bad guy. Some tools are too expensive and I don't have the extra cash to get what I need. I wasn't lying when I said every independent contractor has bought a tool that may or may not have been hot so if you're busting me, you're going to have start busting everyone."

"Seems kind of risky for a business owner," Luna said.

He agreed. "Yeah, but sometimes you have to take chances when the risk is low. To be honest, people rarely register their tools. Like I said, a guy like Roger Leicki, he could afford to replace anything that was stolen. I never meant anyone to get hurt. I'm just trying to make a living."

She didn't want to feel sorry for him, but times were hard. The economy was trash. Everyone was feeling the pinch in some way. Even the department—downsizing, staffing issues, it was all there. But that was no excuse for turning to crime.

Luna closed her notebook. Aside from finding this Johnny Richards, at least it was somewhere to start. You never knew where the most critical lead was going to pop up.

"All right, if your story about Johnny Richards checks out we'll see about talking to the judge about your charges. But if you're lying to me again, I will bury you in this place and no one will ever remember your name, got it?"

Mark looked scared, but maybe that's what he needed to turn his life around. *We'll see.* People rarely changed their ways, even after experiencing a come-to-Jesus moment.

Luna left the county jail and headed back to Cottonwood. She wanted to talk to Benjamin even though she knew he'd be annoyed that she talked to Mark without him.

But leaving without him seemed the same as forgetting something important. Benjamin felt like her partner even though he wasn't.

Maybe she wouldn't call him tonight. If she wasn't careful about the cord between them, it might become a lifeline, and she couldn't afford that kind of tether.

Not when Benjamin wasn't planning to stay.

As the day came to an end and he hadn't heard from Luna yet, he called her. He had planned to go out to the ranch, but he was embarrassed to admit that he'd chickened out. He couldn't bring himself to walk into that house

alone. He hoped Luna was coming to make good on that
rain check so they could talk about it over dinner.

But when she declined—again—he knew something was
up.

"What's going on?" he asked.

"Nothing. Just tired from a long day. I talked with Mark
Duncan today—"

"Why didn't you tell me?"

"Because I knew county wouldn't let you into the interrogation room without official clearance and there hadn't
been time to create an accredited identification for you. It
was easier and more efficient to handle it myself."

Suddenly, she was all business. "Are you sure everything is okay? You seem…off," he said.

"Benjamin, when I tell you I'm fine, I don't like to be
interrogated like a suspect, okay? The reality is the courtesy I extend to you for this case was an inconvenience to
accommodate today. I'm trying to solve your sister's murder. That takes precedence over feelings and is something
we need to remember."

Her words stung, even if he understood them. "Yeah, of
course," he said stiffly. "That's all you had to say." He waited
for a beat, then asked, "Are you coming over for dinner?"

"No, I don't think that's a good idea."

"Why?"

"You know why. Lines are getting blurred and I can't afford to lose focus. This is a protection for you as much as it
is for me. In the tidal wave of our shared grief, I think we
lost sight of the potential implications of our entanglement
and we need to pull back."

Even if there was a certain level of logic to her explana-
tion, he struggled not to react emotionally to his hurt feelings. It'd been a long time since he'd let anyone get close
enough to wound him. "Seems kinda abrupt," he said. "Can't
help but take what you're saying personal."

"I'm sorry. I shouldn't have let things go this far. I take full responsibility for—"

"Bullshit," he called her out. "Do me the courtesy of honesty. I'm an adult. I can handle it. It's okay to have feelings, Luna. You can tell me that you're hurting and confused. If you'll let me, I'll be there for you." The heavy silence on the other end felt like a brick wall. "Luna? Don't shut down on me. Talk to me."

"I don't know what else there is to say," she admitted in a mournful tone. "We both knew this was a mistake and we did it anyway. All we did was kick the can farther down the road. Nothing actually changed. If anything, it got worse. Charlotte—"

"Loved you," he finished for her because he believed it. "And she'd never begrudge you happiness, no matter where you found it."

"But she's not here to test that theory and it feels wrong."

"If this is the end of whatever is between us, don't do it over the phone. Come talk to me."

Benjamin was prepared for her to shut him down but when she sighed and agreed, he took the win.

"I'll be over in a bit."

He clicked off, mollified that she was coming over. They weren't a couple, but feelings were involved. He liked to believe that they were mature enough to handle whatever needed to be discussed.

Like adults.

Luna was a complicated woman—and he liked that about her.

Maybe a little too much.

Chapter 19

"Thanks for coming over," Benjamin said to Luna as he let her in. She was dressed down in her civilian clothes, so she must've changed at the station before arriving, but her hair was still in a tight bun.

The bun mirrored the unyielding guard she had around herself as she perched on the sofa, looking more professional than personal, and it pinched at his pride that it seemed easy for her to shut the valve off between them when he was struggling.

No sense in beating around the bush. "I'm just going to come out and say it. Did I do something?" he asked. "Something had to have flipped your switch and I need to know if it was something I did."

She assured him with calm sincerity, "You didn't do anything, it's…it's that we're getting too close, too fast." Luna paused before sharing her concerns. "My judgment is becoming clouded when it comes to you and that's not going to help solve Charlotte's case. You have to understand, neither of us can let personal feelings get in the way of finding who killed Charlotte or else we would always carry that guilt and I can't handle that idea."

"Do you regret sleeping with me?"

"Yes."

Ouch. "Why?"

"C'mon, Benjamin. Think about it. What we did wasn't right or professional. I've never in my life done something like this and it's eating at me. It doesn't matter that you think Charlotte would be okay with what we're doing, she's not here to confirm that theory and whether we had her blessings or not, it feels wrong. We shouldn't be enjoying each other's company when Charlotte and her family are gone. When I'm with you, I feel like a terrible person because I shouldn't be that happy."

"Happiness isn't a crime," Benjamin said, trying to understand. "If anything, with cases like this you have to cling to whatever bit of happiness you can get because otherwise it will destroy you. Survivor's guilt is something I'm pretty familiar with. Trust me, you can't live in perpetual darkness or it will swallow you whole."

"It's more than survivor's guilt," she said. "It's every level of guilt on the spectrum. When I'm with you, it's too easy to slip into a relaxed state of mind and until this case is solved, that kind of sloppy behavior is how people get killed."

It was more than guilt—Luna was afraid. He tried reaching for her but she stiffened and he pulled back. "No one would ever accuse you of sloppy police work, Luna. You work harder than anyone I've ever known."

"And yet we're nowhere closer to finding who did this and someone tried to kill one of us."

"We still don't know that's what happened," he said, trying to ease her fears. He'd keep the mystery drive-by to himself for the time being. "For all we know that could've been a bunch of stupid kids goofing off."

"And accidentally shooting out a window?" Luna countered dryly. "Not likely."

"You don't know how stupid teenage boys can be."

She didn't argue that point but her frustration showed. "Benjamin, when you downplay stuff, it has the opposite effect on me. My gut tells me that was no accident, which only increases my anxiety that I'm no closer to solving the case than at day one. I can't fail in this. I just can't. I definitely can't handle the thought of putting you in danger. If you would try to see things my way, you'd understand where I'm coming from."

"I understand. I have a different perspective."

"Which is?"

"Charlotte was a kind, genuine person. If she thought we could find happiness together, she would've been fine with us spending time together," he assured Luna, but the crease in her forehead deepened into a more rigid frown as she shook her head. He tried harder. "I can promise you, Charlotte would've been fine with whatever is happening between us. She might've even been thrilled."

Luna shook her head again. "But she's not here and it's not right that we're snuggling, laughing and eating spaghetti like nothing horrific happened to her family. Don't you see? It's like bad karma or something to feel this good together."

"I didn't realize you were superstitious."

"That's the thing, Benjamin, you don't know me at all. We've only been spending the last few weeks together, which doesn't tell you anything about my past or my likes and dislikes or anything more personal beyond what we've experienced sexually together."

"I want to know you better," he said. "You're a fascinating woman."

"What would the point of getting to know me be?" she asked. "You're not staying and I'm not asking you to stay.

The reality is that all we're doing is delaying the inevitable and the longer we play this game, the more deeply it will hurt when it ends. Benjamin, my life is already full. I don't have time for additional drama, so it's best to pull the plug now."

He wanted to appreciate her solid points of logic and reason, but the fact that she tried to preemptively shut down what they were doing made him angry—or maybe his hurt feelings triggered his anger—but either way, his words came out sharp. "I never took you for a quitter."

"I beg your pardon?"

"You're quitting because it might be uncomfortable when it ends? Why start anything if that's your fear? All things end at some point. You can't build a life with the fatalistic opinion that there's no point in starting anything when it's destined to end anyway."

"No, I'm saying I don't want to start anything with *you* because I know you're leaving," she returned, her eyes flashing with heat. "Look, I get it, being with me was a nice way to push aside the uncomfortable feelings that have inevitably bubbled up since coming home to Cottonwood but I'm not your emotional support dog. I have feelings, too, and I'd really rather not be devastated when the time comes for you to go back to Arizona."

Benjamin throttled down his temper, taking a minute to breathe through the storm. She didn't want to be hurt, which meant, like she'd said, she had feelings, too. That put a different spin on things. "Neither of us meant for this to happen but it did and I don't regret it," he said. "I don't know what Charlotte would've thought but I'd like to think that she would've been okay with it because she loved us both."

Luna conceded his point with a noncommittal shrug. "Yeah, probably," she said, but added, "but she's not here and it just feels wrong to be…happy."

The mask dropped for a moment. Sadness and confusion conflicted with each other, and he wanted to reach out and hold her, but he didn't. She had such a good heart and a solid moral compass, he could only imagine how this must've been tearing her up inside. "Charlotte would've been mortified to think that her best friend was stifling her happiness on her behalf. My sister was the ultimate romance cheerleader. She loved *love* and wanted people to find their soul mates. I used to tease her all of the time about her always trying to play matchmaker with all the wrong people."

Luna's grudging smile gave him hope. She shared, "She was so over-the-top when it came to trying to match people up in town. One time she thought Bonnie Turford and Nelson Hough would make a good match and she spent so much time and energy trying to throw them into social situations until it became embarrassingly obvious what she was doing and Bonnie and Nelson begged her to stop." She chuckled at the memory. "As it turned out, Bonnie was gay but hadn't come out yet so there was no way Bonnie would've ever looked Nelson's way. We all had a good laugh about it later, though."

He could see it. He didn't know how given their childhood, but somehow his sister had been a romantic at heart. "That's another reason I have a hard time believing that Charlotte would've cheated on Roger. He might not have been my choice for her, but she seemed head over heels for the guy."

"She really was," Luna agreed. "And he was for her, too. They were very sweet to each other. I don't believe Brianne's story about Charlotte and Scott Johnson. I think it's exactly as Scott said—he tried something but Charlotte shut him down." She sighed and sank into the sofa as if she'd used up the last of her energy for the day, sharing, "The other thing that's been eating at me for a few days is that I can't get past the brutality of what happened. You don't imagine something so horrific happening to someone as kind and gentle as Charlotte and Roger. They were genuinely good people. Who does that? And the fact that they're still here somewhere? Lurking? Watching and maybe even enjoying the trauma they've caused our community? It messes with my head. I have to find out who did this so it never happens again."

The desperation in her voice tugged at his heart. He had to help, even though his way might be coloring outside the lines. Now was the time to share about Codi.

"I have something to tell you that you're probably not going to like, but I think it's our best chance to find what Roger was up to."

Luna was emotionally exhausted, but Benjamin's announcement grabbed her attention. "What do you mean?"

"A friend of mine I served with in Afghanistan works in the private sector in financial security. If I can get some personal information like Social Security, birth date and things like that, she can trace his financial trail."

"She's a forensic accountant?"

"Not exactly. She's more of a sophisticated hacker who uses her talents for good rather than evil, but she knows how to navigate the tricky waters used by those trafficking the deep web."

Luna was confused. "How can she help us track Roger's financials? And how would we use any of the information if she manages to find something?"

"Okay, that's the sticky part but we've got nothing to go on right now. We don't even have a direction to head in. We need a light in the dark. Codi will get us that."

Luna didn't want to encourage Benjamin to do anything illegal, nor did she want to know anything about this Codi person breaking the law to find information. Still, sometimes you had to look the other way for the greater good of a situation. Detectives bent the rules all the time with confidential informants. How was this different? She warned herself that that was a slippery slope, but she was curious what his friend could find. Maybe if Codi found the right clue, they could follow up through the proper channels.

It was worth a shot.

She cracked a yawn. It felt good to be here, even though she ought to leave. Her stomach yowled like a cat in heat. Damn it, she'd forgotten to eat lunch again.

In true Benjamin fashion, he offered to feed her. "I've got some leftover Chinese I could heat up for you."

The temptation to cave was the fuel she needed to stick to her guns. "I appreciate the offer but I should go." If she stayed a moment longer, her willpower would crumble. It was already too enticing to fall back into the comfort of his arms and she was determined to see this through.

Benjamin didn't hide his disappointment but he didn't continue to press. It was contradictory but her feminine pride pinched when stopped.

But this was better.

As she reached the door, he said, "I have a favor to ask."

She waited, listening.

"Tomorrow, I have to go to the ranch to find that stuff for Codi, but I don't want to go out there by myself. I know it seems stupid but—"

"It's not stupid. I'll go with you," she cut in quietly, understanding completely and feeling bad that she'd almost made him deal with it by himself. This wasn't pushing a boundary, this was part of her police work. It was only right that she go with him. "What time?"

His voice sounded rough as he said, "Whenever is good for you. Does ten thirty work?"

"Yes, that's fine. I'll clear my schedule and we'll head out there."

He nodded, ducking his gaze, but not before she caught the sudden sheen in his eyes. They never talked about his grief. Luna knew it was there, but she wouldn't appreciate someone drawing attention to her most vulnerable places either, so she didn't bring it up. Maybe that was the wrong way to handle the situation.

"I'll see you tomorrow," she said, forcing herself to leave and ignoring the pull to wrap her arms around his neck.

As she drove home, her thoughts came back around to a jarring realization.

What if the person who killed Charlotte and her family was hiding in plain sight?

What if it were someone no one would ever suspect?

Chapter 20

Benjamin and Luna pulled up to the ranch, and immediately he wanted to leave. Luna sensed his apprehension and reached for his hand. "I'm right here. If you want to stay, we can stay. If you want to go, we can go. I'll follow your lead."

Knowing that she had his back no matter what gave him the strength to nod and say, "Let's get this over with," and exit the car with a strengthened resolve.

"It's a gorgeous place," he acknowledged, almost hating it for its beauty. Nothing should look this good when something terrible had happened behind its walls. "If it were up to me, I'd burn it to the ground."

Luna regarded the sprawling ranchette with the same apprehension. The rigid set of her shoulders mirrored the tension roiling in him. "It likely won't sell locally," she shared. "It'll have to sell to someone looking to relocate to Cottonwood but even then, houses with violent pasts are a hard sell."

"Whether it sells or not, I couldn't care less. The money means nothing to me."

"You could donate the proceeds to a charity Charlotte supported," Luna suggested.

"Not a bad idea," he agreed, considering the possibility. "Charlotte would approve of something like that."

He wasn't superstitious by nature, but he couldn't help but believe trauma clung to the ranch's framework like a hidden virus, lurking in the timbers to contaminate any future joy. He still thought the best course of action would be to burn it down.

But Luna gently rubbed his shoulder, saying, "Someone will buy it and it will be a happy home again. Charlotte loved this house. Just because something bad happened here doesn't mean that it can't be a wonderful place for someone else. My mom once told me that an ending for one person is a fresh start for someone else and I think Charlotte would agree."

"You're right," he conceded but for him, it would always be tainted.

Luna pointed at the gazebo off to the left. "According to Mark Duncan, that's the gazebo he built for Charlotte and Roger and why his prints were all over the garage."

"Do you believe him?"

"I do. He has no motive. I looked into his background and he's not a killer."

Benjamin grunted in agreement, but where did that leave them? With nothing. "Who could have motive to wipe out an entire family? I mean, you've got to be a stone-cold killer to kill two defenseless little kids."

Luna nodded. "Whoever did this is definitely a sociopath."

Upon entry, the smell of bleach and harsh chemicals assaulted Benjamin's nostrils. He rubbed at the tingle in his sinuses. "At least the company I hired to do the hazmat cleanup did a good job." The place was pristine. Any evidence of the tragedy was gone. They'd cleaned away the broken glass, washed the blood, replaced the soiled carpet and put a fresh coat of paint where it was needed. It was showroom ready and looking to seduce future buyers.

He closed his eyes, remembering the last time he was here—Christmas three years ago.

Charlotte, beaming as the consummate hostess, bringing countless baked goodies to the table as if she were feeding an army and not just her family and brother; her joy was contagious.

"I made your favorite—banana cream pudding—and you have to try the macarons. I've fine-tuned the recipe and they're as perfectly French as they will ever be."

He'd chuckled at her determination to master a French pastry. "I'm sure they're delicious. I've never tasted anything you've made that hasn't been perfect."

"There isn't a single dessert my wife can't recreate with the precision of a classically trained pastry chef," Roger had cooed, kissing Charlotte on the cheek, which had elicited groans from the boys that Benjamin felt in his bones.

But now that memory hit differently.

Maybe he'd been a real dick to Roger when all the man had wanted was to be a good husband.

He shook off his thoughts before they ran away from him. "Where should we start?" he asked, clearing his voice, but as he looked to Luna, her hollow expression stopped him. "Luna?"

"I'm fine," she said too quickly to be true. Luna looked away, but not before he saw the pain. He wasn't the only one struggling. Luna had found their bodies. He couldn't imagine the horror of her memories. It was bad enough to find her best friend, but to find the boys, too? Hell, if he'd been the one to find them, he might've lost it completely. She looked to Benjamin, her eyes glassy, admitting in a strangled voice, "It's harder than I thought it would be."

"C'mere," he murmured, pulling her into his arms to

hold her tightly. She trembled in his embrace, and he absorbed the pain rolling through her as if it were his own.

Luna shuddered and reluctantly pulled away, wiping at her eyes. "Sorry, I got overwhelmed. I didn't think it would hit me like that," she admitted, embarrassed.

"No need to apologize," he assured her, giving her distance. The best course of action was to get what they needed and get the hell out. He drew a deep breath and glanced around, puzzled. "So, where should we start? The office, maybe?"

"It's that way," she said, pointing down the hallway.

They walked into the office, expecting the same level of tidiness as the garage, given that Roger liked his space to be organized, but that's not what they saw.

"What happened here?" Luna asked, troubled. "Do you think the cleaners didn't clean in here?"

"No, they were supposed to clean the entire house, top to bottom," he answered, equally troubled.

It looked like a tornado had ripped through the room. Papers were scattered about the floor, books tossed from the bookshelves, and the desk drawers had been emptied seemingly in a frenzy.

"What the hell?" he murmured, shaking his head. "Maybe thieves looking for easy cash?"

But Luna's alarmed expression told a different story. "They're still looking for something that was left behind. Don't touch anything."

Luna and Benjamin donned gloves to protect the scene, and Luna called dispatch to get forensics back out there, but while they waited, Luna pushed everything else out of her brain to focus on the smallest details.

"Whoever came back was looking for something specific, something they thought Roger would have in his office, which tells me it was something business-related," Luna said, thinking out loud. "One of the original items missing was Roger's laptop, so whatever had been worth killing over must not have been on the laptop, which sent them back to the ranch to look."

Benjamin nodded, following her bread crumbs. "So, something they assumed would be on the laptop... Financial information maybe?"

"If not an electronic device, then something written in longhand," Luna processed, slowly circling the room as she searched her brain. A childhood memory jumped out of nowhere. "Charlotte used to journal," she remembered. "But she used to have to hide the journals from your dad. She'd hide them in the floor vent."

This was news to Benjamin, but he quickly followed Luna and ran up the stairs to the master bedroom. She systematically went to each vent, carefully pulling it free from the ceiling and feeling around for anything that didn't belong. Finding nothing, she went to the last vent on the floor, nearest the bed. She pulled the vent and exclaimed as she lifted a small notebook from the closed-off vent.

"Holy hell, you found something?" Benjamin said in shock. "What's it say?"

"I don't know. Let's find out." She flipped the notebook open and started skimming the contents. It felt like an invasion of Charlotte's privacy to read her journal, but it couldn't be helped.

Luna read a passage out loud.

Roger thinks he's found a way to get us out of this terrible mess, but I don't see how it's going to work. We could lose everything, but we'd be alive. Roger says not to worry, that he's got a plan, but I'm real scared. I wish we'd never agreed to take on The Book. The money isn't worth the risks we're taking.

"What book?" Benjamin asked, confused.

"I don't know," Luna murmured. "Maybe like a black book or something? A ledger of illegal activity?"

He nodded. "That makes sense. If Roger was doing the books for shady people, the black book would be a dangerous weapon in the wrong hands."

"It would also be the most incriminating piece of evidence that people would do anything to protect," she said.

Luna skimmed down farther, her heart jumping into her chest at the last entry.

Me and Roger got into an argument tonight. He won't let me tell Luna what's going on, but I know she'd find a way to keep us safe if she knew what was going on. He said we can't take that chance. He assured me he has a way out, but I have to be patient. How can I pretend everything's okay when I'm scared to death most days? Maybe I should put the boys in the car and just drive away. I can't take much more of this stress. This isn't how it was supposed to be. Not ever. What am I going to do?

Luna closed the journal, her throat closing. "That was her last entry," she said, her voice hoarse. *Damn it, Charlotte, why didn't you tell me you were in trouble?* She looked to Benjamin, her heart breaking. "I would've done anything in my power to keep her and the boys safe."

"I know," he said, stricken. "And she knew that, too. She put her faith in Roger and it cost them."

Luna wiped at her eyes. "We have to find this book Charlotte was talking about. Whatever is in that book is what got them killed."

"And whoever killed them thinks it's still in this house."

Luna didn't have the resources to post a patrol outside the residence, but she couldn't afford to let whoever killed

Charlotte waltz in and out of the ranch at their leisure while they continued to look for The Book.

"We don't have the manpower to post an officer 24/7," she said. "I'll have to stay out here and keep the place locked down."

"Hell no, that's not happening. You'd be a sitting duck out here in the middle of nowhere with no backup available if you got into trouble."

"What choice do I have?"

"Then I'm staying with you."

"I can't let you do that," she protested.

"There's no discussion that ends with you staying in this giant house by yourself," he said firmly. "If you can't get your department to cough up the extra dough for another patrol officer out here, you'll have to make do with me."

Luna didn't want to stay in the house alone but was it right to ask Benjamin to put his life on the line for her? No, it was not.

But he wasn't going to budge. She could see from the set jaw and hard press of his lips that it would take an act of God to get him to change his mind, and that wasn't likely to happen.

"Fine but I don't like it," she said with a glower.

"That makes two of us," he said. "But I'll be damned if I'm going to let anything happen to you. At this point in my life, you're the last person who means anything to me and that's just the facts."

Luna blinked back the sudden tears. It was possibly the sweetest and most messed-up thing anyone had ever said to her, and she didn't know if she ought to be flattered or angry.

Maybe a little of both.

But the truth was, she wasn't going to get a wink of sleep if left alone in that house.

It wasn't that she believed in ghosts, but this would be a hell of a time to discover they were real.

They could use some luck right about now.

Luna worried they were running out of time to solve this case.

Chapter 21

Luna was surprised the police chief found some extra resources for additional patrol at the Leicki ranch, which ne-
gated her having to do the patrol herself. She wasn't going
to argue the unexpected win, relieved that she wasn't going
to have to spend the night out there.

Benjamin was also relieved, but they were both privately
shaken by the reveal of Charlotte's journal.

While they hadn't found anything else in the house that
might've led them to this mysterious Book, Benjamin managed to find the personal documents his friend Codi needed
to do her deep web sleuthing, which freed them up to handle some personal details.

For Luna, it was spending some time at home with her
family.

Sayeh, ever the restless one, was no longer content to sit
at home and wait out her downtime while Internal Affairs
sorted out her assault charge on a fellow agent.

Now, she was digging into things that needed to be left

alone—the death of their parents, which seemed like un-necessary drama as far as Luna was concerned and she'd voiced her opinion as such.

Sayeh didn't agree. *Shocking.*

"I'm doing it anyway," she'd declared and walked out of the room, ending any further discussion.

Luna tried to get Kenna's support but Kenna didn't want to get involved and ran the other way as soon as Luna brought up the subject.

Having both sisters home again was loads of fun.

A part of her wanted to bring up the subject of her last conversation with her dad but she was too chicken and put it off. With nothing to distract her, her thoughts stubbornly returned to Benjamin and how she was struggling with her own decision to keep her distance.

Damn, she missed him. There was something com-forting about his presence that she'd come to rely on and everything about this case had her nerves on edge. What she wouldn't give for a night snuggled up to his big, strong body enjoying a beer on the patio.

Knock it off, already. There is no future that includes that scenario.

A deep sigh rattled out of her mouth as she dropped onto the sofa just in time for Ty to wander in looking like some-one had just kicked his puppy. "What's up, buddy?" she asked. "I thought Grandpa was taking you for more driving lessons in the old truck."

"He had to cancel," Ty answered with a glum expression.

Luna frowned. "Grandpa isn't home?" she asked, real-izing she must've assumed he was tinkering in the shop.

"No, he left in a real hurry. Didn't say much more than he'd have to take a rain check for our driving time."

That's odd. "He didn't say where he was going?"

"Nope." Ty brightened. "Do you think he could bring pizza home tonight?"

"I don't know, maybe," she answered on autopilot, more troubled by her dad's behavior. Since retirement, her dad had had two speeds—slow and stop—and he didn't rush off anywhere. A sense of dread settled in her chest. "You sure he didn't mention anything? Did he get a phone call or something?"

"Oh yeah, on his cell phone," Ty remembered. "But it wasn't a long call or nothing."

Whoever had called her dad had upset him enough to send him running off somewhere. Luna didn't like this one bit.

Was her dad keeping secrets? Or was he losing his mind?

At this point, she didn't know which was worse.

Benjamin was surprised to see Luna at his door but happy to let her in.

"Is everything okay?" he asked with concern as she blew by him, a pensive frown on her face.

Luna didn't hesitate, jumping right into what was eating at her as if trying to purge it from her system. "No, it's not," she answered. "I'm sorry, I shouldn't have come but I feel if I don't vent to someone, I might explode."

"I'm happy to listen," Benjamin offered.

Agitation rippled around her. He wanted to hold her but he wasn't going to do anything that might push her away. For now, he was willing to listen. He followed her to the sofa and waited for her to begin.

"I *never* talk about the things that are bothering me. I stuff it down so I can focus on what needs to be focused on in the moment and nothing gets settled and nothing else gets fixed. I just keep soldiering on to keep the peace because that's what needs to be done."

"What needs to be fixed?"

She threw her hands up. "At this point, I'm not even sure where to start."

"Just say whatever you need to say. I can promise you, I'm in no position to judge."

Luna flashed a brief smile before continuing. "Sayeh has issues with her childhood and I've never really understood why. Bill and Nancy were wonderful parents. Aside from changing our last names, Nancy did everything she could do honor our heritage. I was grateful for everything they did for us and I have no complaints but Sayeh doesn't see it that way. Sayeh always thought that something was taken away from us when they changed our names and she's always held it against our parents."

"Seems like the easy answer for your sister would be for her to change her name back. She's an adult, she can do that without much trouble."

Luna frowned as if she'd never considered that possibility but said, "But why is it necessary? I feel Sayeh pulls this crap because it's incredibly hurtful for no purpose. She's doing all the same things she's always done whenever she's home and right now I don't have the mental bandwidth to deal with it."

Benjamin shrugged. "So don't deal with it. She's an adult. Let her deal with her own shit."

"It's not that easy," Luna returned with an edge of frustration. "I'm the big sister. I'm supposed to be the one who's wiser and more mature and able to handle this kind of stuff, but right now I don't feel like I can handle anything."

That last part cut him. He hated seeing her so broken up over some perceived failure that wasn't true. "Give yourself some slack. No one would blame you for not wanting to take on anything extra, particularly in your family. Family stuff is exhausting."

"You have no idea," she muttered, rubbing her temples. "And that's not even the half of it."

"What else is going on?"

"There's my sister, Kenna, too, who is very sweet but

she's definitely hiding something. I can feel it. Am I a terrible sister because I haven't dug into the reasons she ran off in the middle of the night from an abusive situation that was so bad that she won't talk about it? I should be digging for more information. I should know what happened but I can't even bring myself to press her for details. I just don't have it in me to dig."

He sighed. "One thing I've learned is that when people don't want to share, they find ways to hide the information. If your sister wanted to tell you what happened, she would. You digging isn't going to make it any better, it's just going to make her withdraw from you and that's probably not what she needs right now."

Luna nodded, her expression mired in misery. "There's more."

"More?"

"Now my dad is acting weird and I don't know if it's symptoms of dementia or if he's hiding some kind of secret."

"What secret could your dad be hiding?" he asked, nonplussed.

"I don't know," she admitted in a wail. "But he's definitely acting out of character and I don't know what to do about it. I feel like a bad daughter for not chasing my dad down for answers but when I think about it, I get very uncomfortable and I push it down to the bottom of the list."

"Okay, let's triage this situation," he suggested. "You have such a kind, loving heart but you take on more than you should. It's not your responsibility to be everyone's solution to their problems." He reached for her hand, drawing a deep breath before sharing. "Charlotte always took on more than she could handle because she wanted everyone to be okay, but at the end of the day, who was taking on that burden for Charlotte? My sister is dead because she couldn't ask for help."

Luna blinked back tears, appalled. "I hadn't thought of it that way. I'm so sorry. Here I am talking about my bullshit and you've got your own pain to deal with."

He shook his head, adamant. "No, that's not the point. I *want* you to ask for help. I want you to know that I'm here for you. I wish Charlotte had asked me for help. I wish she had called you. I wish she would've called someone, anyone, because maybe if she had she'd still be alive. She'd still be alive to be a pain in my ass like she should've been, pestering me like a sister should."

"It's not natural for me to burden other people with my problems," Luna said quietly.

"I get it. Look, I'm going to share something I learned from my own therapy that's helped put a lot of things in perspective. Sometimes the coping mechanisms we pick up along the way work in the moment but they're not sustainable. I cut a lot of people out of my life, not necessarily because it was the right thing to do but because it was the only thing I could handle at the moment. It's taken me a long time and a lot of mistakes to realize that instead of cutting people out I should've gotten the help I needed for myself. Your sisters are grown-ups. Let them deal with their own stuff. The same thing goes for your dad. If he wants to tell you what's going on, he will. Unless things get worse, there's not much else you can do. Give yourself permission to focus on what you can handle. You have enough on your plate, wouldn't you say?"

Luna wiped at the tear snaking its way down her cheek, accepting his advice. "You're pretty smart."

He chuckled. "Not really, I've just made a shit-ton more mistakes in my life. They say wisdom is earned. Well, I've definitely put in my time."

Luna's warm, appreciative smile reached into his soul and squeezed with greedy hands. He could feel the bond between them growing, but he didn't do a thing to shut it down.

Chapter 22

Wes dropped a report on Luna's desk with a heavy sigh. "Just seems like things are getting worse and worse."

She looked up. "What do you mean?"

"Seventeen-year-old kid died two weeks ago of an apparent drug overdose. Someone dropped the kid off at the emergency room and split but the kid was already dead by the time they dropped him off. Surveillance cameras show a dark, older sedan but whoever dropped him off was wearing a hoodie and a ski mask so they knew the cameras were there and avoided showing their faces."

"Do we know anything about the kid?"

"Not much. Name's Dougie Branch, in and out of juvie for minor offenses, a short stint in foster care, and didn't seem to be going anywhere but prison if he'd kept on the same path but fate got to him first."

She opened the file, quickly skimming. "So, accidental overdose. Seems cut and dry. Why's it on my desk?"

"Medical personnel found a packet of white powder in

his pocket when he was brought in. They tested the substance and confirmed it was methamphetamine but it was also laced with fentanyl. They turned over the packet for further testing and forensics came back with something unusual on the packaging."

"What do you mean?"

"A howling wolf, only visible under a black light, which is pretty sophisticated for a backyard operation. No one's going to that kind of packaging trouble for a small batch of product. That made me look into the database and see if that particular packaging has popped up before and it has."

"Oh? Where?"

"All up and down the Midwest and as far as New York. Whoever is behind the howling wolf production line, it's pretty extensive."

A sophisticated drug operation running close to Cottonwood? Or was it bad luck that Dougie Branch had happened to get his hands on product that came in from out of town?

"Seems like bad business to cut product with a lethal ingredient," Luna mused. "Can't count on a repeat customer if they're dead."

"My guess is that somebody inexperienced cut the meth with too much fentanyl not realizing just how deadly that shit is. It's not like these drug dealers are hiring chemists to mix these deadly compounds together. It's basically a paint-by-numbers: mix the green with yellow and you'll get blue. They don't know what the hell they're doing and that's how dumb kids like Branch end up dead."

Luna thought of Roger and his mystery money source. Was it possible Roger had been mixed up in some drug network? "Thanks, Wes," she said, deciding to look a little more deeply into the howling wolf drug emblem. "Can you pull up last known associates of Dougie Branch?"

"Sure thing," Wes said, leaving to do as requested.

She was only a few minutes into her research when Bonnie Turford surprised her with a knock on the doorframe.

Luna bit back her irritation, only because Bonnie had been less aggressive since the bigger networks had split town for bigger news. "What can I do for you, Bonnie?"

"Maybe the question is, what can I do for you?" she countered, sliding into the chair opposite Luna.

"What do you mean?"

"Imagine my surprise when Sayeh Griffin came around asking to take a look at the archives, going back thirty years to when an explosion on the reservation killed four people and orphaned three little girls."

Luna sighed, returning to her paperwork. "Yes, Sayeh is doing some personal research into the deaths of our biological parents. That's entirely her project, not mine."

"Any reason why she's looking into that old case?"

"Not that I can tell."

"Is it related to the Leicki murders in some way?"

Luna's expression mirrored her tone. "What? Why would it? They aren't related at all. Sayeh is bored and looking to satisfy some personal questions. That's all."

"Must be hard on the family," Bonnie said. "Very painful."

"Yeah, it's not fun," she agreed wryly. "But Sayeh has always done whatever Sayeh wants to do."

"Hmm, tension at home, huh? That's rough. But it must be hard to not have answers."

"That's where we disagree. I have all the answers I need about that situation," she returned, hoping Bonnie would take the hint. She looked pointedly at Bonnie, saying, "Was there anything else you needed…?"

"You really have no idea why Sayeh would be digging into that cold case?" she asked, surprised.

"Other than personal curiosity, Sayeh has no reason to be digging and I have no reason to care. I'm satisfied, she's not, but I have bigger fish to fry than the prospect of chasing ghosts."

Bonnie understood but added, "I was new to the *Tribune* staff but I remember the explosion being big news even here. A few people actually heard the explosion, according to interviews. There were quite a few conspiracies."

The reservation wasn't far from Cottonwood, so that wasn't surprising. "Sound travels," she said, shrugging, but her curiosity got the better of her, and she asked, "What conspiracies?"

"Mostly aliens."

That made her laugh. "That's refreshing."

Bonnie smiled as she rose. "In all seriousness, what happened to your parents—"

"—Biological," she gently corrected.

"Right, biological parents, was a tragedy but it's a miracle you and your sisters weren't in that trailer that night. It was a stroke of pure luck or divine intervention that Chief Paul was able to put you and your sisters with your dad that night."

Luna looked up, confused. "What do you mean?"

Bonnie seemed delighted to have something of value to share. "Because there weren't any tribal police available that night, Cottonwood Police Department took the assist call on the reservation. Chief Paul was covering the night shift when the regular shift deputy got called away for an emergency."

Luna shifted with discomfort. She'd never heard that version of the story, but then it wasn't something her parents liked to talk about. Nancy had consistently downplayed talk about the incident, saying it only brought up sad memories, and they were trying to move forward, not backward.

That statement had always seemed sensible, but now it hit differently.

Maybe she ought to take a look at the archives, too.

She bit back an unhappy sigh. Might as well add that to the growing list of things she had to talk to her dad about. "Thanks, Bonnie," she said, mulling over the information. "I appreciate the stop by."

"Of course. Actually, since I'm here, I was wondering if there's been any new news on the Leicki investigation that you can share."

"Not really," she said. "I promise, you'll be the first to know if that changes."

Whether or not Bonnie believed her, she didn't say, but she waved and let herself out, leaving Luna to circle back around to Bonnie's little tidbit about the past.

It wasn't a big deal that Chief Paul had been involved with their rescue, she told herself when it continued to strike an odd chord. Cottonwood had an assistance agreement with the reservation to help when the need arose, seeing as there were only two tribal police for the entire reservation. The explosion would've attracted a lot of attention, and the need for assistance would've been an obvious choice.

Luna remembered very little about that actual night, and the details she did remember she was happy to forget.

She remembered being cold and afraid, huddled with her sisters on an old musty couch that smelled like stale cigarettes and spilled beer.

She remembered the loud boom that shook her small bones and the way little Sayeh had wailed while four-year-old Kenna vibrated with silent terror.

But she didn't remember anything past that moment; it seemed someone had taken an eraser and wiped away the memories that followed until Bill and Nancy appeared, wrapping them in warm blankets and tucking them into soft beds for the night.

Yeah, there was a reason she didn't like to go down memory lane; it sucked.

Shaking off her thoughts, she gathered her stuff to meet

Benjamin for lunch. He had information to share from his friend Codi and didn't feel comfortable sharing at the station, which sounded cryptic, but Luna needed a break from the station anyway, so she'd agreed.

Benjamin wanted to meet at Branson Park, an older, secluded park that'd fallen into disrepair over the years when a newer park opened across town. He figured they'd have some privacy for what he had to share, and it was a pretty place for a bite to eat.

"We couldn't meet at the café?" Luna asked, eyeing the graffiti marring the cement walkway and weeds choking the metal play structure. "At night this place is a popular hangout for the local hooligans."

"Call me paranoid but I don't know who might be listening," he said, adding wistfully, "I remember being one of those hooligans back in the day."

She chuckled. "That sounds ominous," she said, half-joking as they sat at the picnic table. The old wood creaked beneath their weight but seemed solid enough. Luna got right to business. "What do you have?"

Benjamin pulled the hoagie from the bag and handed Luna her half. "Codi called me last night. She went down a rabbit hole after I gave her the personal info she needed to start the search. You're not going to believe what popped up."

Intrigued, Luna took a bite while she waited for him to continue.

"Roger Leicki was purposefully keeping his deposits under ten thousand per deposit so the bank didn't report the deposit to the federal government. He knew to keep a low profile as far as the government goes so it was important for him to go unnoticed."

"Is there any way to trace where the money came from?"

"Sure, if we had a lot more time. It would take capturing a digital footprint of the cash deposits and matching it to deposits made from other places."

She frowned. "I don't understand."

He explained, "Micro similarities in the ink, paper and environmental contaminants—as I said, it would take way more time and resources than we have available. Codi is doing me a favor but I don't want to overtake her life."

"Got it, but this doesn't feel like much of a win," she said.

"On the money angle, true, but that's not all she found. Codi found financial records from a deep web search indicating Roger Leicki was in business with a company called HW Inc. But a deeper dive revealed the company wasn't real in spite of owning several properties."

"Why would anyone do that?"

"Lots of reasons but I think the biggest and most plausible reason—money laundering. Or tax evasion, either one would work."

"And you think Roger was involved with something like that?" she asked, trying to wrap her brain around the idea of mild-mannered Roger Leicki as some criminal mastermind.

"He was definitely involved on some level, but whether or not it was willing remains to be seen. I keep thinking of what we read in Charlotte's journal about Roger wanting out. That tells me either he was getting cold feet or he was scared."

"Seeing as they all ended up dead, seems like his fear was justified."

Benjamin nodded. "He could've gotten spooked by something and that's why he was trying to distance himself from the operation but he should've known that once you get in over your head, there's no one to save you from drowning."

Luna's frustration showed as she wiped her mouth. "It was probably his damn pride that kept him from coming to me for help and Charlotte was trying to stand by her man so she kept all this to herself, too. This could've been avoided. My sister works for the FBI. I could've brought the feds in to help."

Benjamin wanted to believe it could've been prevented, too, but hard to say. "The feds don't usually get involved unless they can get something out of it. They might've been on their own."

"A kid here in Cottonwood died from an accidental overdose—fentanyl cut with the meth—but the packaging came up with a howling wolf printed in invisible ink, which has shown up in the database quite a few times—all the way to New York. Got me to thinking, why is product from a sophisticated drug network showing up here? It seems almost as out of character as an entire family getting murdered in their own home."

"Codi did say that if Roger was involved with private security doing something illegal, there was a good chance drugs were involved."

"And everyone knows there's the potential for a lot of money in the drug trade," Luna said, thinking out loud.

"Have you asked your sister about it? Didn't you say she worked in narcotics?"

Luna chewed her bottom lip, admitting, "No, I haven't had the chance to talk to her about it but that's a good idea. She might know something that could help."

"Is there anything about the kid that stands out?"

"Not really. Just your garden variety messed-up kid who drew the short straw in life. I plan to talk to a few of his associates and see if they remember where he might've gotten the drugs."

"Good luck with that. They're going to scatter in the wind the minute they see a cop show up."

"I have to try."

"Fair enough. In the meantime, I'll keep after Codi and see if there's anything else she can find."

Luna nodded but seemed distracted, which was odd given the information he'd shared. He broke into her thoughts to ask, "Is there more?"

She shook her head. "Not on the case, something personal. Bonnie Turford told me before I came to meet you. She said that Chief Paul was the one who found me and my sisters the night of the explosion but I don't remember that at all. You'd think I would remember that my dad's best friend was the one who rescued us that night. But my mind is blank. Like the memory was erased or something."

"It's normal to have gaps in your memory when something traumatic happens. You see it all the time with combat veterans. Why does it bother you that you can't remember it was him?"

"I don't know, something feels off about it. I want to talk to my dad but…" She trailed off and Benjamin filled in the blanks.

"One problem at a time," he reminded her gently.

"Yeah," Luna agreed, shaking off her thoughts. "I don't know what Sayeh hopes to find but it's disturbing how the dust is already being kicked up over the smallest details. Worries me."

Benjamin wished he could help somehow, but he knew this was something she had to figure out with her sisters, and it was best to stay in his lane. He wanted to invite her over but didn't want to add to her stress either. He wanted to rub the tension bunching her shoulders and creasing her brow but tried to follow her lead, even if it was maddening as hell to hold back.

Luna cast a brief but warm smile his way. "I appreciate your advice. You always seem to know what to say to make sense of the chaos in my head."

He'd gladly take that compliment. "Anytime."

From the way Luna lingered, her gaze holding his, he thought she might broach the subject of coming over tonight but she didn't. Instead, she thanked him for the sandwich and left to return to the station.

He didn't let his disappointment show. He wasn't supposed to feel this much for a woman he hardly knew. It didn't make sense but he was getting real tired of not having her in his arms at the end of the night. He needed to decide how much longer he would stay in Cottonwood, especially when it didn't feel like they were any closer to solving Charlotte's murder.

If he weren't careful, he'd end up living here again—and that wasn't an option.

Chapter 23

Later that night, Luna approached Sayeh. "Do you have a minute?"

Sayeh eyed Luna warily, saying, "If this is about me going to the archives—"

"No, something I need your help with," Luna answered, hoping Sayeh was feeling in a helpful rather than adversarial mood because Luna didn't have the energy to fight.

Sayeh relaxed. "Oh, sure. What's up?"

"A case came across my desk, a kid who overdosed on drugs mixed with fentanyl."

"Always tragic," Sayeh murmured, shaking her head. "But not uncommon these days."

"True, but when forensics went over the packaging they found a howling wolf printed in invisible ink and that particular label is showing up all over the database. Have you heard anything about this?"

Sayeh perked up with immediate interest. "A howling moon? Yes, it's a growing network of drug distribution that has so far managed to avoid getting busted. If it wasn't so damn dangerous, I'd be impressed by their slippery connections."

Luna frowned. "How have they managed to elude the FBI?"

"It's very sophisticated and they are good at slipping away. They have friends in high places. It always seems like they're one step ahead of the investigators. I wasn't on the team chasing after the network but I know a few people who are."

"Do you think the operation is based out of New York?"

"We don't know. The base of operations could be anywhere in the world. All we know is that the Howling Wolf has become one of the most powerful drug networks since the Mexican mafia got into the game and started running the border trade."

"Damn, that's scary," Luna said, troubled that something so big had made its way to Cottonwood.

"You said a kid died?"

"Yeah, a seventeen-year-old boy."

"Might've been a bad batch," Sayeh said. "Did you run a check on fentanyl-related deaths in the area?"

"Not yet. We're not used to having these kinds of problems here."

"Welcome to the big time. Fentanyl is a growing problem. It's shocking how many people have died and yet people still keep taking it. Talk about survival of the fittest," she quipped, adding with a regretful exhale, "If I were still at the office I could run some numbers for you but as it is right now I'm dead in the water, and if I go anywhere near a case file while I'm suspended, my ass could be bounced for good."

"Yeah, I wouldn't want you to do anything to jeopardize your job," she said quickly. "I'll have Wes run some numbers tomorrow and see if anything pops up locally.

Is there anything else you can tell me about the Howling Wolf network?"

"I can tell you whoever is running the Howling Wolf distribution chain is sophisticated as hell and when you have this level of sophistication there are many layers of protection. It's not like it's going to be one person in charge. They run these networks like corporations with a distinct chain of command."

"Yeah, but somebody has to be the boss."

"That's true, but finding that boss? Damn near impossible. People end up conveniently dead before they can testify."

Luna rubbed at her forehead, trying to figure out if the pieces connected to the Leicki case or if the Howling Wolf showing up in her area was a different problem altogether.

Sayeh regarded Luna with rare understanding. "Sorry to hear about the kid. It's never easy to hear about a young kid dying over a bad choice."

"Thanks," she said with a brief smile. "I plan to talk to the parents tomorrow, see if I can get any information on the boy's crew. Whoever dropped him off at the hospital dumped a body. The kid was already dead. I need to make sure there aren't more kids in danger of dying like Dougie Branch because of the drugs they're doing."

"Drugs are a pervasive problem everywhere, even Cottonwood."

Luna nodded. She ought to leave it at that but was still thinking about what Bonnie had shared about the explosion and was curious to find out what Sayeh had found out.

"So, I've been thinking about your decision to dig into our past… Even though I don't understand it, I won't stand in your way of finding the answers you need," she said. "All I ask is that you try to be kind. Dad's not young and he hasn't been the same since Mom died. I'm not sure how much he can take with this kind of stress."

At first, Sayeh started to bristle, but she backed down with a short nod. "Okay, fair enough."

It was the best possible outcome between them, and both silently agreed to the terms.

"I was thinking of taking a drive out to the reservation tomorrow. Do you want to come with me?"

It was on the tip of her tongue to decline, but something had her agreeing. Sayeh, surprised but glad, smiled with genuine happiness, and Luna felt terrible for always seeming like the overbearing older sister. "Any particular reason?" she asked.

"I want to see the property where we used to live, maybe talk to a few people."

"It might be difficult to find anyone who remembers anything about that night," Luna said.

"I know but it's worth a shot," Sayeh said. "Plus, I don't know, I have this need to connect to my roots. Cottonwood never felt like home and it's always been a challenge for me to admit that because it made me feel guilty."

"You mean, I made you feel guilty," she clarified quietly.

"Yeah," Sayeh admitted with a slight shrug. "But I don't know, maybe going out to the reservation will give me the closure I need to move past whatever is keeping me stuck."

"Maybe."

They shared a tentatively warm moment—the first in so long that Luna didn't know how to proceed—but before she could inadvertently break the fragile peace, Kenna, carrying groceries, walked in with Ty as she announced with glee, "I have a job interview!"

And Luna gratefully turned her attention to her middle sister's welcome news.

Tomorrow she and Sayeh would go to the reservation for a trip down memory lane that Luna had been avoiding her entire adult life and didn't have time for.

Yay me.

* * *

Since Luna would spend the day with her sister at the reservation, Benjamin decided to meet the Realtor out at the ranchette to discuss putting the property up for sale.

The dry heat was already crisping the air before noon as he waited for the Realtor to arrive. Since the last time he and Luna were here and discovered someone had been rifling through the house looking for something, the chief had found extra money for a patrol officer to remain stationed at the property for a few days, but that funding ran out quickly. The house was vulnerable again, but the situation wasn't easy to solve. He didn't want Luna out there by herself and he didn't want to be there either.

He figured maybe the problem would solve itself if he could get it sold.

A sleek Mercedes rolled up the drive, and a man in a sharp suit and designer sunglasses exited the vehicle with an appreciative whistle at the ranch. "Roger always had excellent taste," he said, reaching out to shake Benjamin's hand. "Preston McGovern, Cottonwood Realty. We're here to make this process as painless as possible. I know it can't be easy to have to deal with this situation."

"It's not," Benjamin agreed, gesturing for Preston to follow. "Well, let's get this over with. I'm sure you know the property specs and all that. Your office said to leave the furniture for now, something about dressing the house makes it easier to sell, but I'm going to need to box everything up. We've had some issues with vandals camping out in the house with it fully furnished."

Preston nodded, accepting the lie without question. "Sure, sure, no one would begrudge you any request, Mr. Reeves, given the circumstances."

"Great. I don't care about the price. Sell it for the lowest possible amount. I just want it gone."

"I certainly understand your need to move the property

but let's not allow grief to color your business sense. This property is worth a lot of money to the right buyer and I wouldn't be doing my job if I didn't caution you against making decisions based on emotion."

"Look, I'm not trying to be rude or ruffle your feathers or anything but I know the real reason you don't want to undercut the price and it has nothing to do with your need to make sure I'm getting a fair deal. The more money in the sale, the fatter your commission, I get it, but I don't want this house sitting in the hopes of landing a better deal. I just want it gone. If I could burn it to the ground, I'd do that."

Preston looked appalled but didn't push Benjamin any further. He admitted, "In that case, I might have a buyer."

Benjamin did a double take. "Already?"

"It's a seller's market right now and the buyer is motivated. I think we could've went higher on the price, which is why I didn't say anything right away, but seeing as you're eager to unload the property, there's no reason to wait."

"Who's the buyer?" Benjamin asked.

"You might know him. Scott Johnson. He owns the Johnson Ranch."

"I know of him," Benjamin said with a frown. "And why does he want to buy this place when he's got his own fancy ranch?"

"Well, the actual Johnson Ranch is owned by his father, so while he's set to inherit the ranch, that's not likely to happen anytime soon as old man Johnson is pretty hale. Scott thinks the Leicki ranch would fit his needs perfectly and he's not squeamish about the circumstances of the sale."

Benjamin kept the growl behind his teeth. He shouldn't care that Scott Johnson wanted to buy the property, but he did. "I was told it was unlikely a local would want to buy the ranch because of what'd happened here. Don't you think it's a little weird that it doesn't bother Scott?" he asked.

"Not my place to question people's motivation," Preston said. "Frankly, this is a blessing because you're right. Not a lot of locals would want to take on this house with its baggage—no offense—but Scott is willing to look past the ranch's circumstances, which would help you as well."

Benjamin didn't like how it made him feel that Scott Johnson was riding in to save the day. Maybe it was unfair of him to feel that way, but he didn't appreciate that the man had tried to put the moves on Charlotte knowing she was married.

Preston was surprised Benjamin wasn't more receptive to Scott's offer. He frowned, perplexed. "Is there some reason you wouldn't want to sell to Scott?"

His misgivings weren't grounded in anything but emotion, and that was the last thing he needed to stop this sale. "No reason. Give me a few days to think it over," he said.

"Sure," Preston said with a quizzical frown. "I'm sure Scott will understand. He's a good guy."

Yeah, real good guy.

Preston clapped his hands together, ready to do a quick once-over on the property, but halted as he stepped on the porch. "Everything is…clean, right?"

"Yes," he growled, walking past Preston. "I hired a professional company to take care of the biohazards."

"Ah, excellent," Preston said with a relieved smile. "All righty then, let's take a look at this gorgeous place and see what we're working with, just in case the deal with Scott falls through."

Benjamin bit down on his urge to fire the Realtor and find someone else. It wasn't Preston's fault that he was a cranky ass when it came to this house, and he couldn't blame him for doing exactly what he wanted the man to do—sell the property. But the longer he stayed in this house, the more he really did consider the idea of it mysteriously going up in flames during the night.

Chapter 24

Luna had spent the better part of her life burying memories from the time spent at the reservation, but now, she was bothered by the conspicuous gap in what she remembered. She was only six years old; she should've remembered Chief Paul being there, but she didn't.

And she couldn't bring herself to talk to her dad about it either.

Somehow it seemed disrespectful to start questioning Bill about the past as if he were guilty of anything other than being a wonderful father to three little girls who'd been all alone in the world.

"Do you have the address?" Luna asked.

Sayeh double-checked her phone. "Yeah, 5750 Flying Hawk Road. It'll be just outside of the reservation proper."

Luna put the address into the GPS, and they hit the road. It wouldn't take long to get there, but it felt awkward to fill the silence with stilted conversation, so Luna decided to enjoy the summer sun on her face and the breeze in her hair.

But it was Sayeh who broke the silence.

"Did you know around the same time of the explosion, authorities arrested a member of the Mexican mafia who'd been part of a massive recruiting ring involving four other reservations throughout Montana and Wyoming?"

Luna shook her head. "I was too young to pay attention to that stuff when it happened."

"Same, but when I went through the *Tribune* archives there was a write-up about it and it seemed interesting that the incidents happened around the same time."

"Sounds coincidental to me," Luna said. "What would our biological parents have to do with a Mexican drug ring?"

"It's not that baffling to connect the dots, Luna. As you're fond of pointing out, our parents were drug addicts and their trailer blew up mixing deadly chemicals. What if they were involved with that particular drug ring?"

Luna struggled with the idea that their parents could've been involved with something that deeply corrupt. Somehow it seemed less threatening to believe they were guilty of poor life choices, not some big, interconnected drug dynasty. But then, she was struggling to grasp the idea that Roger may have been involved in something illegal that ended up killing his whole family. Thus far, this case had revealed her professional prejudice that nothing truly bad happened in Cottonwood.

"I think it would be difficult to prove," she murmured as tension began to build at the back of her neck. She absently rubbed the muscles with her free hand, wishing she'd had the forethought to take ibuprofen before leaving.

Sayeh surprised her by digging into her purse and dropping two into her hand. At Luna's questioning look, Sayeh shrugged, saying, "I hold tension in my neck, too. I never leave anywhere without my arsenal."

Luna accepted the ibuprofen and washed it down with a swig from her water bottle. "Thanks."

"Don't mention it."

A thought occurred to Luna. "Was there any mention of the Howling Wolf drug network in that article?"

Sayeh shook her head. "I think it predates the Howling Wolf," she said. "Howling Wolf didn't start showing up in the FBI database until about five years ago."

Roger Leicki left Asset Protection three years ago. Why did that pop into her head? Probably nothing. Her head was full of odds and ends these days, making it more difficult to sift through what was important and what wasn't.

They drove through the heart of the reservation, a collection of storefronts and a town plaza of sorts, with many of the reservation's tribal offices clustered together, including the tribal police office. As a courtesy, Luna pulled in to let them know they were on the grounds.

The tribal police office was housed in the same building as the tribal liaison. The building was old but still holding up, the tile floors dull but clean.

Luna and Sayeh found their way to the tribal police office, and Luna knocked on the doorjamb. An older man with his long salt-and-pepper hair pulled into a queue at the back of his head and secured by an intricately beaded band looked up, surprised at their appearance. "Can I help you?"

"Detective Luna Griffin with the Cottonwood Police Department. This is my sister Sayeh Griffin—"

"You might remember us as Luna and Sayeh Proudfoot," Sayeh interjected.

The man narrowed his gaze as if trying to discern whether or not Sayeh was being truthful. "Proudfoot... That's not a name I've heard in a long time." He rose and shook Luna's hand, still regarding them warily. "I'm Tribal Officer Joe Dawes. What can I do for you today?"

"We're here for personal reasons," Luna admitted, looking to Sayeh. "We were hoping to drive by the place where our biological parents—Mika and Darryl—died, 5750 Flying Hawk Road."

Joe Dawes frowned. "There's nothing out there. Just a patch of dirt and overgrown weeds. What are you hoping to find?"

"Closure?" Luna answered, unsure. "My sister thought it might be good to see where we used to live."

"I don't know what good that will do you, sister. Nothing left out there but sad memories."

"Did you know our parents?" Sayeh asked.

"I knew Mika. She was a sweet woman, deserved better than Darryl ever gave her," he said, glancing at Sayeh as he gestured. "You're practically her twin."

That took Luna aback. She'd never thought about who they might favor but hearing that Sayeh looked like their biological mother twinged in a place she didn't know existed.

"Really?" Sayeh said, her eyes lighting up. "Can you tell us more about our parents? We don't have any pictures or any details because our adoption was sealed and the records were somehow lost."

Luna looked sharply at Sayeh. That was new information. She filed that nugget away for discussion later. Sayeh was too eager to hear more, and Luna hated to admit she wanted to know more, too.

Joe looked unsure what was safe to reveal. Luna made it easier for him. "We know our parents had a drug problem—"

"At least that's the story we've been told," Sayeh quickly corrected, shooting Luna a look. "But we'd like to know more about them from someone who actually knew them."

"Are you sure? Restless spirits are best left alone," he warned.

"We've spent our whole lives in the dark about our heritage. I need to know if there's more to their story than what we've been told," Sayeh said in earnest.

"I suppose if that's what you want." Joe shook his head, exhaling loudly before continuing. "Darryl was always trouble. Good-looking boy but his heart was weak. He didn't have an ear for wisdom. Always looking for the easy way. I always want to believe that people can turn their lives around if given the right motivation but I don't think the road would've ever been long enough for Darryl to find his path."

Luna's eyes stung for no good reason. Why did it bother her that their biological father had been a loser? This shouldn't have been a surprise given how they died but somehow, having it confirmed hurt differently.

"But Mika, she wasn't like Darryl. At least not at first. She was a good girl with a giving heart. A strong woman who believed in standing behind her man, even when her man wasn't worthy of her loyalty. She tried so hard for you girls. I know that. But sometimes the fork in the road leads to a dead end."

A shiver danced down Luna's spine. She didn't know how to feel about this new information. She felt like a traitor to Bill and Nancy for wanting more. *This is for Sayeh*, she reminded herself. "Can you tell us more about how they died?"

"The explosion killed both your parents," he answered with a sad expression. "Drugs have taken their toll on our people."

"Was there any forensic testing done at the explosion site?" Sayeh asked.

"There was no need. Barrels of toxic sludge were found on the property confirming they were manufacturing methamphetamine."

"Yeah but anyone could've planted those after the fact,"

Sayeh pointed out. "Forensics would've confirmed that the blast was caused by the chemicals in question."

"I was a young officer at the time and it wasn't my call. We didn't have the resources for that kind of investigation and we still don't. As it was, we had to bring in federal agencies to dispose of the sludge left behind and now that property is uninhabitable until the soil tests clear of contaminants but we don't have that kind of money to follow up. Not that it matters—no one wants to live there. The elders have determined the land is damaged at its heart. Best to let it heal naturally."

Luna didn't believe in any of that, but it felt jarring to know that her parent's death was considered some bad juju to the locals.

"But it's safe to go out there, right?" Luna asked.

"To walk around, yes. To dig a well to tap into the ground water, no."

"Thank you, we appreciate the information," Luna said, preparing to leave, but Sayeh wasn't finished.

"Did our parents have a drug rap sheet?"

Luna paused, interested, too.

"Darryl certainly did. Possession for sales, paraphernalia, restricted possession of ephedrine, assault, and the list goes on. To my recollection, Mika was busted for a misdemeanor possession of paraphernalia but she was caught under the influence a few times."

Luna shared a look with Sayeh. She hoped this was all Sayeh needed to let this go. "Thank you, Officer Dawes. We appreciate your time."

But Sayeh had one final question. "Where were we found when the trailer exploded?"

"There was another trailer on the property. You three were found there. Thank Great Spirit."

Luna paused. The hazy memory resurfaced—the cold, the

smell of stale, moldy furniture, Sayeh screaming "Mama!" over and over again. "Were we alone?"

"Yes."

Why were three little girls left in an old trailer while their parents were elsewhere?

Luna hated to ask but had to. "When the bodies were recovered… Was there an autopsy to confirm it was the blast that killed them?"

Officer Dawes shook his head. "It was pretty obvious how they died. Their bodies were burned to a crisp. There wasn't much to autopsy."

An efficient way to cover up a crime, too, Luna thought. Was she going there? A part of her wanted to shut down the questions starting to stack up, but another part of her couldn't stop thinking Sayeh might've been right.

Even if Mika and Darryl were guilty of being drug addicts and dealers, that didn't mean they weren't also victims of a crime.

But why?

On a whim, she asked, "A few weeks ago, a man named Roger Leicki and his family were murdered in their ranch home in Cottonwood. Does the name sound familiar?"

To her surprise, Joe's expression registered cognition.

"You know him?"

"Both him and Charlotte, good people. They were working with the volunteers down at the Macawi Tribal Center to help get updated medical equipment to the clinic, something about getting used equipment donated through the Soroptimist organization. I took a fishing trip on the Yellowstone River and only just got back. I hadn't heard they were killed." His mouth compressed into a tight line. "Do you know who did it?"

"No," Luna answered, shaking her head. "We're still investigating the case."

Her mind was swimming. Why would Charlotte and Roger be volunteering at the reservation? And why didn't they tell anyone? Charlotte was known for rallying the troops, so to speak, gathering people to every cause, and yet not a peep was uttered about her work at the reservation?

What were they into, and what did it have to do with the reservation?

"Can you tell me who Charlotte and Roger were working with at the clinic?" she asked.

"Sure, the clinic director, Dr. Susan Leggins. She's in charge of everything that happens at the clinic."

Luna thanked the officer again and everyone hastily said their goodbyes. A different fire was under her as they returned to the car.

Sayeh chewed her bottom lip, thinking and feeling a little overwhelmed. Luna understood because she felt the same. Sayeh turned to Luna. "No autopsy, kids were put someplace else before the blast, and there was no forensics taken at the site to confirm the chemicals were used. I've never seen such an obvious cover-up in my life."

Luna couldn't deny something shady had gone down, and no one had thought to ask questions. Or they were told to let the questions die with Darryl and Mika?

But her brain was chewing on the bomb about Roger and Charlotte.

"I need to talk to the clinic director about Roger and Charlotte," she said.

"And I need to get someone out to the blast site to take soil samples."

Luna looked at her sister. "How? You're going to need permission from the Macawi Tribal Council and that's not going to be easy."

"I don't care."

The stubborn set of Sayeh's jaw was all Luna needed to see. Sayeh wouldn't stop until she got what she was after.

"Okay, I'll see what I can do to help," she said with a sigh. "But there might not be anything left to find after all these years."

Sayeh understood but said, "I have to try."

Luna wouldn't stand in her way. She nodded and put the car in Drive. Time to talk to the clinic director about Charlotte and Roger's clandestine volunteer work at the reservation.

Chapter 25

It was late when Luna and Sayeh returned to town but Luna couldn't keep her thoughts from turning in a circle after what they'd learned at the reservation. She wanted to tell Benjamin in person but she'd settle for a phone call.

After she rattled off everything she'd learned, Benjamin was suitably stunned by the information as well.

"Charlotte and Roger were working at the reservation to get better equipment for the clinic? That seems on par for something Charlotte would do but it's weird that she would keep it to herself. Something feels off."

"That's exactly how I felt. Charlotte was never one to be silent about the causes she was championing. That was one of the best parts about having her on a volunteer committee. People flocked to be wherever Charlotte was. The fact that she didn't tell anyone that she was working with the reservation gives me a bad feeling. Like it was a secret or something."

Benjamin said, "On the surface it wouldn't seem that

would be a bad thing but given the fact that Charlotte and Roger were murdered and no one knew what they were doing at the reservation, it seems suspect."

"I'd like to think there's really nothing there but intuition says I need to dig a little deeper. Except I don't know where to dig. How do I question someone's philanthropic actions when they're no longer here to explain themselves? Not to mention, I'm not trying to question it was a good thing they were trying to do but my question is why were they keeping it a secret?"

Benjamin soothed her fears. "I know Charlotte was a good person but we already know she was involved in something bad. Learning that she was also involved with a secret project at the reservation just seems to further point to the fact that they were possibly caught up in something they shouldn't have been."

"Does it, though?" Luna asked, unsure. "Why would helping the reservation be a bad thing? Maybe Charlotte was waiting to do a big reveal? Like when she'd managed to secure the equipment or something?"

Benjamin murmured in agreement, but Luna was already changing her mind. "No, what if someone at the reservation was going to help them if she could get the clinic equipment? Like a tit-for-tat thing?"

"What was your impression of the clinic director?"

"She seemed like your typical clinic doctor—goodhearted but overworked and underpaid," Luna answered, sipping her wine. "Definitely not a criminal mastermind if first impressions are to be believed."

"Okay, so maybe they were simply doing a good thing and wanted it to remain private," Benjamin suggested.

"Maybe. Still feels weird. Just when I think this case can't get more twisted, some new lead pops up and I feel like we're right back to square one."

Benjamin drew a deep breath, adding his own two cents

to the mix. "Speaking of twisted. I met with the Realtor today and it appears I already have an unofficial offer before the ranch has even been listed. And it's from a local."

Luna didn't bother hiding her shock. She honestly thought the ranch would never sell, at least not so soon after the Leickis were killed. "How is that possible? I mean, I guess it's a blessing but it's surprising that anyone would buy it given the circumstances."

"Yeah, well, I don't want to take the offer."

"Why not? Have you changed your mind about selling?"

"Hell no. I just don't want to sell to *him*."

"Him, who?"

"Scott Johnson."

"Scott Johnson?" she repeated, flabbergasted. "Why would *he* want to buy the ranch?"

"According to the Realtor, the big ranch belongs to his dad and Scott wants his own piece of property. Call me a cynic but I'm not buying it. Why this property when there are so many other properties available? I think there's something he's not telling us."

Luna chewed on that for a minute. She had to tread cautiously with Scott Johnson after using her one shot to haul him in for questioning had ended up with nothing but a pissed-off chief. However, she agreed with Benjamin; Scott's interest in the Leicki ranch felt off. "I've been told under no uncertain terms that I'm not to go near Scott Johnson unless I have concrete evidence that he's done something wrong. I can't even look cross-eyed in his direction without something to build a case on."

Benjamin understood her dilemma, admitting, "And I don't have the answer as to how to approach that situation without making it worse. All I know is that it feels wrong to sell the ranch to him. I've been trying to process my thoughts about it since this morning. It could be that I know Scott kissed my sister and she wasn't happy about it. Maybe it's my latent way of trying to protect her even though I know that doesn't make any sense."

"Grief doesn't have to make sense, nor does how we grieve, but I think it goes deeper than just your protective feelings toward Charlotte. Selling to Scott feels wrong, and I don't know why either. When did you say you'd give the Realtor an answer?"

"I told him I need a few days to think about it and he gave me the typical Realtor spiel that I shouldn't wait too long or I might lose the sale but I'm not pressed about losing Scott's offer. You already know how I feel about that house and what I feel would be appropriate."

Luna chuckled. "Watch yourself. I don't want to have to turn you in."

"A fact I told myself as well," he said. "Our situation is complicated enough. No sense in adding arson to the list."

She chuckled, even though her heart winced at being classified as a *situation* but what could she expect? She'd been the one to pull the hand brake.

"You sound like there's something else eating at you," he said.

She closed her eyes at the soothing tone of his voice in her ear. There was something about the timbre of his voice that calmed her nerves and set her on fire. What was she supposed to do with that? It was on the tip of her tongue to blurt, "I miss you," but she didn't. Maybe she hoped for points in heaven for reining in her baser needs when it came to Benjamin but she only won a hollow victory when she managed to say goodbye without losing her resolve.

Too bad that hollowness started to feel like her chest caving in.

Aside from the stunning revelation about Charlotte and Roger working secretly on the reservation, Benjamin had a sinking feeling that Luna wasn't going to budge. She was holding firm in her decision to keep things professional between them and it hurt.

He should've been grateful. At least one of them was thinking clearly and it wasn't him. He wanted Luna in his arms. Every night.

What was wrong with him? He'd stepped into Cottonwood and lost all the good sense he used to have.

Maybe it was time to start thinking about his return to Arizona. He'd planned to stick around until the case was solved but he'd underestimated how complicated this case would become. The truth was, it could be years before this case was settled and he couldn't stick around that long.

He had a life back in Arizona that he missed—friends and a routine that made sense—and he couldn't give all that up to chase Luna and this case around. That was no kind of life and eventually, it would crumble, leaving him and Luna in an even worse situation than they were in now.

The answer was clear as the nose on his face: regretfully, it was time to wrap things up in Cottonwood.

But first he had to decide what to do with the ranch. Should he sell to that douchebag Scott Johnson or hold out for a different offer? On principle alone he wanted to tell Scott to stick his thumb up his ass and spin on his offer but that was his anger doing the talking.

The memories of Cottonwood were messing with his head. Luna was the only bright spot in his mind about this place.

But she shone like a damn beacon.

Argh, leaving her will be the death of me.

Chapter 26

Since discovering yet another mystery surrounding the Leickis after the reservation trip, Luna couldn't help but wonder if everything that'd happened—from the explosion that killed her parents to the Leicki murders—was connected.

But how?

The easiest line to draw was the drug connection, but the Mexican mafia had supposedly cleared out of the reservations years prior to the Howling Wolf network appearing on the streets.

Not that she had any proof that the Howling Wolf operation was responsible for the Leickis' murders, but the fact that product from a well-established drug network had appeared in Cottonwood seemed suspect.

The problem was there were too many gaps in the information she had to work with. She exhaled a long breath. There was no going around it; she needed to talk to her dad about the night of the explosion. She needed more details.

Luna made Sayeh promise she'd let Luna do the talking to their dad because Luna knew Sayeh would come at the situation with a sledgehammer and likely shatter their poor father's heart.

Meanwhile, Sayeh was chasing down ways to get a soil sample from the blast site by negotiating with the Macawi Tribal Council. Luna could only hope Sayeh handled that situation with more finesse than she usually handled things.

Luna found her dad in his shop tinkering on a project. She felt bad for disturbing his peace, but this couldn't wait.

"Dad, can I talk to you?" she asked.

"Sure, what can I do for you?" he answered, smiling as he wiped the sawdust from his overalls. This was the dad she knew—kind, generous and always ready to help. Her heart hurt for the painful conversation she was about to have with him, but it couldn't be avoided.

"I need to talk to you about something that you're not going to like but I really need your help to understand some things and I have no one else to ask."

His expression turned serious. "Is there something wrong with Sayeh or Kenna?" he asked, instantly concerned. "I know Sayeh can be a handful but she's got a good heart. You just need to be more patient with her."

Her dad was immediately ready to defend Sayeh, which only made Luna want to forget this whole mess but she knew she couldn't. "No, they're both fine. It's actually about the night my biological parents died."

Suddenly Bill's energy became less warm and interested. She could almost see the curtain closing on his willingness to talk. She rushed to keep him from completely shutting down. "Dad, I would not ask if I didn't need to know. I have no interest in hurting your feelings or being disrespectful to the life that you and Mom gave us but I've come across some information that doesn't make sense and I need you to help me understand what actually happened."

"Why? That's all in the past—best to leave it there."

"Because there's a chance the explosion and the Leickis' murders are connected but I can't figure out how because I don't have all the pieces from the past."

"They're not," Bill answered sharply, his bottom lip trembling a little. "You're grasping at straws and barking up the wrong tree, sweetheart. There ain't nothing but pain and heartache that far back and there's no way the two incidents could be connected."

"Dad, as much as I hate to admit it, the Leickis might've got caught up with some bad people and I think drugs might've been involved."

"Do you have proof?"

"Well, no," she admitted.

"Then don't go saying things like that—it's dangerous."

At the rebuke, she stared in shock at her dad, her feelings a little bruised. Suddenly, she felt ten years old again and somehow she'd disappointed her beloved father. "But Dad, if there's even a chance, I can't let it go. There are too many missing pieces of the puzzle and I need your help. Can you just tell me what actually happened that night?"

Confusion settled on his features. "What do you mean, what actually happened? We've told you the facts of what happened that night and it's not something I enjoy going over again. It was an awful tragedy."

"Yes, it was, but there's a possibility that they were murdered and their deaths covered up."

At that, Bill's agitation grew. "Why can't you let this go?" he asked, almost pleading. "Nothing good can come of digging into that situation."

Luna and her father had always been close. She couldn't remember a time when he hadn't been there for her. He was the most generous individual she'd ever known in her life, and the fact that she could see the pain in his eyes at the mere mention of the death of her parents made her sick to her stomach, but she couldn't stop.

"Dad, how did Chief Paul know we were in the trailer that night?"

He rubbed his forehead as he recalled, "Well, he was called by the tribal police for an assist. I've told you that."

"Yes, but how did he know we were in the other trailer and not in the trailer with our parents? The story that I remember was that we were with a babysitter but as it turns out there was no babysitter. We were alone. It's true, I remember very little of that night but why wouldn't I remember Chief Paul being there to rescue us?"

Bill looked flustered. "Honey, it was a long time ago. I don't remember the exact details of how everything went down. I just know that there was an incident on the reservation. Chief Paul was covering the night shift and took the call. He came back with three little girls who were scared out of their minds and your mother and I fell in love with those girls. We were lucky enough that Nancy was your biological mother's only living kin, which enabled us to adopt you."

"But did Mom know Mika? I know they were distant cousins but did they ever know each other?"

"Only by name. Nancy's family left the reservation when she was born so she was never raised the tribal way. I don't understand where any of this is coming from. Your biological parents died almost 30 years ago and whatever problems they had in their life are done. They're at peace now. Let the past remain in the past."

"But there's a chance they were murdered, Dad."

"No," he disagreed firmly. "It was a terrible accident. They were mixing highly volatile chemicals. It's all in the report."

"Yes, but there was no forensic testing done at the site.

There wasn't even an autopsy done on their bodies. How does anyone know what actually happened if there's no science to back up the reports? You, of all people, should know that the investigation was done in a way that would not be tolerated if it had happened anywhere but the reservation."

"We were only called in to assist. The investigation was handled by the tribal police," he said. "It wasn't our jurisdiction to question how they proceeded with the details. And even if you're right, we can't change the past. Digging into the details is only going to make a mess out of things that can't be changed. Please let this go."

Luna flushed with anger that her dad was asking her to go against everything she'd ever believed was right, the way he raised her, to look the other way. "I can't," she said. "And Sayeh can't either. Right now, Sayeh is getting permission from the Macawi Tribal Council to take a soil sample from the blast site. She wants to see if the chemical compounds match what the accelerant would have been in the event of a chemical explosion."

"Why? Even if it's discovered that something happened to your parents there is nothing that can be done to bring them back."

"Don't they deserve justice?"

Bill looked caught between a rock and a hard place, stating stiffly, "They were deeply troubled people. I'm sorry but they were drug addicts who put your lives in danger every single day. I'm not saying they deserved to die, I'm just saying that sometimes God takes care of those who need taking care of."

She stared in disbelief. "Dad, I can't believe you just said that."

Bill crumpled with shame. "I'm sorry, that was out of line."

"For Sayeh, it's personal, but for me, I have to make sure

the two incidents aren't connected. My gut says to keep digging and that's what I'm going to do. I hoped I would have your support."

"I would support you in everything and *anything* except this," he said. "I can't."

A chill traveled down her spine. "Dad, what are you telling me?"

"I'm telling you there are some things in life that aren't worth chasing," he answered quietly.

She blinked back tears, whispering, "I don't believe that's true." It was like watching her idol crumble before her eyes, and she couldn't stand the pain of it. "If you can't tell me the truth about that night, I will find it a different way, but don't ask me not to do my job because I simply can't."

"Luna—"

But Luna had had enough. Her heart couldn't take another minute.

Benjamin was a big believer in going to the source. He had questions that needed answering. He needed to ask Scott Johnson point-blank what his intentions were and let the chips fall where they may.

"I'm just gonna cut to the chase. Why do you want to buy my sister's ranch?" he asked, squaring up to Scott, arms folded, meeting his stare, man-to-man. "'Cuz I gotta be honest, it don't sit well with me."

Scott's brows rose at the question, taking a minute to digest the energy Benjamin was coming at him with before answering. "I swear, you and your sister are a lot alike."

"Meaning?"

"It means, she kept me on my toes, too. I never knew what to expect when Charlotte came at me with something and I liked that about her. People are usually predictable. I enjoy the challenge of someone who is not."

Benjamin found Scott's answer patronizing. "Is that your answer?"

Scott chuckled, amused by Benjamin's hard stance. "Look, I could offer the socially acceptable thing and say that I wanted to do something posthumously for Charlotte by helping you off-load a house that harbors nothing but bad memories but I'm not that altruistic. The truth is the property is prime, and Charlotte had a good eye for design. The house would make a good investment. Tragic as they are, I'm not squeamish about the circumstances, so when I heard you were eager to dump the house, I put my offer in to Preston."

"So it doesn't bother you at all that Charlotte—a woman you admitted to being attracted to—was brutally murdered along with her entire family in that house?"

Scott was unapologetic, shrugging. "Not the first time I've been accused of missing an empathy chip but no, it's just a house. I don't believe in ghosts either. I believe in good investments, the flow of money and hot sex with willing women. Everything else is just noise."

Benjamin appreciated the candor, but he was also proud of his sister for seeing through this douchebag and running when she had the chance. Any woman with the misfortune to get tangled up with this guy was likely to end up with emotional damage.

"So it's just a good investment to you?" he summarized.

"Exactly."

Benjamin probably should've left it at that. Scott had answered, and Benjamin should've been happy to let him have the house.

But he couldn't leave it alone. "In the spirit of full disclosure, I'm not sure whoever killed Charlotte got what they were looking for."

Scott frowned. "What do you mean?"

"Someone returned to the house after the fact and tossed

Roger's office, clearly looking for something. I feel it's only right to share that they might keep returning until they find what they were looking for."

Scott relaxed, chuckling at Benjamin's warning. "Once I take ownership, no one's going to mess with me or the house. I'm not worried, but I appreciate your concern and your honesty. You're a good man. I should probably take a lesson," he said with a wink.

Don't punch him in the face. "Yeah, well, thanks for your honesty. I'll let my Realtor know my final answer in a day or two."

"Take your time."

Benjamin turned to leave, but as he approached the door, he asked, "Can I ask you something?"

"Anything."

"What'd you think of Roger? Do you think he was capable of doing something dangerous?"

"Roger? Dangerous? Look, he was a good man. Maybe he wasn't the most masculine—I think he might've been a buck eighty soaking wet—but he was a solid guy. Someone you could really depend on. He always knew what to do to get things done. Smart as a whip that guy."

"Did you work with him?"

"No," Scott clarified quickly, "he just seemed that way from what I heard around town. Nothing but good things said about Roger. Your sister picked a good one."

Benjamin nodded and let himself out.

How was it possible for the guy to say all the right things, yet Benjamin still wanted to toss him in a lake? It wasn't anything he could put his finger on, but he didn't trust Scott Johnson any more than he'd trust a hungry bear coming out of hibernation not to chow down on a fresh haunch of deer meat.

But nothing tied Scott to Charlotte's murder, and being

a rich asshole wasn't a crime, so was he going to decline Scott's offer because he didn't like the guy?

Maybe.

Irritation with nowhere to go left him growling for no good reason. He needed to get the hell out of this godforsaken town. He purposefully grabbed his cell and called up the Realtor before he could change his mind. "Get the paperwork ready. I'm ready to take Johnson's offer."

Chapter 27

Luna met Sayeh in town for lunch. She was still hurting over her conversation with her dad and needed to get some fresh air, and Sayeh, always thinking with her stomach, suggested they meet at the café so she could get a sandwich and a milkshake.

Luna wasn't hungry and had only picked at her club sandwich. Her thoughts were a tangled mess, and she didn't know where to start. Finally, after some prodding, Luna shared with Sayeh the details of her conversation, still feeling miserable and out of sorts.

"I don't know how to process this information," Luna admitted. "I never in a million years would've believed that our parents were murdered but it would seem that may be the case. But even worse, what if our own father knew something about it? I can't tell you how this is messing with my mind and I can't focus for shit."

Sayeh, for once in her life, was understanding. "I know I'm always being the difficult one, but I've never once believed that our dad wasn't a good man. However, if there's one thing I've learned through my time with the FBI is that I've seen hundreds of good people make shitty decisions for what they thought was the right reason. Maybe he wasn't involved but he looked the other way, plausible deniability. Or maybe he thought he was doing the right thing and justified his actions. Have you tried talking to Chief Paul? Is he still alive?"

Luna sighed. "He is still alive but his brain is tapioca pudding. He's in a memory care facility in Billings. He barely remembers his own name these days. I doubt we would get anything of value out of him. Certainly nothing we could trust."

"Not necessarily. Long-term memory is the last to go. He might remember something about that night."

"I thought of that, but I checked with the facility and he's nonverbal at this point. There's literally nothing going on upstairs anymore."

"Okay, so basically we have to keep digging and let the evidence speak for itself. Eventually, something will turn up. That's the nature of these things. Nothing stays buried forever."

"Well, this particular secret has been buried for thirty years," she pointed out derisively. "Not quite sure what kind of clues we're going to find after all this time."

Sayeh was undeterred. "Speaking of, I got ahold of a company that's willing to go out and take soil samples. Because I don't have any jurisdiction and I'm definitely going rogue I'll have to pay for the sampling myself. I've got some money in savings and it doesn't look like I'm traveling to Aruba anytime soon so I'm willing to dump some cash into this project."

"Are you sure? This could be a dead end. An expensive dead end at that."

"It's worth it. Otherwise the questions in my head will

never stop and I might go insane. Considering I am dangerously close to that borderline anyway I figure we should probably not push it."

Sayeh was joking, but these days everyone's mental health seemed to be hanging on by a thread, including Luna's. Her thoughts circled back to Charlotte and Roger. "I don't know what to do with the information about the Leickis either. Why would they be doing secret volunteer work at the reservation? The only reason it feels bad is because it was a secret. On the surface, it seems like a wonderful way to pay it forward but sometimes when people keep secrets they are doing something they don't want people to know about. Do you see the circular logic I'm stuck in? I don't know where to go with this. A part of me, the weak part of me, wants to drop it all but I can't—especially if there's any chance the Leickis' murders are connected."

Sayeh's expression softened with kindness. "If our parents taught us one thing it's this: doing the right thing is never easy and sometimes doing the right thing will create new enemies but you have to keep doing it because it matters. Doing the right thing matters. I know you can figure this out. You're smarter than you give yourself credit for. And I've never known anyone with a stronger moral compass than you."

Sayeh's quiet confidence in her meant more than she could say. Luna momentarily choked up. When she could speak again, she said, "Who are you and what have you done with my sister?"

"Watch it," she growled. "I'm trying to be genuine with you."

Luna immediately sobered, realizing Sayeh was right. Now wasn't the time for jokes. "I'm sorry I didn't treat your concerns with the respect they deserved. I'm a big enough person to admit that I was wrong. I should've been listening to you all this time instead of brushing you off and judging you for things that weren't your fault."

Sayeh blinked rapidly as her throat worked convulsively. A long minute passed before she could respond. Finally, she said, sniffing back tears, "I appreciate that. I have your support now and that's all that matters."

They both took time to find their composure, then Luna tentatively dove into something even more personal. "So any suggestions on how I should handle the fact that Benjamin is leaving town soon?"

The fact that Luna was asking Sayeh for romantic advice was huge and not lost on her sister. "I'm probably not the best person to ask for romantic advice but I love that you are. Here's the thing—first you have to ask yourself how do you feel about the guy? How does it feel to know that he's leaving?"

"It feels awful and I feel stupid for letting myself get this attached. We were open and honest with ourselves from the very start and I always knew he wasn't going to stay. And yet here I am wanting to burst into tears at the thought of not sleeping beside him every night. How stupid am I?"

"You're not stupid," she vehemently disagreed. "You're a closet hopeless romantic and it's part of your charm. I actually don't know how you've managed to remain unmarried all this time. You are definitely a 'mater' not a 'dater.' You weren't made for the casual hookup scene." At Luna's grimace in agreement, Sayeh said, "So who's to say you have to stay in Cottonwood? It's not like if you leave this place you're going to turn into a pumpkin. Where does he live? Arizona? Yikes, very hot, but you never know, maybe you would love it."

"Nobody loves Arizona."

"Not true. Retired people love Arizona."

"They also love Florida and I'm not moving there either."

"In all seriousness, I think you fell in love with him and there's nothing wrong with admitting that," Sayeh said.

Luna protested. "Except that it was a dead end and stupid to fall in love with him. I basically just self-sabotaged myself into total misery. And here I thought I was well-adjusted."

Sayeh hooted in laughter. "Oh girl, there is no way you are well-adjusted in any way, shape, or form given the way our foundation started but that doesn't mean that you aren't capable of creating a love worth holding on to."

"I'm in the middle of an investigation. It's not like I can just leave."

"So don't leave right away. Maybe you guys have a long-distance relationship for a while. You are allowed to have a personal life. I doubt Charlotte would've wanted you to make her investigation your new personality. There has to be balance. In fact, if Charlotte were here she would probably be like, 'Go get your boy!'"

Luna laughed because it was true. "At first I wasn't sure but now that I've had time to think about it, I definitely think Charlotte would have been overjoyed at the idea of me and her brother becoming a thing. She was such a matchmaker," she recalled fondly. "I think at some point she even tried to match me with her hairdresser."

"Did she think you were gay?"

"I think she wasn't sure and she was trying to be supportive. I mean, after my breakup I didn't date for a really long time she probably started to wonder. I had to assure her that I was very much straight, but I wasn't ready to date."

Sayeh laughed. "I wish I would've known her better. She sounds like a kick-ass person."

"She was," Luna agreed sadly. "I wish I would have made our friendship more of a priority. You never realize when time is going to become your enemy. I always thought we had more time."

"Isn't that the point? We don't know how much time we have. What if you're giving up a future with Benjamin thinking that you have more time when you don't? You're head over heels for this guy. Don't let him walk away without a fight."

"I don't know what I could offer him. I'm not moving to Arizona and he's not moving to Cottonwood so where does that leave us?"

Sayeh sighed, conceding, "I don't know. I'll be honest, you're right it sounds hopeless but if anyone could make it work it would be you. You're the most amazing problem-solver I've ever known—and I'm not just saying that because you're my sister."

"How so?"

"Do you remember that time I was determined to play on the boys baseball team because I didn't wanna play softball? And the school refused to let me because of the whole gender discrimination thing?"

Luna recalled that kerfuffle with an eye roll. "Yes, it caused a complete riot at the school. I think that incident gave Mom a few new gray hairs as she tried to defend you every time people started whispering about you behind your back."

"Yeah, well you were the one who came up with the solution. You told me to go to the school board with case files of other schools and how their refusal to let me try out was opening the school up to a discrimination lawsuit. You said, if I exhibited the ability to play at the same level as the boys I should be allowed to compete on the boys' team. You helped me create an argument so airtight that they had no choice but to let me try out."

"That's right and you made the team. I forgot about that."

"Well, I have never forgotten. You showed me in that

moment that giving up isn't an option. Winning requires thinking outside of the box. Going around the obstacle. I don't always have that skill. I charge right through something if it's in my way, but you find ways to get where you need to go, even if you have to go around the obstacle. That's a skill set that anyone would be lucky to have."

"Thank you." Suddenly Luna saw her sister in a different light, and wondered how long she'd been blind to how strong and wise her little sister could be. For so long, all she had seen was Sayeh's hot temper and how it often caused trouble. "It means a lot to me that you feel that way."

Sayeh drew in a deep breath, wiping at her own eyes before saying, "All right, so the problem is you have to find out why Roger and Charlotte were playing secret benefactor to the reservation clinic. You've got to start pounding the pavement, knocking on doors, asking questions. Someone has to know what they were up to. You have to play the law of averages and find them."

Luna realized Sayeh was right. Her mind started to click. She had to stop looking at the obvious. "I need to find somebody behind the scenes, somebody who wouldn't be noticed but who might know or hear the gossip. Sayeh, you're a genius."

"I learned from the best."

Luna threw down some cash to cover their lunch and scooted from the booth. "I have to go. Let me know what you find out about the soil sample company. I need to make some calls. I'll see you tonight at the house."

And with that, she left.

Chapter 28

Benjamin agreed to go with Luna back to the reservation for a second conversation with the clinic director, Dr. Leggins, but he also wanted the chance to talk to her about his decision on the ranch.

"I met with Scott Johnson the other day," he started while they drove.

"Yeah? Why'd you do that?"

"I wanted to look him in the eye and ask him why he really wanted to buy my sister's house."

"Did you tell him it felt weird?"

"I did."

"And?"

"And he said it wasn't emotional. He thought the ranch was a good business investment and he never let personal feelings get in the way of good business," Benjamin shared.

Luna whistled beneath her breath. "What a heartless prick."

"Yeah, he's a real cold fish and while that might make me want to punch him in the nuts, it doesn't make him guilty of anything. I didn't see any other reason not to sell to him so I made the call."

Luna looked sharply Benjamin's way. "You did? You're going to sell to him?"

He shrugged. "Seems that way. I gave Preston the all clear to start the paperwork."

Luna digested that information, remaining silent for a moment. Benjamin wasn't sure how she felt about it, and his uncertainty made him anxious. "Do you think I shouldn't have sold to him?" he asked.

"I think it's your decision and you have to do what you think is right," she said.

"That's not an answer."

"It's the only answer that's appropriate."

"Don't give me that. Be honest. Tell me how you feel."

Luna sighed. "Okay, I probably would've let emotion get the better of me. I wouldn't have sold to him. He's a slimy jerk who uses people. He acts nice and congenial until you realize he only treats people as well as they benefit him. People like Scott Johnson are dangerous, not because I think they're capable of murder but sometimes it doesn't take pulling a trigger to ruin a life."

"I can call Preston and call the whole thing off," he said. "It wouldn't hurt my feelings to screw with Johnson's good day."

She chuckled. "No, you're probably right and this is the best option. Do you know what you're going to do with the money?"

"Not yet. I was hoping you could help me find a Charlotte-approved charity to donate the proceeds of the sale to."

"Are you really sure you want to donate all of the money?" she asked.

"Yep," he answered without hesitation. "That money feels tainted. If I can do something good with it, maybe that'll help wash away the stain. I can't imagine benefiting from my sister's tragedy."

"Of course, you're right. I'd be happy to help you find a good cause to donate the money to."

He smiled, grateful for her presence in his life. Damn, he was going to miss her. "So, now that I've decided to sell, it won't take long for the paperwork to go through. Preston said escrow will close in thirty days, but I don't need to be here for that. I know I said that I would stay until the case was solved but that might've been an unrealistic promise. The reality is that I can't stay here indefinitely."

"You have a life to get back to," she said with understanding, adding with forced cheerfulness, "You must be relieved to get out of Cottonwood. You probably miss Arizona."

A little. Surprisingly, he hadn't missed his place as much as he thought he would. He knew that was 100 percent because of Luna. But why make things more painful than they needed to be? He lied, "Yeah, I'm itching to get back into the shop and tinker in my friend's bike garage. It's always a good way to unwind and, as my therapist used to say, it'll help with the mess going on upstairs. I need to hit the open road for a few days. Go on a road trip." He glanced her way. "Have you ever been on a motorcycle?"

"Me? Oh gosh, no. I've seen too many road casualties to put my life on two wheels," she answered with a shudder. "I prefer an armored metal tank to surround me. Feels safer that way."

He laughed. "Depends on the driver. I can promise you I've never taken road safety lightly. You'd be safe with me, sweetheart."

The endearment slipped from his mouth, but it fell so quickly and naturally that it happened before he could stop it. He swallowed and met Luna's gaze. Hell, were either of them going to admit how they felt about each other, or were they going to dance around the truth for the rest of eternity?

When she said nothing, he followed her lead and changed the subject. "You still feel the doc is solid?"

Luna contemplated the question, answering, "Honestly, she seems like a good person. Overworked, underpaid and with a good heart. She wants the best for her people and it's hard to get quality care to the reservation. She hadn't heard about Charlotte and Roger so when I broke the news, she was upset, which seems a natural response to such horrible news."

"And what are you hoping to discover from a second meeting?" he asked.

"I don't know. Maybe more information about the equipment, who was their contact and if there was anyone else involved with the project. I'm kinda feeling around in the dark, hoping to connect with something."

"Sounds like a plan," he said, dropping off into reflective silence. He'd expected more of a reaction when he told her he was planning to return to Arizona. Was it immature of him to hope that she would voice some objection? Yeah, probably, but maybe he wasn't above hoping the most intriguing woman he'd ever met would want to fight to hold on to what they had. He swallowed his ego, realizing that was no way to act like an adult, mainly when they were too old for those kinds of games.

That's the thing—he didn't want to play games, but he didn't want to stay in Cottonwood either. Hell, this was unhealthy. Stick to the plan. Don't make it sad and traumatizing. It was good while it lasted.

Luna ignored the pull to tentatively broach the subject of trying long-distance dating instead of saying goodbye permanently as if none of this had happened between them. When he didn't respond with even a hint that he might be open to that suggestion, she shut it down hard. One thing she'd never be was desperate to hold on to someone. If they wanted to leave, she'd show them the door with a smile.

She had plenty in her life to keep her occupied—relationship drama had no place in her day-to-day.

But boy, she'd miss him. How quickly he'd become a fixture in her life that felt like a piece of her. Not sure how that'd happened, but she couldn't deny that it had.

Now she had to find a way to get over it.

They parked in front of the Macawi health clinic and walked inside. Luna had scheduled an appointment, knowing how busy the doctor was and not wanting to jam up an already hectic schedule.

The waiting room was filled with people of all ages and needs, from sniffling children suffering from summer colds or allergies to the elderly of the tribe needing medical attention of some sort. Luna was struck by how privileged she was to enjoy quality health care when the Macawi people were funneled into a single building, cramped and overcrowded, with far too few resources to possibly adequately care for its patients. She could easily see why Charlotte would champion a cause on the reservation because the need was apparent, but why would she keep it a secret?

"Thank you for agreeing to meet with me a second time Dr. Leggins. I appreciate that your time is very valuable," Luna said.

The older woman nodded and gestured for them to take a seat. "I'll admit I was surprised to hear back from you. I'm not sure what else I can add to what I initially told you but I'm happy to help in any way that I can. Charlotte was a wonderful woman and we are devastated to learn of her death."

Luna gestured to Benjamin. "This is Charlotte's brother, Benjamin Reeves. He would love to hear more about what Charlotte was doing to help the clinic."

Dr. Leggins looked to Benjamin, surprised. "I wasn't aware Charlotte had a brother. How wonderful of you to be interested in knowing more about Charlotte's project."

Benjamin smiled. "Pleasure to meet you. It doesn't surprise me that Charlotte chose to champion a worthy cause. That was who she was at heart. Can you tell me how far along you were in the process of getting the equipment donation?"

"Not as far as I'd hoped but these things move slowly. As I mentioned to Detective Griffin, Charlotte was hoping to get an equipment donation from the local Soroptimist International. Apparently there are programs where the Soroptimist organizations donate used equipment to developing countries. While we are not considered a 'developing country,' we are a sovereign nation. She was hoping that maybe she could make the case that we would qualify for a donation under the auspices of that program. Albeit, it would've been a broad interpretation of the program parameters."

Benjamin nodded with interest. "And what kind of equipment are you needing?"

"We really could use an updated mammogram machine, ultrasound and X-ray machine. Those are big-ticket items that we don't have the resources to acquire on our own. But we would happily take gently used equipment. Most of our equipment is used anyway."

"That's admirable. Was there anyone Charlotte was working with on this project? Do you have her contact's info with the Soroptimist?" Luna asked.

"I do, I can get you that information."

Luna smiled. "Excellent. That would be very helpful. Maybe we can pick up where Charlotte left off and see that the donation still happens in her name."

Dr. Leggins's eyes lit up with hope. "Do you think that's possible?"

"I'll be honest with you. I don't know but I'm willing to try," Luna offered.

The doctor's joyful smile made Luna's day. "That would be amazing. We would be happy to help in any way possible if we could make this happen. Many of our people are reluctant to go anywhere off the reservation and most can't afford to go elsewhere anyway. That means most of their care is overlooked until it's too late. We are really working on improving preventative care for our people in the hopes of improving quality of life but change comes slowly and many of our community are wary of big changes."

"Is there anyone else Charlotte was in contact with on the reservation?"

Dr. Leggins considered the question, frowning. "Not that I'm aware of. I'm pretty sure I was her formal contact, particularly with the clinic, but I don't know who Mr. Leicki might've been in contact with as he wasn't always present for our meetings."

Luna and Benjamin shared a look. "Oh? And where was Roger when you were meeting with Charlotte?" Luna asked.

"I don't know. I think he had business to take care of elsewhere and sometimes he dropped Charlotte off and then picked her back up again when she was done. Kind of like killing two birds with one stone."

What business could Roger possibly have had on the reservation that had nothing to do with the clinic? Luna forced a smile. "And you have no idea who he could've been talking to?"

Dr. Leggins frowned, trying to remember any detail. "Sorry, I wasn't very close to Roger. He seemed like a nice man but most of my conversations were with Charlotte."

"Of course, I understand. If you remember anything would you mind giving me a call?" Luna asked.

Dr. Leggins nodded. "I would be happy to do anything

that might help you keep this hope alive. May I be frank with you?"

"Please do."

"News of Charlotte's death was devastating but losing hope of getting that equipment was a terrible blow to our community. I don't mean to make light of her tragedy but my people need help and help from the federal government is slow to get here. I can't tell you how exciting it was to find someone who truly wanted to help and work to make things happen in real time."

"Charlotte was an amazing human being," Luna agreed. "May I ask how she came to champion this cause? I confess, we didn't know anything about it until the other day and usually Charlotte was very vocal about the causes she was involved with."

Dr. Leggins shook her head. "I can't say for sure but I think Charlotte was worried that people might not be willing to help if they knew the donation was for the reservation. Some people have a very poor opinion of our community."

"What do you mean?"

"Our people have struggled. I'm not going to say that drugs and alcohol have not taken their toll on the Macawi people much like many of the Indigenous tribes but we've had our share of crime and corruption on the reservation that has become a stigma that's been challenging to overcome."

"I wasn't aware of the stigma. Can you elaborate?"

"There have been rumors that drug manufacturing has taken over Indian Country because of the sovereign nation protection but the actions of a minority should not color the character of an entire people. I see good honest people every single day in my clinic who are trying to survive with so little. Our people shouldn't be punished for the actions of a few bad apples."

Luna swallowed, thinking of her parents. "Thirty years ago there was a supposed drug explosion on Flying Hawk Road. Were you around when that happened?"

"Yes."

"And you don't think it was drug-related? That was the report at the time."

Dr. Leggins chose her words carefully. "I know what was said and I know what was reported. I also know that our tribal chief of police at the time made some questionable decisions regarding the reservation. And that's all I'll say about that."

A shiver went through Luna. "And who was the tribal chief police at that time?"

"He died many years ago and we're happy to let the past remain the past."

Luna bit down on her frustration. "Of course, thank you for sharing. I'll let you get back to work. I appreciate you taking time out of your schedule to meet with me again."

"Please let me know if you can help us with that equipment donation," Dr. Leggins said.

They left the office, and Luna felt sick to her stomach. "Why is it every time I turn around I find something more disturbing about the night my parents died?" she asked Benjamin.

In a surprise move, Benjamin pulled her into his firm embrace, his scent enveloping her like a comforting blanket. "I can only imagine how tough this must be for you. I wish I had the answers," he murmured.

She buried her face against his chest, taking a moment to collect herself. When she felt she could face the moment, she pulled away. "I don't know what I should be chasing or who I should be questioning. Everything seems so damn complicated and somehow interconnected that I don't know which end is up anymore."

"You'll figure it out. I have faith," Benjamin said.

But did Luna share his confidence? Maybe she was in over her head. Perhaps she wasn't cut out for this level of corruption.

She didn't know anymore.

Chapter 29

Luna wanted to spend the night at Benjamin's but knew she needed to put that distance between them. Better to start the process now than suffer an abrupt ripping off of the Band-Aid at the last possible second. Besides, she was terrible company tonight.

Sayeh was out for the night, and Kenna was in her room, but Luna's nephew, Ty, wandered in and sat next to her, clearly something on his mind. Luna felt bad for neglecting her only nephew in all the commotion and ruffled his tawny mop. "You settling in okay?" she asked.

"Yeah, it's fine. Different than the city but I like driving Grandpa's truck. He's teaching me to work a stick shift, and he says it's a lost art nowadays. Kinda like cursive, but I don't know what that means."

She chuckled. "Cursive is a form of writing that's become obsolete. You'll likely never learn it because you'll never need it."

"Will I need to learn a stick shift?"

Luna considered Ty's question, answering, "Well, if you plan to drive a race car or high-performance vehicle, it might come in handy, but by the time you're driving, everything will probably be automatic."

"Then why am I learning?" he asked, confused.

"Because chicks dig boys who can drive a manual transmission," Luna quipped, tickling Ty in the ribs.

Ty laughed and undoubtedly believed his aunt Luna was loony tunes, but that was okay. It wasn't likely Luna was ever going to be a mother, but she'd happily be the best aunt ever. Kenna never talked about why she'd bailed from the city, aside from saying she was running from an abusive ex, but the fact that Ty wouldn't talk about it either worried Luna.

From a law enforcement perspective, Luna wanted to ask Ty for details, but as his aunt, she wanted him to feel safe to move on. She figured Ty was bored and wanted to be entertained, but he surprised her with his question.

"Auntie, some guys were talking to Grandpa and they seemed real mad. Is Grandpa in trouble?"

Luna stilled. "What do you mean? What guys? When did this happen?"

"Yesterday. When everyone was gone. It was just me and Grandpa at the house. They didn't see me. I couldn't hear everything they were talking about but I could hear their voices and it wasn't good."

"What did they look like?"

Ty shrugged. "Regular guys. I dunno, just regular."

That wasn't helpful. "Tall, short, fat, skinny?" she supplied, trying to jog his memory.

"Um, no, regular, but strong. They looked like they could punch your lights out without a problem."

Good Lord, why were people showing up at the house

and intimidating her dad? "Did Grandpa seem scared?" she asked.

"Yeah," he answered in a small voice. "He kept saying he was sorry and then they yelled at him some more and told him to 'handle it.' What did they mean by that?"

"I don't know, buddy, but I'm going to find out," she promised. "Is there anything else you can tell me about Grandpa's visitors? How many were talking to Grandpa?"

"I saw three."

"And they didn't see you?"

Ty shook his head. "I stayed hidden in the shop while Grandpa talked outside."

"You were smart to stay hidden."

"I know."

That one statement hurt her heart. How many times had Ty been instructed to hide or stay hidden because of whoever Kenna was running from? *A heartache for another day*, she promised. "Hey, I think Auntie Sayeh bought some more ice cream sandwiches. You want to run and check the freezer for me?"

Ty eagerly jumped from the sofa and ran out to the outside freezer, where they kept the frozen foods. When he returned with two ice cream sandwiches, she smiled with approval. "Excellent. I can always count on Auntie Sayeh for the sweet tooth supplies."

Luna pretended to happily munch on the ice cream bars with her nephew, but she couldn't taste a thing. Her mind was paralyzed with fear that someone was terrorizing her dad, and he hadn't told her. Why? What was he hiding? Did this have to do with Charlotte and Roger or her biological parents' death?

It could be either.

She had cause to question her father's integrity for the

first time in her life, but that didn't mean she wouldn't fight like a badger to protect him.

Where was her dad tonight?

"Do you know where Grandpa went?" she asked Ty casually.

He shrugged, licking the quickly melting cream from his fingers. "Dunno, he said something about needing supplies for his woodshop. You think he can make me a bow and arrow? I saw one in the sports shop but Mom said it was too expensive and maybe Grandpa could make me one. I haven't asked him yet, though."

"I bet he could, buddy," she answered absently, her mind churning. *Dad, where are you? And what have you gotten yourself into?* Luna smiled briefly down at Ty, trying to remain calm for the sake of her nephew. He'd had enough turmoil and fear in his young life. She wasn't going to add to it, particularly when she didn't have all the facts.

Ty finished his ice cream, and Luna reminded him to wash his hands before he touched everything with his sticky fingers. He rolled his eyes. "I'm not a baby, Auntie Luna."

And she quipped, "Then why do you have an ice cream mustache, buddy? Go wash."

He groaned but went to do as she asked.

He was a good kid. She was glad he was here now. Maybe he and Kenna could build a new life and start over. Lord knew her sister's first attempt at adulting had crashed and burned. If it weren't for Ty, she wasn't sure where Kenna would be.

Kenna had certainly made her share of costly mistakes in her life. Now that Luna had mended fences with Sayeh, she would have to make a concentrated effort to be there for Kenna as she began her new life.

Fresh starts sounded like a breath of much-needed oxygen in this family for all of them.

But first, she had to figure out why the hell their dad was keeping dangerous secrets.

Benjamin drove out to the ranch, possibly for closure or to prove to himself that this house didn't have any power over him or his decisions.

The place would forever feel like a tomb to him, but if some good could come out of this tragedy, he'd call it a win and be done with it.

The house would fetch a lot of money. Maybe he'd donate the money to the reservation clinic in Charlotte's name and give them the purchasing power to buy the used equipment they needed.

The thought warmed his heart. That felt right.

The last time he saw his nephews, they'd been running around like wild-eyed heathens, half-naked Liam wearing nothing but his underwear and a blue cape trailing after him as he hollered like a beast after his big brother, tackling him to the plush carpet. He remembered remarking proudly, "That boy is going to make a good lineman someday. I'll have to teach him the ropes when it comes time," because Lord knew it wasn't as if Roger had an athletic bone in his body.

He swallowed the lump in his throat at the memory. Goddamn, would the pain ever end? He'd tried to be a good uncle, but he'd traded gifts for time spent. Sure, he'd never missed a birthday or holiday gift opportunity, but he'd run away from most of Charlotte's attempts to get him to come home to visit.

He'd justified his absence by saying that the boys only cared about the presents, anyway, and that was okay with him. He remembered being a kid, too. Cool presents were way better than talking to some old guy they barely knew.

But he'd give his right arm now to be that old uncle

boring his nephews to death with stories they couldn't care less about.

He hadn't told Charlotte, but he'd made grand plans to someday buy his nephews their own bikes. He'd wanted to teach them the joys of the road, and he'd only trusted himself to do it.

That was all gone now.

Moisture crowded his sinuses, and he pinched the bridge of his nose, sniffing back the tears. What was the point of coming out here again? *Oh yeah, closure. So, let's do this and get it over with.*

Benjamin climbed the porch stairs and unlocked the front door. His footsteps echoed on the hardwood. He clicked the lights on and wandered into the kitchen. He opened the refrigerator and saw it empty. The cleaning company had emptied all the perishables, and everything gleamed clean and move-in ready for whoever came next.

He closed the fridge door and climbed the stairs, heading for the master bedroom where Charlotte died. A part of him needed to say goodbye to her ghost. He wasn't particularly woo-woo, but it seemed important.

But as he climbed the final stair and started to turn right to head down the hallway, an unfamiliar sound pricked his ears. Immediately on high alert, his every sense tensed as he listened for the sound. There it was. He crept to the wall, hugging the shadows. The sound was coming from the boys' bedroom.

He had nothing to defend himself with, but the US Marine Corps trained him, and if need be, he'd defend himself to the death with his bare hands.

Benjamin slowly peered through the cracked door and saw a hooded figure pulling the boys' books and toys from a bookshelf, clearly looking for something. Rage blotted out his good sense, and he charged the man without thinking twice. He knocked the man to the floor with a hard grunt and landed a solid right hook to the man's jaw, but the man recovered fast enough to drive a knee straight into his groin. Benjamin groaned as he rolled to the carpet, his nuts throbbing as his gut threatened to unload his dinner. He swiped at the man scrambling to his feet to run and managed to send him sprawling to the floor, but the man was wily and quick. Springing back to his feet with the agility of a cat, he ran down the stairs.

"What the hell are you doing in my sister's house?" he roared, chasing after the man, but he'd jumped into a waiting truck, which had been hidden from view when Benjamin pulled up, and sped off, spitting gravel in its wake. "Damn it!" he yelled, grabbing his cell phone from his pocket with trembling hands to call Luna. When she answered, he shouted, "Someone broke into Charlotte's house again! I caught them trashing the boys' room. They were definitely looking for something. I landed a punch, but he got away. I want you to arrest every goddamn son of a bitch sporting a shiner!"

"Are you okay?" Luna asked, ignoring his rage and going straight to concern. "Did he have a weapon?"

He did a quick inventory. "No, I'm fine. No weapon. But I need you to get out here quick and bring your forensic kit. The guy wasn't wearing gloves and he was touching everything."

"Okay, don't touch anything until I get there," she advised. "I'll be there in fifteen minutes."

He clicked off, his adrenaline still pumping. He was pissed at himself for not seeing the groin shot coming. He was rusty. It'd been a while since he'd done any hand-to-hand combat, and it showed.

He bounded back up the stairs, only this time, he did a more careful search of the house before heading back to the boys' room to survey the damage. Much like in Roger's office, he'd tossed the room looking for something. Something that would've been easily hidden in a bookshelf. What could Roger have that would keep them desperately coming back to find?

Something worth killing for, that's for sure.

He glanced at his knuckles, the reddened flesh torn in places. Was it possible he had some of the guy's DNA embedded in his skin? God, he hoped so. He was careful not to wipe his knuckles just in case.

I'm going to find you and nail your ass to the wall, he vowed.

So much for bailing on Cottonwood and heading back to Arizona. He returned his gaze to his knuckles with a mean, hard-ass stare. With any luck, this was exactly the break Luna had been hoping for to crack the case wide open.

Chapter 30

Luna's dad had returned home just when she got the call from Benjamin about the break-in at the ranch. Fear for Benjamin's safety and frustration that her conversation with her dad would have to wait galvanized her into driving with lights and sirens blaring as she called the incident in to the station.

A forensic team would take too long to get there from the neighboring county, so Luna prepared to collect the evidence herself. She pulled up in a spray of gravel and grabbed her kit, practically running to Benjamin, her heart pounding.

She found him sitting in the boys' bedroom, far enough away from the disturbing scene not to contaminate anything, but she felt his agitation like vibrating energy pulsing from his body. She knelt beside him. "Are you okay?"

"I'm fine," he bit out, admitting with heavy shame, "I let him get away. I should've had him."

"You didn't let him do anything. You were attacked and

you're lucky to be alive," she admonished, putting on her gloves and removing her collection kit materials to start gathering DNA evidence. She carefully swabbed his torn knuckles, hoping for DNA left behind. "What happened?" she asked.

"It sounds stupid but I came by the ranch to say my goodbyes," he said gruffly. "But when I came upstairs, I heard something. I found the guy rifling through the boys' bookshelf, tossing shit around like he was looking for something. I tackled him and landed a punch to the jaw but he got me with a power drive straight to the nuts and dropped me like a damn stone."

She heard the embarrassment in his voice. Benjamin was the least tangled in toxic masculinity of any man she knew, but she could almost feel his humiliation at being bested.

"Stop." Luna bandaged his ripped knuckles the best she could, wishing she could kiss his injuries. "You were caught off guard and you could've been killed. You should've called me the minute you realized someone was in the house. You're lucky all he bruised was your ego. What if he'd had a gun?"

Now probably wasn't the time to school him but her heart had nearly stopped. What if something had happened to him? She rose and surveyed the damage. "Same pattern as the office. He was definitely looking for something small enough to be hidden in a bookshelf."

"That's what I was thinking, too." Benjamin watched as Luna meticulously dusted for prints and took a ton of samples. Then she did a careful search for anything else that might've been missed. "I should've called you," he admitted.

She acknowledged his admission with a smile, accepting his apology, nothing more needed between them. Luna took pictures of the mess from every angle. She regarded

Benjamin with question. "Do you think they returned because they heard you're selling the house?"

"It's possible," he agreed. "Whatever they're looking for must still be here."

"What could it be?" she mused, mostly to herself. "The original items listed as stolen included Roger's laptop, but clearly whatever they were looking for wasn't on the laptop. Otherwise they wouldn't still keep returning."

"What if they're looking for The Book as Charlotte called it in her journal? What if it's an electronic copy? But it wasn't on the laptop... Something small, portable—"

"A flash drive," Benjamin said, snapping his fingers. "I bet they're looking for a flash drive."

Luna agreed, nodding, and returned to survey the room, thinking aloud. "Why would they search the boys' room? Something they thought they knew... A new clue? Something that tipped them off?" She did a slow turn around the room, narrowing her gaze at everything, looking at it with new eyes. "Where would Charlotte hide something small and important? Somewhere no one would look?"

"She wouldn't hide it in the boys' room," he said, shaking his head. "She would never want to draw danger to her kids but it would have to be someplace close enough that she could keep track of it easily."

"Her room," Luna guessed, gesturing for Benjamin to follow. She tried to think as Charlotte would. Where would Charlotte hide something important yet easy to grab and go, if need be? "We already found her journal in the vent, but there was nothing else there." She walked into the bathroom, opening drawers, looking for anything out of place. She opened the top drawer in the bathroom, and a variety of lipsticks rolled out. Luna frowned. "Did Charlotte wear a lot of lipstick? I don't remember her wearing anything brighter than tinted lip gloss."

Benjamin wasn't sure. "You'd know better than me," he admitted.

Luna checked each lipstick, finding them new and untouched until she found the last one. She pulled the top and gasped. A secret flash drive. The stroke of luck was astounding. "Benjamin! This is it! This has to be what they've been looking for!"

"Are you kidding me?" Benjamin's gaze widened with shock and surprise, but he quickly recovered. "Whatever is on that flash drive killed my family. Let's get the hell out of here and see what was worth killing for."

Luna nodded and carefully bagged the drive. They locked up the house and took separate cars to the station.

Was it possible she'd found the answer to this nightmare? God, she hoped so.

Benjamin sweated. Luna might've found the key to this case. It'd been right beneath their noses the whole time, and to think the company he'd hired to empty the house of its personal effects was coming in a day or two, and would've made them lose any chance of finding the drive.

What happened now? What could be worth killing for on that drive?

He didn't know. He couldn't imagine. Nothing in this world would've been worth the lives of his sister and her family.

Even Roger's.

He pulled up to the station, right behind Luna. They tripped over themselves to get to her computer. Luna made quick work of logging the portable drive into evidence, so there was a record, and then she plugged it into a dummy computer used solely for this purpose.

The computer began to whir and read the drive, but a passcode popped up, stopping them from seeing anything.

"Damn it," Luna swore under her breath, disconnecting

the drive. "We'll have to wait until the IT team can unlock this encryption in the morning."

"To hell with that. I'll call Codi," he said, grabbing his cell, but Luna stopped him.

"We need to follow protocol on this. If this drive has what I think is on it, we will want to be able to submit it to the courts as evidence. We can't afford monkeying around with the rules right now."

Of course, she was right, but his anxiety was climbing through the roof. He had to know what was on that drive.

Luna took a deep breath and calmed him with a hand on his chest as she met his gaze. "We have the drive in custody. No one can take that from us now. It'll be safely logged into evidence under lock and key. No one is going to get their hands on it. I promise. We'll come back fresh in the morning, okay? It's been an eventful night."

He nodded reluctantly, loathe to let that drive out of his sight, but, again, she was right. They couldn't do anything about the drive tonight, and it was better to come back with a clear head. But one thing he knew for sure—Luna was coming home with him tonight. *To hell with the rules.* "Stay with me," he said, not asking.

Luna held his gaze. Her lips parted, as if to shut him down, but she couldn't bring herself to do it. A wordless exchange passed between them.

We shouldn't.

I know.

What if—

I need you.

Benjamin felt it in his soul the minute she gave in. There was no denying what was between them. Keeping each other at arm's length had only made the yearning turn into a wild, snarling thing that listened to no one. She nodded, saying, "We need to swing by my place first. I have to talk to my dad about something."

He'd drive her to the moon if she asked. "No problem," he said, itching to feel her in his arms. The adrenaline rush still pulsed through his veins, sharpening every emotion to a fine edge. He didn't want Luna out of his sight and he wanted to feel his body pressed against hers, to hear her moan in his ear and shudder beneath him. "Let's get out of here," he growled.

They would leave Luna's car behind and take Benjamin's, but as he went to open her door, she wrapped her arms around his neck and kissed him hard and deep. His arms curled around her with all the hunger he'd been suppressing for days, drawing her more deeply into the cove of his chest, needing to feel her against him. His hands roamed her backside, squeezing her plump behind and groaning as he suddenly strained against her. This wasn't the time or place but throttling down that wild need was almost more than he could stand. This woman had attached herself to his soul and he was helpless to stop what was happening between them, no matter the wreckage of the inevitable crash.

It is what it is—but what if it turns out to be everything?

Somehow the heat between them cooled, and they remained a long moment holding each other with unspoken words flowing like an unchecked river, swollen with the spring thaw. *I love you, sweetheart*, were the words he wanted to say but didn't. How could he say that when he knew it could go nowhere? Instead, he pressed a small kiss on her forehead, and she pulled away so he could open her door. She slid into the seat, and he closed the door behind her.

"What do you need to talk to your dad about?" he asked once they were on the road.

She rested her head on her hand, using the window to brace herself. "Right before you called, my nephew told me something upsetting. It seems my father has someone threatening him. I need to find out who and why."

"Do you have any idea who might be doing it?"

"No, but I have a bad feeling it has something to do with my biological parents' death thirty years ago."

"How is that possible?"

"I don't know," she admitted with a heavy exhale, "but I need to find out. I'm not about to let someone bully my father but he needs to be honest with me so I can help him."

He nodded, resolving to play the part of whatever Luna needed tonight. She directed him to the driveway, and they pulled up. An unknown truck was parked off to the side, partially hidden in the shadows. A warning tingle started at the base of his skull. That truck looked oddly familiar. He started, "Luna, wait—" but she was already out of the car, heading for the house.

"Damn it, Luna!" he called out to her in a harsh whisper, but she was moving quickly. Something had caught her eye, and she was hustling to get into the house. He reached her just as she opened the door. The sharp bang of gunfire erupted, and something sizzled through his shoulder. Familiar pain awakened his nerve endings, and he went down, memories of sniper fire blazing through his brain as his pain receptors fully engaged that he'd been shot.

When he realized he wasn't in Syria, but right here in Montana, his first thought was that Luna was shooting at whoever had taken the shot. Someone screamed, "Dad!" as more shots rang out.

Luna screamed, "Get Ty out of here!" Then more shots.

Benjamin tried to roll to his feet, but the pain was excruciating. He attempted to apply pressure with his opposite hand to the gushing wound, but he nearly blacked out from the agony. All he could do was lie there and hope Luna was okay and that he didn't bleed out in the meantime.

It felt like an eternity before the shooting stopped,

and Luna ran out to find him, gasping as she called 911 with shaking hands. "I need immediate assistance at 1916 Ponderosa Drive! Shots fired, three victims, one with a gunshot wound to the shoulder, the other 10-55 with a possible—"

But before she could finish, another voice rang out, clogged with tears. "Luna! It's Dad, he's not breathing, hurry!"

"I called the ambulance," she said, her voice shaking, looking down at Benjamin, her eyes swimming with tears. "I called the ambulance…"

And he knew, just as she knew… Her father was dead.

Chapter 31

Luna couldn't breathe.

Her brain wouldn't function.

Everything had happened so fast.

Somehow Kenna and Sayeh helped her to her feet as the ambulance arrived to load Benjamin into the rig while officers flooded the house to find the gunman that Luna had shot and to look for her father, who'd been gunned down seconds before.

Wes came over, his gaze stricken as he tried to do his job for one of their own when he was still so new on the job. "Luna, um, can you tell me what happened?"

The ambulance took off, sirens blazing, and she swung her gaze to the young officer, blinking as her brain froze. What happened? *I don't know.* What happened? Gunfire. Screams. Fear. Everything congealed into a gooey mass in her brain.

Sayeh took action on Luna's behalf. "The gunman entered the house and held our father at gunpoint. He was demanding that our father find a way to get his hands on something the man wanted or else he was going to ruin my father's family."

"Do you know what he was talking about?" Wes asked.

Luna swung her gaze back to Wes with a dull nod, answering, "A flash drive. We found it at the Leickis' ranch tonight. We think whatever is on that drive is what killed them. I logged it into evidence before we came here."

"What does your father have to do with the Leickis?"

"I don't know," she answered truthfully, looking to Sayeh and Kenna. Suddenly, she realized with a jolt that her nephew was missing. "Is Ty okay?"

Kenna assured her with a shaky nod, "He's fine. Shook up but okay."

At that, tears started to fall as she blubbered, "Is Benjamin going to be okay? I should go to the hospital. Can someone drive me, please?"

Sayeh rested her hand on Luna's shoulder. "I'll drive you," she promised, but her eyes sparkled with tears. "Luna… Dad didn't make it."

"I know," Luna said, biting back a sob as the river of grief threatened to drown her. "I took the shot but it was too late. He killed our dad. I couldn't stop him. I don't understand. What was Dad involved with? Why didn't he tell me he was in some kind of trouble? I would've helped him. I would've done anything to protect him."

Sayeh nodded, understanding how Luna wanted to curl in on herself but was trying to hold it together. "Do you know who the gunman was?" she asked Luna.

Luna shook her head. "But we took a DNA sample from Benjamin's fist. He might be the same guy who was searching the Leicki ranch tonight. Benjamin caught him and they fought but he got away. I took the samples. They're waiting at the station for forensics."

"Good thinking," Sayeh said. Looking to Wes, she said,

"Can this wait? I need to get her to the hospital and I don't think she needs to be here when the coroner arrives."

Wes nodded. "Sure, go ahead."

A part of her wanted to see her dad, but she knew that would end badly in her current mental state. Sayeh read her thoughts and agreed. "Let's go to the hospital, okay? Benjamin needs you right now."

Nothing could be done for their dad, but Benjamin was still here. She jerked a short nod and struggled to her feet, handing over her sidearm as was customary in an officer-involved shooting when a death occurred.

Wes accepted her piece and slipped it into an evidence bag while Sayeh helped Luna into the car. Kenna ran back into the house to get Ty, and they all left for the hospital.

Every detail kept playing in her head with agonizing repetition, but there was no way to see how it might've ended differently. Maybe if she and Benjamin hadn't taken the time to make out in the parking lot of the station, they would've had those precious moments needed to save her father's life.

Or maybe if she'd been quicker up the steps, she would've caught the gunman before he'd taken that first shot.

Sayeh's quiet voice interrupted the loop of intrusive thoughts. "Stop doing this to yourself. You couldn't have changed what happened."

"How do you know?" she asked, her voice hoarse.

"Because you couldn't have predicted that Dad was going to try and reach for the man's gun when he should've just remained still and played the accommodating hostage. He tried to be the hero because we were being threatened. Lord love the man but he should've just let the situation play out."

Tears blinded Luna. "He was trying to protect his family."

"From what? What kind of leverage did they have on him?"

"I don't know," Luna answered with a hiccup as pain burned beneath her breastbone. Her dad was dead. He wouldn't be able to finish teaching Ty how to drive a stick shift. He wouldn't be around to tinker in his woodshop, doing terrible projects. No more mornings with burned blueberry pancakes that he slathered with maple syrup he always ordered from his favorite place in Vermont. "I don't know."

She dropped her face into her hands and sobbed. Her grief had no words.

"You did what you could," Sayeh promised her in a fierce tone. "Dad would've been so proud. If you hadn't shown up, we'd all be dead."

Luna knew how devastated Sayeh was that she'd been equally as helpless to save him, but she didn't have her sidearm either due to her suspension. They'd been sitting ducks.

"Benjamin is going to be okay," Sayeh assured her. "The shot looked like it was a through and through. A quick surgery and some rehab, he'll be good as new."

"Stop," she begged with a weak voice. She knew Sayeh was trying to help, but it was scraping on Luna's raw nerves. "Just stop."

Sayeh didn't take offense. The rest of the drive to the hospital finished in silence. As soon as Sayeh parked, Luna burst from the car and ran through the emergency bay doors. She went straight to the nurse's station, flashed her badge, and demanded to know Benjamin's status.

"He's in surgery, Detective Griffin. We'll let you know as soon as he's out."

Luna blinked, shaking her head. What more could she do? Nothing. Again, Sayeh was suddenly at her side, holding her up. "Let's get some coffee, okay?" she suggested. "It's going to be a long night."

Luna looked with gratitude at her little sister and sagged

against her, the tears falling without a stop gate. "He has to be okay, Sayeh," she begged, her knees threatening to buckle. "He has to be."

"He will be. The man survived how many tours in the Marines? He'll be fine and he'll have a new scar to tell stories about when he's old and decrepit, which isn't far off."

Somehow that made Luna laugh—a silly, hysterical bubble of a laugh—but it was enough to create a break in the tears. She wiped at her running nose and met her sister's soft gaze. "He's not old," she rasped.

"Agree to disagree but then, you're old, too, so you're not a very good judge."

Luna offered a watery chuckle, realizing everyone in the lobby was staring at them. "Let's get that coffee," she said, nudging Sayeh. "I'm going to need it."

"Maybe they can add a little amaretto to mine because I think I'm going to need booze to get through this night," Sayeh quipped with just enough dark humor to betray her pain.

Luna slipped her hand through Sayeh's. "Maybe so." Then, she remembered Kenna and Ty and felt terrible all over again. "What about Kenna and Ty?"

"They're staying at a hotel room for the night. No one wants to sleep at the house right now."

"Good call," she said, grateful for Sayeh's foresight. "Thank you."

Sayeh nodded, her own eyes red but dry. The tears would come later—of that, Luna was sure—but for now, Sayeh would grieve in her way, which included not crying but holding it together so Luna could break apart.

Benjamin's eyes fluttered open to the sound of beeps and blips, a sound he knew well.

He was in a hospital.

Despite the drugs flowing through his system, his sluggish brain pieced together the events with surprising clarity, and he forced his eyes to focus. He saw Luna curled up in the seat beside his bed, her long legs looking uncomfortably bent as she snatched a few hours of sleep while he recovered.

"Luna," he called out, his voice hoarse from the anesthesia.

Immediately she startled awake, going to his side, and her hand curled gingerly around his, careful to avoid his IV port. "Hi," she murmured, tears leaking from her eyes. "You're awake."

"Barely. How long was I out?"

"You were in surgery for a few hours last night and then you went into recovery before they brought you to your room. You've been here about four hours. Surgery went well. You're going to be okay but you'll need rehab once you're well enough to move your shoulder. Are you in pain? I could call the nurse if you are. Just let me know."

It was too many words all at once, but he appreciated that she'd been paying attention to the doctor on his behalf. Then he remembered. "Luna," he said softly, his heart breaking for her. "Your dad…"

She nodded, the tears falling faster. "He's dead. Um, I couldn't reach him fast enough."

Benjamin took a minute to let the cobwebs clear from his brain. His mouth was dry, and his tongue felt furred. "Do they know who the gunman was?"

She nodded. "He was identified as Lyle Negan, a ranch hand with the Johnson Ranch. He was the same guy you fought with. They matched his DNA with what we collected from your fist."

"A ranch hand? What the hell does he want with a zip drive?" he asked in fuzzy confusion.

"I don't know," she admitted. "But we're going to find out."

Benjamin sagged against the stiff bedding, relieved.

"Thank God." At least one good thing had come from this nightmare situation. "What was the connection to your dad?"

"I don't know that either. We're still waiting for the IT team to unlock the encryption but we've got a warrant for Scott Johnson's ranch and they're serving it—" she paused to check her watch "—right now."

"You should be there. This is your case," he said.

"I'm right where I want to be."

He closed his eyes as tears burned against his lids. "I'm sorry," he whispered.

"Don't be. None of this is your fault."

She leaned over and brushed a soft kiss across his lips. He felt her body tremble, and he wanted to hold her tightly, but he was as weak as a kitten. "You should go home and get some rest," he said.

"I'm not leaving your side."

"Okay." He wasn't going to argue. His lids were dragging again. "I love you, Luna," he said, the words trailing as fatigue and drugs pulled on his consciousness.

But he heard, "I love you, too," just as he went under.

Chapter 32

It'd been a month since the night her dad died and Benjamin took a bullet to the shoulder, but much had happened in that time—so much so that it was enough to frazzle the brain.

The search warrant on the Johnson Ranch recovered Roger's stolen laptop with Scott Johnson's prints all over it. Scott Johnson was arrested that day on suspicion of murder and possession of stolen property, but prosecutors weren't confident it was enough to hold Scott until IT could break down the encryption on the zip drive.

Then all hell broke loose, and the most extensive drug network in recent history was laid bare.

Roger had been planning to go to the DEA with the evidence he'd been quietly collecting against the Johnson family and their connection to the Howling Wolf drug network that'd been building an empire on the bones of the Mexican mafia connections beneath the radar of law enforcement for decades.

Roger had been lured away from Asset Protection into keeping the books for the Johnson Ranch, only to discover he wasn't only keeping the books for the ranch but the drug network. By that point, it was too late to get out.

The flash drive had been his ticket to safety for his family, but before Roger could take his evidence to the DEA, someone on Scott's payroll at the reservation saw Roger having secret meetings and reported it to Scott. When questioned, Roger's stammered excuses set alarm bells off in Scott's head and he ordered the hit on the family.

It wasn't until Scott had the laptop that he discovered The Book wasn't on the hard drive and that Roger must've off-loaded the evidence to an external drive. This pressed Scott to find it before law enforcement did.

When he realized the flash drive had to be in the house still, he made the offer to buy the house with the bullshit reason that it was a good investment, which almost worked, if it hadn't been for the bumbling attempts of Lyle Negan to recover the drive that night.

Lyle, knowing that Scott was likely going to have him killed if he didn't find a way to get that drive, made the desperate attempt to squeeze Luna's dad using information he'd acquired from an acquaintance at the reservation who'd known the previous tribal police chief.

Using the framework of the Mexican mafia's operating plan with some improvements, the Howling Wolf network used tribal land to circumvent the usual checks and balances within law enforcement, greasing the wheels with much-needed money within an impoverished community. The Johnson Ranch recruited ranch hands from the reservation and roped them into the lifestyle to keep the drugs moving, using the ranch planes to fly the cargo at night off tribal land.

Luna was still trying to wrap her head around how sophisticated the network was, and now that the DEA, FBI and the Bureau of Indian Affairs were all involved, she was no longer in charge of the investigation.

And she was glad.

Sayeh, on the other hand, wasn't as happy.

"You did all the work, you deserve the credit," Sayeh groused.

"I don't want credit. I want life to return to some kind of normal," she said quietly.

Not that life would ever feel normal without her dad, but she had to start somewhere.

"How's Benjamin doing with rehab?" Sayeh asked.

"Good. I'm supposed to see him this weekend."

They were doing the long-distance thing. So far, it was working. Benjamin was warming to the idea of returning to Cottonwood, but Luna was also considering finding a new place to retire to. She'd always liked the idea of Washington or Oregon. Benjamin was open to either. They would cross that bridge when they came to it. For now, long-distance worked for them.

But she missed him terribly when they were apart. That much was true for both.

Sayeh was getting ready to return to New York. Her Internal Affairs investigation was nearly complete, but surprisingly, she wasn't eager to put Cottonwood in her rearview mirror. Not yet, at least.

"Any word on those soil samples yet?" Luna asked.

"No, apparently these things take a long time, even when you're private paying for their time," Sayeh said with a glower. "I don't understand how hard it is to look at a clump of dirt under the microscope and determine what chemical compounds are present but I'm no scientist so what do I know?"

Sayeh was still determined to chase down the mystery of their parents' death. Now that they knew about the

Howling Wolf network and how it'd enslaved parts of the Macawi reservation, she couldn't let go of the possibility that perhaps their parents had also been unwilling victims and potentially murdered.

It wasn't as ludicrous a theory as Luna had previously thought, and she was determined to be supportive, no matter what Sayeh dug up.

Now that both their mom and dad were gone, all they had was each other.

There was some promising news for Kenna, though. She managed to land the job at the local vet's office, which was a good fit. She loved animals, and each day she seemed to get a little stronger, her smile a little less haunted, even though she still refused to talk about her abusive ex.

Ty, on the other hand, worried Luna.

Seeing his grandpa get shot seemed to mess with him. He was acting out a bit. Nothing they couldn't handle as a family but Luna had suggested counseling, which Kenna quickly shot down, saying she'd handle it.

"He just needs time to grieve. That's what we all need," Kenna had barked, ultrasensitive to the suggestion. So, Luna let it go but made a mental note to be watchful.

The department also got the K9 grant they'd been hoping for. The new K9 officer, Lucas Merritt, was scheduled to arrive in Cottonwood in a few days, and Luna was excited to see the program brought back to life.

But from all of that, what hurt the most had been discovering the secret their father had been desperate to keep hidden.

Bill and Nancy had known that their friend Chief Paul had bent the rules to push their adoption through, and they'd said nothing, more interested in having the girls than following the rules, which, knowing their dad, had probably eaten at him for decades.

But it certainly wasn't worth dying over.

There were still troubling questions that bothered both Sayeh and Luna. Why were three little girls in a separate trailer on the night Darryl and Mika died? How did Chief Paul know they'd be there? Had their dad known more about what was happening on the reservation than he wanted to share?

Those answers were frustratingly out of reach, which only sharpened her confusion and her grief.

If her dad had been honest with her, she would've done everything to help, and she certainly would've forgiven him.

But he was gone, and she had to find a way to move on.

And she was determined to do that.

Her phone rang. She smiled instantly when she saw it was Benjamin. Sayeh rolled her eyes as Luna stepped outside to the porch to talk in private.

"Hey you," she said. "Ready for this weekend?"

"Doc says I shouldn't stress my shoulder too much. You might have to do all the work," he teased, causing an all-over blush to creep up her face. They were planning their first romantic night since the incident. They were nervous and excited. "You don't mind, right?"

"I don't mind," she agreed with a subtle purr. "Just as long as you promise to keep your stamina up. I've missed you."

His voice dropped an octave. "Sweetheart, you have no idea. The weekend can't come soon enough. What time's your flight?"

"I arrive at 2:00 p.m."

"I'll be there with bells on, baby."

"Ohh, that sounds interesting," she said with a giggle. "Do I get to pick where to put the bells?"

"You can do whatever you want to my body."

"I'll hold you to that promise," Luna murmured, her breath catching. "Okay, enough of this. I have to get to work. I have to turn down an offer to work for the FBI."

"My woman is a badass," he said with pride. "Go get 'em, baby. I love you."

She laughed. "I love you, too. Now rest up. I'll accept no excuses for this weekend."

"Yes, ma'am." His low chuckle sent shivers down her spine as she clicked off.

For a long moment, she held her phone and smiled, even though her heart still hurt and probably would for a very long time.

She glanced up at the brilliant blue sky, hoping Charlotte was happy with how things had ended. Shortly after Scott Johnson was arrested, Benjamin ditched his Realtor and found a buyer for the ranch on his own, selling it for a ton of money, then donated every penny to the Macawi health clinic just like he'd said he would. They were planning to use the money to buy a lot of much-needed equipment, and Luna had convinced the local Soroptimist organization to make the big-ticket purchases, just as Charlotte had been trying to do. It would take a while for the wheels to turn, but they were set in motion, and that was the best thing one could hope for in these situations.

As it turned out, Charlotte and Roger were also working with someone in the Macawi BIA office to bring down the Howling Wolf connections within the reservation and had needed a reason to be at the reservation without question. Charlotte had found a cause to champion that worked as a convenient cover.

When Luna discovered the full breadth of Charlotte and Roger's attempt to bring down the Howling Wolf network, it made her incredibly proud of her friend.

Also, it was gratifying to learn that Charlotte was as good as Luna and everyone else had believed her to be.

That meant something.

Now, Luna was ready for quiet—and her first bike ride.

No one, least of all Luna, could've ever imagined life would turn out this way.

Epilogue

Luna shook her hair free from the helmet and drank in the arid scenery of the crystalline lake stretching out into the distance below. The brilliant blue water reflected the clear skies of late autumn as if deliberately defying the imminent arrival of cooler temperatures.

"See? Arizona isn't that bad," Benjamin teased, coming to stand beside her, looking out across the vista. He gestured with a smile. "This is one of my favorite views."

"It's gorgeous," she murmured in agreement, her heart full even if her behind was a little sore from riding all morning on Benjamin's Victory. As Benjamin stepped away to unpack their picnic, Luna cast a glance at the man she'd spent the last few hours clinging to like a spider monkey, and realized any discomfort was worth it.

She breathed in a deep lungful of clean, warm air, watching as Benjamin unpacked their lunch from the small travel cooler anchored to the back. Life was different with her father gone—grief still found her in quiet moments—but healing came in fits and starts and Benjamin had been her rock through it all.

Sitting side by side, eating hearty sandwiches with the man she loved, enjoying every second, couldn't have felt more like heaven.

The long-distance thing was working but she already knew she'd follow this man wherever he wandered because he had become her home, instead of a place.

If it came down to it, and leaving Cottonwood was the right thing to do, she'd pack with a smile because Benjamin was her partner for life.

"You're real quiet," Benjamin teased as he swigged his water. "Everything okay? If you want we can find a hotel and call it a day if you're not ready for another couple of hours on the bike."

She smiled at the thought. "A soft bed, room service and a naked you is hard to pass up but I'm good to push on if you are."

Benjamin matched her smile and brushed a kiss across her lips, murmuring, "And a naked you is even harder to pass up. Maybe we need a break after all."

Instant heat curled between them as the kiss deepened. Within minutes, they had to remember they were in broad daylight, parked alongside the highway in plain view of God and country.

"Yep," Benjamin decided, stowing their trash and handing her her helmet, "hotel it is."

Luna giggled and snapped her helmet into place as she climbed onto the bike behind her man and they roared back onto the highway.

A smile found her as her arms circled his waist. Benjamin was definitely her home.

For now and forever—no matter where they eventually landed.

* * * * *

Get 4 FREE REWARDS!

We'll send you 2 FREE Books plus 2 FREE Mystery Gifts.

FREE Value Over **$20**

Both the **Harlequin Intrigue®** and **Harlequin® Romantic Suspense** series feature compelling novels filled with heart-racing action-packed romance that will keep you on the edge of your seat.

HARLEQUIN
PLUS

Announcing a **BRAND-NEW**
multimedia subscription service
for romance fans like you!

Read, Watch and Play.

Experience the easiest way to get
the romance content you crave.

Start your **FREE 7 DAY TRIAL** at
<u>www.harlequinplus.com/freetrial</u>.